MW01632063

THANKFUL IN GOOD HOPE

CINDY KIRK

Copyright © Cynthia Rutledge 2019

All rights reserved.

No part of this book may be reproduced in any form or by any electronic or mechanical means, including information storage and retrieval systems, without written permission from the author, except for the use of brief quotations in a book review.

This is a work of fiction. Names, characters, places and incidents are products of the author's imagination or are used fictitiously. Any resemblance to actual events, locales, organizations, or persons, living or dead, is entirely coincidental.

ISBN: 978-1-7329601-8-3

CHAPTER ONE

Cheers and clapping filled the Ding-A-Ling bar in Good Hope. The election results were in, and Trinity McConnell's brother Wyatt had lost.

As Greer Chapin—the winner—was Wyatt's fiancée, Trinity joined in the applause. She'd been eager to see her brother, but wished she'd come at a different time.

She hadn't planned to arrive on election night, or to find Wyatt and his opponent sharing an election night watch party at a bar on the edge of town. After driving almost ten hours to surprise him, she'd been the one surprised.

"A free round for everyone," a tall man with dark hair and a confident air called out. "In honor of my sister, the next mayor of Good Hope."

"Congratulations, Greer." Trinity forced enthusiasm into her voice. If Wyatt wasn't upset about the loss, she wouldn't be either. "I'm sure you'll..."

Her voice trailed off as she spotted a man standing alone by the bar, dressed all in black. Once, long ago, Trinity had been punched in the chest so hard it stole her breath. She remembered that feeling. She felt the same way now.

Perhaps that wasn't Ryder, simply a doppelgänger. Didn't they say everyone had one somewhere? Even as the thought surfaced, she pushed it aside. This was the man who haunted her dreams. He was as handsome as she remembered, with eyes the color of rich Venezuelan chocolate and hair as dark as midnight.

Dressed in black jeans and a shirt of the same color, he couldn't have looked any more masculine. Trinity already knew this guy was all male, with and without clothing.

Her heart picked up speed as she narrowed her gaze. "Who is that man?"

Thankfully, her voice came out casual and offhand, reflecting none of her inner excitement.

"Ryder Goodhue. He owns the Daily Grind coffee shop." Greer paused, her gaze openly curious. "Have you seen him before?"

Trinity saw no need to keep their acquaintance a secret. "We've met."

Before Greer—or Wyatt—could ask any questions, calls of "Speech, speech," rang out.

Trinity listened with half an ear while Greer addressed her supporters. Someone pressed a beer into Ryder's hand.

He lifted the bottle to his lips, and his gaze met hers.

Ryder was waiting, she realized, for her to make the first move. It was a considerate gesture and in keeping with the person she'd gotten to know last month when they were both stuck at O'Hare.

The intense connection between her and the sexy businessman had taken Trinity by surprise. A shared meal and an evening of conversation on a rainswept night had led to her inviting him up to her hotel room. Though the impulsive behavior had been out of the norm for her, Trinity didn't regret that night. Now, their paths had crossed again.

Had Ryder even said where he lived? They'd talked a lot about her, briefly touching on her short-lived marriage in her early twenties and about California, where he'd lived before moving back to Wisconsin. After he'd come to her room, there hadn't been much talking.

With her heartbeat swift and tripping, Trinity wove through the crowd, most of whom were listening to Greer's acceptance speech or grabbing a free drink. They paid little attention to her, so it didn't take her long to reach Ryder.

"This is a nice surprise." She smiled and, lifting the bottle from his hand, took a drink.

"An amazing surprise." He took the bottle back, and when his mouth touched the rim, she felt a surge of heat.

After he lowered the bottle, those glittering dark eyes met hers. "How are you?"

"I'm well. Yourself?"

His lips lifted in a sardonic smile. "We're very polite."

"Extremely." She reached for his bottle again.

This time, he held it out of reach. "Why are you here?"

"In Good Hope? Or at the Ding-A-Ling?" Trinity was having difficulty reading him. Was he upset to see her? Or merely startled?

"Let's start with the Ding-A-Ling."

Trinity inclined her head. "Why are you here?"

He gestured with the hand holding the bottle to her brother and Greer. "The election watch party is the big event in town tonight. I'm acquainted with both candidates." The smile he flashed reminded her of the man she'd met in Chicago. "Now you. What brings you to Door County?"

"Wyatt is my brother." Trinity paused when Greer handed the microphone to her fiancé. When Ryder opened his mouth, Trinity held up a hand, wanting to hear Wyatt's speech.

When he said that Greer might have won the election, but he'd won when she agreed to marry him, Trinity's heart swelled. Wyatt had come a long way from the bitter, cynical boy she'd first met in foster care.

Trinity sighed when Wyatt and Greer embraced. "I'm happy for him."

Ryder took another pull of his beer, his assessing gaze never leaving her face.

"I quit my job," she said. Over the dinner they'd shared, she'd mentioned her concern about an impending takeover of the clinic where she practiced.

"How do you feel about that?"

"I feel good." Once she'd resigned, the tension had disappeared.

"I'm happy for you."

This was the man Trinity remembered, the one who'd appeared genuinely interested in what she had to say.

"What made you decide to cut the cord?"

Somehow, without her realizing how it had happened, she found herself sitting across from him at a small table near a karaoke platform. Thankfully, the stage was closed for the evening.

Ryder indicated to the server to bring him another beer and one for Trinity.

"I can't sit long." She slid a glance in the direction of Wyatt, who was still surrounded by friends. "My broth—"

"—is occupied."

While Trinity stared, Wyatt lifted his gaze over the group and caught her eye. She knew he worried that he was neglecting her, even though she'd crashed his party.

She gave him a broad smile and a thumbs-up and refocused on Ryder.

Ryder studied her with brown eyes so dark they looked black in the dim light. A lazy smile played at the corners of his lips.

The server, a pretty girl with auburn hair, brought the beers along with a basket of bar mix.

"How long will you stay?" Ryder scooped up a handful of nuts, never taking his eyes off her.

"I'm not sure. At least a week." The way Trinity looked at it, even if the job opportunity Wyatt had told her about ended up being a bust, this was her chance to get to know his fiancée.

Her older brother—by three months--was the only one of the McConnell tribe to get this close to the altar so far. The rest of them, including herself, tended to be wary of putting that much trust and faith in anyone else.

"Perhaps we can do dinner while you're here." Ryder's gaze was watchful, as if he was unsure of how his invitation would be received.

"I'd like that." Trinity decided to address the elephant in the room so they could get on with their conversation. "I don't see any reason to keep the fact that we had dinner in Chicago a secret. The fact that we slept together, well, that's our private business."

"Agreed." He grinned. "Though I don't recall much sleeping getting done."

Trinity laughed and clinked her bottle against his. "Touché."

~

Ninety-seven-year-old Gladys Bertholf stood with her two besties, Katherine Spencer and Ruby Rakes, out of the main crush of people in the bar. She loved parties and most of the people in the room, but what she had to say was private, and she wasn't in the mood to shout.

She settled her gaze on Good Hope's soon-to-be mayor and her fiancé. Gladys couldn't stop the smile from lifting her bright red lips. "We did it again."

Before she could say more, Oaklee Marshall, pushed through the throng to join the threesome. At twenty-one, Oaklee was young enough to be their granddaughter, or even their great-granddaughter. Since her arrival in Good Hope earlier in the year, the young woman had proved to be a kindred spirit.

Yesterday, Oaklee had had the sides of her hair cut short, just shy of being shaved, while the top had been left long. The short strands were now platinum, while the mohawk top was a vivid jet black.

On anyone else, the style would look ridiculous, but on Oaklee it worked.

Oaklee narrowed her gaze. "You were going to cut me out of the action."

Bringing one hand to her chest, Gladys widened her eyes. "What are you talking about? The girls and I merely moved so we could hear ourselves think."

"Seriously? You expect me to believe that?"

Gladys chuckled. "Not really."

Oaklee's gaze swept the room. "Who's the next target?"

"That's what we were about to discuss." Ruby, a petite woman with hair the color of champagne, smiled at her.

"Maybe we should find a match for you." Katherine's clear-eyed stare might have intimidated someone else, but Gladys knew it held no power over Oaklee.

"Ha-ha. Good one, Kate." Oaklee's use of the nickname Katherine couldn't abide told Gladys the girl hadn't appreciated the comment, even made in jest.

Oaklee met Gladys's gaze. "You've got someone in mind. I can tell."

Gladys didn't. That was the trouble. Normally, she and her matchmaking buddies had some idea who would be the next couple on their list. Though there were plenty of singles in Good Hope—many of them in the bar tonight—no one jumped out at her.

"Do any of you know the woman with Ryder?"

The second the question left Gladys's lips, the three women with her turned to search the room. Gladys groaned. What had happened to the art of subtlety?

The only saving grace was, with the bar so packed, the gawking wasn't obvious.

"I can't believe you don't know her." Oaklee's astonishment had Gladys stiffening. "You know everyone."

Gladys prided herself on being knowledgeable about what went on in Good Hope. The fact that she didn't have a clue who the blond beauty was stung. "I know she's not from around here."

"Wyatt knows her. He hugged her," Ruby reminded the group. "There's a connection there."

"The connection isn't a romantic one." Katherine's expression grew thoughtful. "The hug was more like what one friend would give another."

"Since he's engaged, that's for the best." Gladys lifted a glass of wine to her lips. "How'd the woman end up sitting with Ryder?"

Her gaze swept the other three women, who either shook their heads or lifted their shoulders in a shrug.

"It's time for a little reconnaissance. You stay here." Gladys fixed a pointed gaze on Oaklee when she opened her mouth to protest. "We're not going to be a herd of elephants tromping over there to pepper the two of them with questions."

"Why is it you who gets to go over there?" Oaklee's tone stopped just short of a whine.

"I'd say age before beauty." Gladys's red lips curved up, and she chuckled at the punch line she had yet to deliver. "Since I have both, let's just say I thought of it first."

CHAPTER TWO

Ryder couldn't take his eyes off Trinity. When they'd parted in Chicago, he'd assumed he'd never see her again. Now, here she was, sitting across from him, even lovelier than he remembered.

"What are you two doing over here by yourselves?"

Stifling a surge of irritation, Ryder pulled his gaze from Trinity. He liked Gladys, but he was hoping for more alone time with Trinity before her brother came searching.

Ryder forced an easy smile. "It's difficult to have much of a conversation in the middle of a crowd."

"Is that what you were doing?" Gladys's gaze shifted from him to Trinity and back again. "Conversing?"

"And," Ryder lifted his bottle, "enjoying a beer."

Gladys cocked her head. "I don't believe I know this young lady."

Before Ryder could perform the introductions, Gladys extended a hand to Trinity.

The former actress-turned-director stood out in any crowd and not just because of her eye-popping purple caftan and dark hair with its distinctive swath of silver. Her regal air and piercing blue eyes said this woman was a force.

"I'm Gladys Bertholf. Welcome to Good Hope."

"It's a pleasure to meet you." Trinity gave Gladys's bejeweled hand a firm shake and offered a warm smile. "I'm Trinity McConnell, Wyatt's sister."

Gladys's eyes brightened with interest. "His sister. I didn't realize he had one."

"He has three." Trinity gestured to one of the empty chairs at the four-top. "Would you care to join us?"

"How kind of you to ask." Gladys paused.

It took Ryder only a second to realize the older woman was waiting for him to pull out the chair. Once he did and she was seated, those piercing blue eyes settled back on Trinity. "Three sisters, you say?"

"Yes, there's three girls and two boys in our family."

Ryder recalled Trinity had mentioned having siblings, but if she'd offered specifics, he didn't recall them.

"Where are they?" When Gladys signaled the server and asked for a glass of white wine, Ryder knew she wasn't going anywhere soon.

"Amber teaches high school in Detroit. The school is a rough one, in a disadvantaged area, but she loves the kids and feels like she's making a difference."

"Our sheriff used to be a detective on the Detroit Police Department," Gladys informed her. "I admire those with a passion for service."

"Our other sister, Sage, is a mixologist at an upscale bar in Chicago." Trinity's lips curved. "I swear she knows every drink known to man."

Gladys's dark brows furrowed. "Mixologist?"

"Someone who specializes in the creation and presentation of cocktails." Trinity chuckled. "Sage laughs and says it's really a fancy word for bartender, but there's more to it than that."

"Interesting." Gladys smiled her thanks and handed a folded bill to the server who brought the wine.

"This round is on Mr. Chapin," the young woman protested.

"Then consider that your tip." Gladys waved the woman away with a sweep of one hand and turned back to Trinity.

Ryder hid a smile. Apparently, the inquisition wasn't over. He didn't mind. He enjoyed hearing about Trinity's family.

"You mentioned another brother," Gladys lifted the glass and sipped.

Trinity's eyes took on a distant glow. "Phoenix is the youngest. He's not a kid anymore, but it's difficult to think of him otherwise."

"Where does he live?" Ryder heard himself ask.

"Nix has lived in a variety of places." She expelled a breath. "Right now, he's living in our parents' basement."

Ryder heard the love in Trinity's husky voice when she spoke about her family. He fought a pang of envy. While he had a brother, he and Rafe had never been close, not even when they were kids.

"What does he—?" Gladys was interrupted when Wyatt and Greer strode up.

Wyatt placed his hand on his sister's shoulder, then turned to Gladys and Ryder. "Sorry for interrupting."

"Excellent speech," Ryder told Greer. "Congratulations on the win."

"Thanks." Appearing happy and relaxed, Greer beamed at him before turning her attention on Gladys. "I bet you never thought you'd see the day we'd be wearing the same color."

Gladys's expression softened. "You're a dull bird that finally burst into color."

Wyatt frowned. "Greer was never a dull anything."

Greer's eyes danced with good humor. "I believe Gladys meant it as a compliment."

"Most definitely." Gladys gestured with one hand toward Trinity. "I assume you've met Wyatt's sister."

"I'm excited she's here and eager to get acquainted." Greer

directed her gaze in Trinity's direction. "Wyatt and I were going to have some photos taken with family for the newspaper. We'd love for you to be in them. I realize you didn't plan—"

"I'd love to join you." Trinity pushed to her feet with an effortless grace, then cast a glance at Gladys. "It was a pleasure meeting you, Mrs. Bertholf."

"Gladys, please." The older woman bestowed a smile on Trinity before shifting her focus to Ryder.

Something in her gaze made him think she expected him to… what? Stop Trinity from going with her brother? Jump up and insist he had to see her again?

Ryder rose to his feet and held out a hand to Trinity. "It was nice seeing you again."

"Again?" Gladys's gaze sharpened. "I didn't realize the two of you were previously acquainted. That's a story I'd love to hear."

Instead of taking his hand as Ryder expected, Trinity wrapped her arms around him in a quick hug.

Then she was gone, shuttled off by her brother and future sister-in-law.

If Ryder had been thinking more clearly, he wouldn't have sat back down. But his mind was on Trinity and the spontaneous hug.

The second he dropped into his seat, Gladys lifted her glass of wine and smiled. "Tell me where you first met Trinity. Don't spare the details."

~

"Gladys."

The older woman turned at the interruption. Though the smile remained on her lips, her expression lacked its customary warmth. "Oaklee. Can't you see I'm busy here?"

"I was headed to the bar, and Wyatt's sister grabbed my arm."

Gladys made a rolling motion with one hand, urging the girl

to get to the point. Probably, Ryder thought, afraid the interruption would give him the time he needed to concoct a getaway story.

Which was exactly what he was trying to do.

After casting an apologetic glance in Gladys's direction, Oaklee turned to Ryder. "She asked me to send you over. If it works for you, that is."

"Thanks, Oaklee." Ryder pushed back his chair and smiled at Gladys. "Duty calls."

Before Gladys could utter a word, he strode off in the direction of Trinity.

Oaklee dropped down into the seat Ryder had vacated and lifted both hands. "Not my fault. Wyatt's sister insisted I deliver the message immediately."

Gladys took a sip of wine, her expression contemplative. "It's as if she knew I planned to grill him and intervened."

"Which sounds," Oaklee kept her voice low as she leaned across the table, "as if the two are more connected than we first thought. What did you find out?"

"You mean, before you so rudely interrupted?"

Oaklee's blue eyes widened. "I wasn't rude—"

"Oh, hush." Gladys patted her hand. "I'm just winding you up. You didn't have a choice, and the positive is that out of everyone here, Trinity picked you to deliver the message."

Katherine and Ruby, drinks in hand, sidled over to sit.

"There's a possibility that Ryder and Trinity McConnell—Wyatt's sister—could be our next couple. Depending, of course, on how long she remains in Good Hope." Gladys twirled the stem of the wineglass back and forward, waiting until she had everyone's attention. "Unfortunately, my interro—ah, conversation with Ryder was cut short."

She slanted a glance at Oaklee, who grinned and made a kissing sound. Gladys hid a smile.

"The two had met before, though I don't have the details.

Whatever their prior relationship, it must have been surface, since he wasn't aware of her brothers and sisters."

"Close enough that she gave him a hug when she left," Ruby pointed out, speaking for the first time since sitting down.

"Yes, indeed." Gladys smiled. "The way I see it, she wouldn't have rescued him if she didn't like him."

Katherine arched a perfectly sculpted dark brow. "Rescued?"

"From me." Gladys brought the glass of wine to her lips. "Asking Oaklee to send Ryder over gave him an acceptable out."

Oaklee heaved a breath that stopped just short of melodramatic. "I was her pawn."

Gladys brushed that away with a sweep of one hand. "I realize now this was confirmation."

Confusion blanketed Ruby's face. "You lost me."

"You don't rescue a man who means nothing to you. Trinity McConnell obviously cares for Ryder." Gladys's lips lifted in a slow smile. "Having that fact confirmed is a most excellent start."

Trinity stood off to the side while a photographer—a woman named Katie Ruth—took pictures of Wyatt and Greer. When Ryder strolled up, she greeted him with a smile. "No need to say thanks."

Ryder cocked his head. "For?"

"Saving you from Gladys." Her husky laugh was like a siren's call. "Greer rescued me. I passed on the favor."

"I appreciate it." Ryder shoved his hands into his pockets and gestured with his head toward Katie Ruth. "This was all a ruse?"

"Not for me." Trinity's expression softened when her brother and Greer faced each other and lovingly stared into each other's eyes. "Katie Ruth wants to do an article on me for some newsletter."

"The Open Door," Ryder explained. "Most people in the area

subscribe. My guess is the election will be front-page news while the two candidates' engagement and your arrival will be in the personal section."

"My arrival is news?"

The skeptical look she shot him had Ryder smiling.

"You're not in the big city anymore. Wyatt McConnell's sister is newsworthy." Ryder placed a hand on her bare arm. Big mistake. The simple touch had memories of his hands on her body flooding back.

"Trinity." Katie Ruth motioned to her. "I'd like to get a couple shots of you with Greer and Wyatt and then at least one with just you."

Katie Ruth smiled at Ryder. "Thanks for keeping her company."

Ryder met Trinity's gaze. "Not a hardship."

He debated whether to wait, but had no doubt that once Katie Ruth finished taking photos, Wyatt would want to introduce his sister to Greer's relatives.

If Trinity wanted to look him up, he'd be easy to find. That was one of the benefits of living in a small community.

He glanced over and saw Gladys and her friends congregated around the table he'd left.

The other beauty of growing up in a small town, he thought as he turned in the opposite direction, was knowing the locations of alternative exits.

It took a little convincing, but Trinity managed to make her brother understand that a quiet evening—alone—in the motel room she'd rented for the night was exactly what she needed after a day spent traveling.

Though Wyatt balked, Trinity knew her brother and his

fiancée had a personal celebration planned once the party ended. A celebration where three was definitely a crowd.

After promising to be in touch tomorrow, Trinity scanned the crowd on her way to the door. It was silly to hope Ryder had stuck around.

When she stepped outside, a smile blossomed on her lips. The man in question stood beside the rail at the edge of the porch, looking impossibly sexy in the shadows. "I thought you'd left."

He sauntered over to her, his eyes never leaving her face. "I have a question for you."

Taking her hand, Ryder tugged her away from the entrance and the bright lights. "Do you believe in fate?"

She wasn't sure where he was going with this, but she'd play along. "Believing in fate is—"

Before she could finish, the front door to the Ding-A-Ling swung open with a clatter. Raucous laughter and boot-tapping music spilled onto the porch. A foursome stumbled outside, talking in loud, excited voices.

As she stood silent beside Ryder in the shadows, not wanting to draw attention, the intoxicating scent of his cologne whispered sweet memories. An intense longing for the closeness they'd once shared rose inside her.

Unable to resist, Trinity turned into him. Resting her hands on his shoulders, she planted a kiss in the hollow of his neck.

His throat worked convulsively, and when he spoke, his voice held a rasp. "Not here."

"Where?"

"Where are you staying tonight?"

"The Sweet Dreams motel." The name made her smile even as her heart hammered.

A spark flared in his eyes. "Not with your brother?"

"Wyatt will be occupied tonight. I didn't want to intrude on his...celebration with Greer." Trinity slid her thumb along the top of Ryder's hand. The man had amazing hands, with strong yet gentle fingers that knew just where she liked to be touched.

"I've thought about you." He cleared his throat. "About that night. The dinner. The conversation. The—"

"Connection," she heard herself murmur.

Ryder inclined his head as he brought their joined hands to his lips and brushed a kiss across her knuckles.

"Seeing you again, it's like fate." His fingers tightened around hers. "With your brother occupied, we have all night."

"Why, Mr. Goodhue, are you inviting yourself to my motel room?" Trinity batted her lashes and spoke in her best Southern belle imitation.

His eyes went molten. "I am."

Before she could say more, Ryder's mouth took hers in a soul-searing kiss.

By the time the kiss ended, Trinity's head spun. Her heart beat a tribal rhythm against her ribs.

"What do you say?" Ryder asked.

She touched a shaky finger to her swollen lips. "I believe I've forgotten the question."

Ryder laughed and gave her hair a playful tug. "Your place or mine. What's it going to be?"

CHAPTER THREE

Sweet Dreams, the small family-owned motel east of Good Hope's business district, offered guests the luxury of being able to park right in front of their unit. Trinity wheeled her vehicle into the allotted space while Ryder parked his truck around the corner.

In a town this small, everyone not only knew you, they knew your car. For Trinity's sake, Ryder didn't want to start the gossip mill churning by parking his in front of the motel.

He rounded the corner and pulled up short when he saw Mavis Rosekranz chatting with Trinity. The portly proprietor of the motel, known for her personal interest in every guest, held a stack of towels in her hands.

"—thought you might need some extra," he heard Mavis say before the gray-haired woman spotted him.

Ryder fought the urge to slink back around the corner. Which was ridiculous. He and Trinity were consenting adults. What they did in private—or planned to do—was no one's business but their own.

Unless, of course, you lived in Good Hope.

"Ryder." Mavis's smile flashed, warm and welcoming.

The older woman was a regular at the Daily Grind-tall latte con panna—with something sweet on the side.

"Mavis." Ryder held out his hands for the towels. "Let me help."

"Oh, no, dear. These are for—" Mavis stopped as if she suddenly realized he hadn't just happened to be walking by her motel at this time of night.

Or maybe she got a jolt from the electricity sizzling in the air between him and Trinity.

Mavis handed over the towels, a twinkle in her eyes. "You two have a lovely evening."

As she hurried off in the direction of the motel office, Ryder wondered if she'd be calling her friends tonight or wait until morning.

"Want to come in?"

While he'd been gawking after Mavis, Trinity had unlocked the door. She stood, leaning against the jamb with a sexy smile that stole his breath.

"Thought you'd never ask." Taking her hand, he pulled her inside. In seconds, the towels were on the dresser, the door bolted and she was in his arms.

Trinity wound her arms around his neck, and Ryder found himself surrounded by the enticing scent that dogged his dreams. Their mouths melded, and his blood turned to fire.

Ryder had dated his share of women over the years. None who scrambled his insides like Trinity did.

Need for her erupted, urgent and demanding, but he would not rush. This reunion deserved better than a quickie.

After a kiss that sent his heart rate soaring into the stratosphere, Ryder rested his forehead against hers. He held her, reveling in the feel of her soft curves pressed against him. "This feels right."

He didn't realize he'd spoken the words circling in his brain until she tilted her head, met his gaze and smiled.

Then she was scattering kisses up his neck, just like she had in Chicago. Being with her that night had felt right, too. But in the morning, they'd walked away and gone back to their separate lives.

They'd had little choice. There had been planes to catch and lives to live in different states.

Now it seemed they'd been given a second chance.

Was it fate?

As her dress fell to the floor and his heart kicked into high gear, Ryder knew one thing: This time he wouldn't be the one to walk away.

The next morning, Ryder's warm lips brushing her cheek stirred Trinity from her slumber.

"I have to open the shop," he whispered in a low voice as he gently pulled the sheet up around her shoulders. "When you're awake, come see me."

Three hours later and fully rested, Trinity reached for her phone. Two new texts.

The first, from Wyatt, asked her to call him. Ryder's text invited her to a morning walk on the beach.

After calling Wyatt and making plans to meet for lunch, Trinity dressed and headed for the Daily Grind.

The beautiful August day brightened her already happy mood. The warmth of the sun on her bare arms and the slight breeze ruffling the hair she'd left down had her smiling. The faint scent of pine and the call of gulls in the distance added to her happiness.

Strangers greeted her as she passed them on the sidewalk. People in this part of the country were a friendly lot, one more plus for Good Hope.

Trinity found the Daily Grind at the end of the block. Excitement had her stomach churning. She hadn't realized how eager she was to see Ryder this morning until she was here.

She stepped into the coffee shop, and her vision of the enthusiastic greeting she'd receive disappeared like an untied balloon. Instead of Ryder, a teenager with jet-black hair and brilliant blue but sulky eyes stood behind the counter.

At least the girl pasted on a smile. "Welcome to the Daily Grind. How may I help you?"

The greeting, spoken in a monotone, had clearly been memorized.

"Good morning." Trinity returned the girl's faux smile with a genuine one of her own. "Is Ryder available?"

The teen's eyes, rimmed in kohl, narrowed. "He's working on payroll."

"If you could tell him Trinity is here to see him, I'd appreciate it."

"He can't be disturbed," the girl began. "He's working on—"

"Ravenna, do you know if—" Ryder, pushing through the swinging door, stopped talking when he spotted Trinity.

"My name is Raven." The girl jerked her head in Trinity's direction. "And you've got a visitor."

"Thank you, *Raven*." He appeared to be hiding a smile as he put the extra emphasis on her name. Then his entire attention shifted to Trinity. "Good morning."

Conscious of the girl's sharp-eyed scrutiny, Trinity simply gestured with one hand. "You have a nice place."

"Thanks." He rounded the counter, and for one crazy second, she thought he might kiss her. "How about a cup of coffee and a kouign amann? Best way I know to start the day."

But the spark in his eyes told her he knew a better way.

"A kouign amann? I'm not sure what that is," Trinity admitted.

Ryder turned to Raven. "Would you explain what that is to Ms. McConnell?"

The girl scowled. "Is this some kind of test?"

"Other customers surely have asked you, especially those not from around here." Ryder's tone was pleasant but firm.

Heaving a barely contained sigh, Raven began, "A kouign amann is like a caramelized croissant. Butter and sugar and layers of puffed dough."

Ryder smiled. "Excellent description."

Raven shrugged, but a slight relaxing of the girl's shoulders told Trinity that Ryder's approval meant something.

The girl fixed her gaze on Trinity. "So, do you want one or not?"

Ryder frowned at Raven's abrupt tone.

Trinity spoke quickly. "I'd love one. Also, a cup of your Indonesian blend."

"You won't regret either choice," Ryder told her.

"I rarely have regrets." She thought of last night. Nope, not a single regret.

Trinity kept her voice low as Raven busied herself with the order. "Do you still have time to show me the beach?"

A slow smile, the one that made him look almost boyish, spread across his face. "I can't think of anything I'd like more."

"Here's your order." Raven rattled off the price.

Trinity reached into her straw bag for the cash, but Ryder shook his head. "On the house."

Her fingers closed over her wallet. "You don't have to—"

"On the house," he repeated.

She released the wallet back into the cavernous depths. "Thank you."

"Take a seat. I'll bring it over." Ryder gestured to a table by the window and seconds later returned with not only her order but a coffee and pastry of his own. "Once we finish, we'll head to the beach. It's close."

"Sounds like a plan." Trinity took a bite of the pastry, then nearly moaned as the caramelized sugar hit her tongue. "This is amazing."

He grinned. "I knew you'd like it."

Trinity gestured to the line forming at the counter. "Are you sure you want to leave Raven alone?"

Ryder glanced at his watch. "I have another employee coming in to help out."

She inclined her head. "Is that your way of saying there's nothing stopping us?"

He grinned. "We just need to get out of our own way."

Ryder didn't make a habit of taking off time during a workday. Especially when he was short of staff. Ravenna—he stopped and did a mental correction—*Raven* was a relatively new employee.

Though she wasn't Cassie—his überefficient former employee—Raven was proving to be a quick study. Besides, it wasn't fair to compare a seventeen-year-old to a woman old enough to be her mother.

As soon as he'd left the motel this morning, Ryder had called another employee to come in. He wanted to be available when Trinity stopped by.

Once they left the coffee shop, Ryder steered her in the direction of the beach. Last night, he'd discovered she wasn't only in town to see her brother, but was considering a position at Connections, a local mental health clinic.

Though Good Hope made its own good impression, he would do what he could to make her see she could be happy living and working here.

Trinity slanted a glance at a dress in the window of a small boutique. "It seems this town has a little bit of everything."

"The tourist trade makes it possible for our small town to have big-city amenities. The Women's Events League, known as the Cherries, plan all the holiday celebrations. There are festivals nearly every month. And no town does Christmas like Good

Hope." He smiled, and when they came to a corner, Ryder motioned her to turn left. "When is your interview with Liam?"

"Today at five o'clock."

"He works a lot with kids. Is that something you're interested in?" The distinct aroma of pizza from Bayside Pizza wafting in the air had Ryder's stomach rumbling. Perhaps, after the beach, he could convince Trinity to stop for a slice.

"I'm more teen- and adult-focused," Trinity told him, "though I have experience in play therapy."

"Sounds as if you two would be a good fit." While the psychologist had lived in Good Hope for over a year, Ryder knew him only casually. Liam wasn't part of his group of friends. Ryder's buddies leaned heavily toward those who'd grown up in Door County. "What do you think of Liam? I can't say I know him well, but he seems like a good person."

Trinity sipped her coffee. "Oh, I've known Liam for years. He and I were friends during our doctoral program."

"Just friends?" Ryder cast a sideways glance at Trinity. "Or friends like we're friends?" he teased, wiggling his eyebrows.

Trinity only laughed. "Strictly platonic. Liam is a great person, and an excellent doctor, but there's never been any spark between us, which bodes well for a good working relationship."

When they reached the wooden steps leading down to the sandy beach, Ryder paused and gestured to a bench off to the left. "We better take off our shoes."

Obligingly, Trinity slipped off her sandals while he removed his sneakers. She slung her purse over her shoulder and let him take her arm as they negotiated the steps.

It was a warm day, and as school wouldn't start until after Labor Day, the beach was crowded. Families sat with umbrellas shading them from the sun, while children played in the sand and frolicked in the water.

A dark-haired woman scolded a boy of about ten because he'd

knocked over his younger brother's sand castle. Nearby, a man slathered sunscreen on a fair-haired little girl.

Ryder gestured carelessly with one hand toward the group. "That'll be your brother and Greer in a few years."

Trinity's toes, painted a bright, glinting silver, sank deep into the sand as she slanted a glance at the family. A smile lifted her lips. "Probably. I can see them having two or three of their own down the road."

He could see it, too.

She glanced out over the blue water, her gaze following a gull as it dove. "The water looks very inviting."

"We can walk along the edge. It's not the same as swimming, but you get the feel of the sand and the water."

They strolled together along the shore of Green Bay, noisy gulls adding to the ambience.

"The water is warm now," Ryder told her. "Another month or so and it'll be a different story. But there's a lot to like about autumn. The tourist trade falls off, and life in Good Hope slows down."

"I'd think as a business owner, you'd want it busy all the time."

He heard the puzzlement in Trinity's voice. "I enjoy the balance. I like when the sidewalks are crowded, and there's excitement in the air. I also like it when I can walk downtown and know practically everyone I pass."

She studied him. "You're painting a pretty picture of life on the Door County peninsula."

"I came back to Good Hope for a reason. This is home to me." He gave her hand a swing. "Given the chance, one day it might feel like home to you."

"The biggest factor is how my interview with Liam goes."

"That'll be a slam dunk." Ryder chuckled at the surprised look on her face. "He'd be a fool to turn you away. While I don't know Liam well, he doesn't strike me as a fool."

"I've got a good feeling," she told him, then shrugged. "After the meeting, I'll know more."

"I want it to work out for you." Ryder hesitated, then pushed ahead. "Seeing you again, being with you, reminds me of the connection we had in Chicago."

Her lips curved. "That was intense."

Ryder squeezed her hand. "The connection is still there."

She chuckled. "After last night, I don't think there's any doubt of that."

"If you stay in Good Hope, I'd like us to spend time exploring the connection more fully."

Her tone turned teasing. "As opposed to simply having sex?"

"I'm serious." Normally, he'd be the one wanting to keep things light, not wanting to get too close, too fast. Pushing for more was unfamiliar territory and as unsteady and shifting as the sand beneath his feet.

Ryder meant what he'd said. He wanted to get to know her better. He wanted to date her. He just needed to know if she wanted that, too. "Look, we know we're a good match physically. Why not see if we get along outside of the bedroom? We can go on dates, hang out, get to know each other better."

"I'd like that." Her gaze lifted to follow a gull winging its way across the sky before she returned it to him. "I have one question."

Ryder braced himself, not sure what was coming. "What is it?"

"As we explore this connection," she cocked her head, "is sex on or off the table?"

CHAPTER FOUR

Trinity knew Ryder would have chucked his plans to spend the rest of the afternoon with her if she'd asked. But he said he understood when she told him Wyatt was expecting her and kissed him good-bye.

She checked out of the Sweet Dreams motel, grateful Mavis wasn't at the desk. Less than an hour later, she'd stashed her bags at Wyatt's house—thank you, key under the mat—freshened up after her beach walk and met her brother for lunch.

"This is the cutest place." Trinity glanced down at the plate of cherry-stuffed French toast she'd insisted on sharing with her brother.

Muddy Boots was every bit as cute as Wyatt had promised, with its shiny wood floors, comfortable booths and an adorable mural on a far wall. "This French toast is spectacular."

"Told you."

When they'd first arrived, deciding what to order had taken precedence. Then she'd asked about his meeting that morning at Cherry Acres.

Orchards and fruit-processing were totally foreign to Trinity, but she found Wyatt's enthusiasm contagious.

"When I spoke with Dad last week, he said he hoped I wasn't the one tending the trees." Wyatt shook his head and gulped down some coffee.

Trinity inclined her head.

"He brought up the time my only chore was tending to the tomato plants."

"Hottest summer on record." Trinity smiled, remembering. "You didn't water them, and they died. None of us kids cared. But Dad, well, the man loves his BLTs."

"I did water the plants," he protested. "Just, apparently, not enough."

She laughed at the memory, then paused. Keeping the smile on her lips and her eyes on him, she lowered her voice. "Why are Gladys and Oaklee staring at us?"

Wyatt turned, ignoring her hiss of protest, to find Gladys and Oaklee, seated in one of the booths by the window, blatantly staring.

Trinity had to give them props. They didn't glance away or pretend they'd been doing anything else but studying them.

Wyatt lifted his fork in a type of wave and smiled.

Only after returning his smile did they shift their attention back to each other.

"Gladys is interesting." Trinity admired a woman comfortable in her own skin.

Wyatt smiled. "Interesting is much too mild a word. The woman is a dynamo. She acts and directs at the community theater, and she's as close to a town matriarch as Good Hope gets."

Wyatt followed his bite of French toast with another long sip of the rich Ethiopian blend that Trinity decided was her new favorite. "Oaklee, well, she's relatively new to Good Hope. But she's jumped right in and gotten involved. Her brother is the minister at First Christian."

"Any idea why they were staring?"

"It's a small town." He shrugged. "You're someone new."

"We're both new," Trinity reminded him.

"Not me, not anymore." Wyatt sat back in his chair, his fingers comfortably encircling the white ceramic cup. "I know them fairly well. Gladys and Oaklee served on an ad hoc committee I recently chaired. We got acquainted working on a project for foster kids."

Trinity shook her head in disbelief. "If I didn't know better, I'd think you've lived in this small town your entire life."

"It's that type of community." Wyatt smiled. "Trust me. If you stay, it won't take long for you to be brought into the fold."

The bells over the door jingled again. Like the rest of the café patrons, Trinity found her gaze shifting to the entrance.

When Ryder's gaze met hers, she felt the familiar punch.

"Ryder." Wyatt surged to his feet and waved him over. "I didn't expect to see you here this morning."

"Unexpected business." Ryder's dark eyes shifted to Trinity. "Hello, Trinity. You look lovely this afternoon."

The look in his eyes told her he noticed she'd changed out of the shirt and shorts she'd worn that morning.

"Thank you." Trinity gestured to her brother. "I admit I was leery about eating at a place called Muddy Boots when Wyatt suggested it, but I love it. Not only the food and atmosphere, but I've found a new favorite coffee."

"The Ethiopian." Ryder's tone remained easy. "We supply it to Muddy Boots."

Wyatt glanced at Trinity. "You should check out the Indonesian blend."

Ryder said nothing, obviously leaving it up to Trinity to decide how much to tell her brother.

"I stopped by the Grind early this morning and had a cup," Trinity told Wyatt. "You're right. I loved it. And the kouign amann was unbelievable."

Surprise flickered in Wyatt's eyes as he set down his cup. His gaze shifted from Ryder to settle on his sister. "I didn't realize you were out and about this morning."

"I had to have my coffee." Trinity lifted her cup. "After making sure I was properly fueled up with caffeine, Ryder showed me the beach. I couldn't believe how crowded it was so early in the day. And the bay, it's beautiful."

Trinity clamped her mouth shut. She'd been babbling. She never babbled.

A thoughtful look filled Wyatt's eyes, and Trinity saw him connecting the dots, one by one.

"That was nice of you to show my sister around," Wyatt told Ryder even as his brows pulled together in puzzlement. "I'm surprised you had time. I know mornings are especially busy for you."

"I wanted Trinity to feel welcome." At the sound of his name, Ryder turned, expelled a breath. "I better go. I'm here to meet with Gladys and Oaklee."

"About?"

"I'm not sure." Ryder frowned. "I received a text from Gladys fifteen minutes ago. Something urgent. I assume it has to do with the foster care committee."

Wyatt frowned. "I thought that was wrapped up."

"So did I." Ryder shrugged. "I'll let you know if it's anything to do with committee business."

Wyatt cocked his head. "She said it was urgent?"

Ryder chuckled. "Yes, but for Gladys, urgent can be a shortage of cherry Danish or a question she wants answered immediately."

Trinity grinned. "I like her more and more."

"She's one of a kind." Ryder's tone was indulgent. "Well, I best find out what she wants so I can get back to work."

"Let me know if it has to do with the committee," Wyatt told him.

"Will do." The smile Ryder shot Trinity had heat surging. "Enjoy your lunch. Good luck with the interview."

Once Ryder had strolled off, weaving his way through the tables, Wyatt's gaze met hers.

"Something tells me I won't be the only one who'd love it if you'd make your home here." At her raised brow, he added, "I saw the way he looks at you."

Wyatt's tone might be casual, but his gaze remained razor-sharp.

Until she knew where this thing, this connection, with Ryder was headed, Trinity decided to keep the explanation simple. "Ryder and I met last month when I had a layover in Chicago. We ended up having dinner together that night."

"I imagine you were surprised when he told you he lived in Good Hope." Wyatt brought the cup to his lips and took a sip, his eyes never leaving her face.

Trinity wrapped her hands around her mug, liking the feel of the warmth through the ceramic. "Good Hope never came up. He mentioned small-town Wisconsin, but since we'd both lived in California for a time, that took up most of our discussion."

"Are you going to be seeing him while you're here?"

"Maybe." Trinity kept her tone offhand, not yet ready to examine her feelings for Ryder. "Maybe we'll have dinner again or something. He seems nice, but we didn't make any plans. Tell me why you like living here."

"I see why you're so effective as a therapist. You're an expert at redirection, and when your eyes settle on me, I want to bare my soul."

She laughed. "Flatterer."

"Life is more relaxed here. The pace isn't as hectic." Wyatt relaxed against the back of his chair. Her eldest brother had always been driven and so very serious. Now, contentment lay around his shoulders like a favorite sweater.

"I'm learning the cherry business," he continued, "and soon I'll be married and building a life with the woman I love."

"I couldn't be happier for you." Trinity lifted her mug in a salute. "Here's to jumping into small-town life with both feet."

Wyatt chuckled. "Spend some time here and you'll understand. There's something about Good Hope. There's such a strong feeling of community."

Trinity gave his hand a squeeze. "I've never seen you this passionate about anywhere you've lived. Do you think it's because your biological family is from here?"

"I don't feel any ties to my grandfather. His house burned down, so there was nothing personal of his left, other than what was in a safe-deposit box at the bank. There were pictures." Wyatt blew out a breath. "A couple of my mom as a happy child. People who remember her say she was never the same after her mother ran off and left her behind."

"You and I, we understand how it feels to be abandoned."

Trinity wasn't speaking to him as an accomplished psychologist, but as a sister who loved him dearly. She understood how those years before his adoption had shaped him. Understood, because she'd been shaped by the same forces. Her childhood before adoption had been equally rocky.

Wyatt took a contemplative sip of coffee.

"Was your mom pregnant with you when she left Good Hope?" When she and Wyatt had discussed this in the past, it had seemed the most likely reason his mom had been on her own, since she'd been eighteen.

"If I have the dates right, she got pregnant a year after she left home." Wyatt set down his cup. "According to local gossip, she and Roy had a big argument shortly after she graduated from high school. She took off and never came back. He didn't look for her, at least not as far as anyone knows."

Trinity only shook her head. She could say that was too bad, but had learned long ago you never knew what went on behind closed doors. "If she was pregnant when she left, you might have had a chance of figuring out the identity of your father."

"Possibly. At this point in my life, who he is scarcely matters."

Trinity didn't argue. Though, like him, she'd struggled with not knowing her own father's identity. "What else was in the box?"

"A copy of Roy's will." Wyatt shrugged. "Some legal papers."

Nothing, Trinity thought, that offered any real insight.

Wyatt's watch pinged.

"If you need to go—"

"What time is your appointment with Liam?"

"At five. I'll need to change and do something with my hair."

"If you're at my house by four, will that give you enough time?"

"Absolutely." She smiled. "What are you thinking?"

"I'd like to show you the cherry orchards and processing plant. I know it doesn't sound exciting, but—"

Trinity placed a hand on his arm. "I was going to ask you to take me to the orchards."

"It won't take long. Then, if there's time, we could drive around the peninsula." He hesitated for a moment. "That ping from my watch was a text from Greer. She'd like to join us."

"I'd love to have the chance to get better acquainted. Based on first impression, I have the feeling she and I are going to be good friends."

"I'm sure you will. Greer is a wonderful woman."

The affection in his voice warmed Trinity's heart. Her brother had so much love to give, and she was glad he'd found a woman worthy of him. "Text her back. I'm ready to go if you are."

In minutes, they were headed out the door. Trinity glanced over where Ryder sat in conversation with Gladys and Oaklee. He must have sensed her eyes on him, because he looked up and shot her a wink.

The silly gesture had her smiling all the way to Cherry Acres.

Wyatt proudly showed her his orchard, with its endless acres of beautiful trees. Would she be here to see them burst into bloom next spring? That depended on how her interview with Liam went this afternoon.

After a tour of the processing plant, Greer took the lead on the tour of the peninsula. As her family had been one of the original settlers of the area way back in the mid-nineteenth century, it shouldn't have surprised Trinity how well-versed she was on local lore.

Trinity found herself making mental notes of places she'd like to visit again. Everything from exploring Cave Point by kayak to taking the Washington Island Ferry.

By the time they dropped her off at Wyatt's house to get ready for her interview, Trinity found herself hoping, really hoping, that the position with Liam's clinic would be a perfect fit.

Connections, Liam Gallagher's clinic, was housed in a modern, single-story structure off Highway 42.

Trinity pulled into the parking lot, then took a moment to study the building. She believed strongly that the feel of the space where services were rendered had an impact on the work done between therapist and client.

This location, on the edge of Good Hope, had a good vibe. It probably helped that the late summer sun shone brightly, and the sky was a brilliant blue. She liked the warm and inviting brick and timber design as well as the large windows that overlooked a garden of wildflowers and rolling countryside.

This building—and the land it sat on—didn't come cheap. That, Trinity knew, would undoubtedly impact how much "buying into a partnership" would cost her.

She told herself she'd worry about the financial aspect once she determined if this was a good fit.

Liam had informed her he'd kept this afternoon free for

paperwork. Trinity assumed that was why there were only two cars in the lot, and no one in the waiting area.

Pausing for a second in the quiet coolness, Trinity found the waiting room as warm and inviting as the exterior. A gorgeous area rug, which appeared to have been made from smaller pieces of various damaged rugs, caught her eye. Trinity wondered if the significance was intentional.

A young woman rose from behind a reception desk built into one corner. In her mid-twenties, she had hair the color of burnished copper and chocolate-brown eyes. The sweetness of her welcoming smile put Trinity instantly at ease.

Score another one for Liam, Trinity thought. Not only had he gotten the aesthetics of the practice right, he'd hired the perfect person to greet clients.

"Welcome. I'm Peyton." The young woman stepped out from behind the desk, and Trinity saw she was dressed simply in a sleeveless cotton dress with brown polka dots. "How may I help you?"

"I'm Trinity McConnell. I have a meeting at five with Dr. Gallagher."

"He's expecting you. I'll let him know you're here." Peyton paused. "May I get you a cup of coffee or a glass of water while you wait?"

"I'm fine. Thank you."

When Liam appeared, Trinity crossed to him, holding out both hands. "It's been a long time."

He looked much the same as he had in grad school. Although his mass of auburn hair was still longish, the wavy strands no longer brushed his shoulders. His smile, open and friendly, reached his hazel eyes.

With him in chinos and a polo shirt, Trinity felt overdressed in her suit. She pushed aside the discomfort, reminding herself that this was a job interview, and she was the one on the hot seat.

"You haven't changed a bit." Liam gave her hands a quick squeeze.

"I was thinking the same about you." She shot him an impish smile. "Except for the hair."

He laughed. "I did wear it long back in the day."

"I envied the curl," Trinity admitted.

Liam grinned and gestured to the receptionist. "Have you met Peyton?"

Trinity offered the young woman a friendly smile. "Not really."

Liam made quick work of the introductions, then took her on a tour. "There's four fully equipped offices. This one is mine."

The space was much like the man himself—warm and approachable. The next one was ultramodern and done all in white, from the large desktop to the overhead and lateral filing system.

"This is where I do most of the testing," he explained, "including neuropsychological assessments."

"Do you do many?"

"The hospital in Sturgeon, as well as doctors in the area, refer a fair number here for memory and concentration assessment." Liam paused for a second. "I thought we could share this office, as well as the one designed for children."

In the next room, lots of bright colors, a chalkboard wall and a corner filled with items for play therapy had Trinity nodding approvingly. "Very nice and functional."

The adjacent door opened to another spacious office. Sunshine flooded the room with bright, cheery light. "This would be your office. It was decorated when the building was built, but it certainly can be redecorated to your taste and specifications."

The space, done in soothing tones, had the same calm feel as Liam's office. Her gaze flicked over the desk and chair. When she was seeing patients, she wouldn't be behind the desk, but rather, in the comfortable seating area. Which, thankfully, was large enough for individual or family sessions.

"It's a beautiful setup, Liam. I'm impressed."

"Impressed enough to discuss the possibility of you joining me?" Liam cocked his head.

"I believe we could work well together." Being in practice with a business partner she respected, while also being near her brother and Ryder seemed like a win-win.

She met Liam's questioning gaze. "Let's talk numbers."

CHAPTER FIVE

That night, over wine and antipasti, Trinity gave Wyatt and Greer a blow-by-blow of her interview with Liam.

"We discussed two possibilities," she told the couple as they sat on the patio. "I could join Connections as an equity partner or as a nonequity one. There are pros and cons to both options."

Greer sipped her wine, her gray eyes thoughtful. As a banker, she would likely be familiar with the advantages of each. "If it were me, I'd run the financials past Prim and Max Brody."

"They're married, and they run a CPA firm here in Good Hope," Wyatt explained, obviously sensing Trinity's confusion. "Prim's dad is married to Greer's mother."

"There isn't anyone I trust more," Greer told her.

"I'll set up an appointment with them." Trinity added the task to her phone's to-do list.

Wyatt picked up an olive and popped it into his mouth. "Did Liam give you copies of the proposed contracts for each option?"

"Yes. He gave me both. One if I decide to go with the nonequity option—which is where I'm leaning—and another if I choose the equity route."

"I suggest having Beckett Cross review the contracts." Greer slanted a glance at Wyatt.

"It'd be a smart move. Beck handled Roy's estate," Wyatt explained. "He's very savvy. He's married to Prim's sister Ami."

Trinity turned to Greer. "Is there anyone in this town who isn't a relative of yours?"

Greer laughed. "I'll let you know if you're about to venture outside the family circle."

"I'll make an appointment with Beck, too." Trinity added that to her list.

"How much does Liam want upfront?" Wyatt asked.

"If I decide to go the equity route, I'll find the money." What she wouldn't do, Trinity thought, was ask her brother for a handout.

Wyatt frowned as if he'd read her thoughts. "There's nothing wrong with family helping family. I inherited a considerable sum. I can give you the money you need and not even miss it."

"That's kind of you, and I'll definitely keep your offer in mind, but—"

"But..." he prompted.

"As I said, I'm leaning more toward going in as a nonequity partner. I'd have the option to switch down the road to equity. Before I invest, I'll be able to see how I like working with Liam. How I like living in Good Hope."

"That makes good business sense." Greer glanced at Wyatt. "But I've got to warn you. Your brother and I are going to pull out all the stops to make sure you love it here and never want to leave."

When Wyatt and Greer decided to watch a movie, Trinity retired to her room. Though her brother insisted he loved having her under the same roof, Trinity believed he and Greer deserved privacy.

Which was why, as soon as she had the job situation with Liam nailed down, she'd start looking for a place of her own.

As it was too early to sleep, Trinity opened a book on her e-reader. Engrossed in the story, she jumped when her phone rang.

Annoyance turned to pleasure when she saw Ryder's name on the screen with a request to FaceTime.

"Hey, you." Slipping off her shoes, she propped up some pillows with one hand, then swung her legs up on the bed.

She hadn't expected to hear from him so soon.

"Am I interrupting?"

"I'm in my room reading. Living life in the fast lane." Her droll tone had him chuckling. "Greer and Wyatt are in the living room watching a movie."

"I wondered how the rest of your day went." The warm richness of his voice wrapped around her like a caress. "Good, I hope."

"Well, once we left Muddy Boots, Wyatt took me to see the orchards. Then he gave me a tour of the processing plant."

"You *are* living life in the fast lane."

She laughed. "After leaving Cherry Acres, we swung by and picked up Greer at the bank, then took a drive around the peninsula. Greer is amazing and quite the historian. There wasn't a single question I asked that she couldn't answer."

"Greer is an expert on all things Door County." Ryder paused. "How did your meeting with Liam go? Think it'll be a good fit?"

"I was impressed." Her former classmate hadn't changed much since grad school. Though he'd grown even more handsome over the years, there was still no sizzle between them. That boded well for a solid working relationship. "Liam is an excellent clinician with a philosophy in sync with mine. He runs a solid operation."

"Is there enough business around here for two psychologists?"

"From the stats he showed me, yes." Trinity had been amazed

by the wealth of data Liam had accumulated. "What impresses me is his commitment to not only run a thriving practice, but to help those who need services but can't afford to pay."

"Do you think you could work together?"

"I do." Her tone turned teasing. "I spent a little time listing all the advantages of staying in Good Hope and realized an added bonus is I'll have easy access to fabulous coffee and pastries."

His dark eyes seemed to bore into her soul. "So, it's a done deal?"

She heard the same hope in his voice she'd heard in Wyatt's barely an hour earlier. "There are papers to review and sign, financial arrangements to be worked out, but..."

"But..." he prompted.

"I'm ready to start looking for a place of my own here in Good Hope."

By the end of her third week in Good Hope, Trinity had met with not only Max and Prim, but with Beck as well. Starting out as a nonequity partner seemed the way to go. At least initially.

Plans were in place for her to start seeing patients at the clinic after Labor Day, once she'd received her Wisconsin license. Eager to find her own place, she'd enlisted the help of top real estate professional Tim Vandercoy.

Tim had been what she'd expected—a polished man in his late fifties, wearing Italian loafers and Oliver Peoples sunglasses. His engaging manner made it easy to understand how he'd risen to be the top real estate broker on the peninsula.

Over the past two weeks, he'd shown her several apartments and condos, as well as a couple of houses. All were perfectly lovely and fit the parameters she'd given him. None felt right.

Now, Trinity stood in front of a large red structure located on the edge of Good Hope.

"The listing just came across my desk this morning." Tim stood beside her outside the first of three possibilities he planned to show her. "What's your first impression?"

"It's a barn. One I've been in before."

The fact that this condominium was minutes from Connections only made it that much more perfect.

Tim snapped his sunglasses into a case. "You know someone who lives here?"

"Ryder Goodhue." Trinity had been to his place more than a few times over the past three weeks.

"That's right. I ran into the two of you at Bayside Pizza last week." Tim's gaze grew sharp and assessing. "Would living near him be an issue?"

"Not at all."

"Good to know." Tim gestured toward the building. "Renovating barns into homes is a trend across the country. This one was made into six condominiums about five years ago. These structures have their own name. Barndominiums."

Trinity had to smile. "You're making that up."

"I'm not." He lifted one hand, his fingers forming the Boy Scout salute. "Ask Ryder if you don't believe me. Or Wyatt. When he was looking for a place to live, he inquired about renting a unit in this building. He was several months too early."

"What do you mean?

"There weren't any open at the time. As I indicated when I texted you, this one just became available." He studied her with intense dark eyes. "Want to check out this unit? Even if you've been in Ryder's, each has its own unique flavor."

"Absolutely."

"Love the positivity." Tim flashed a grin and swiped a card that unlocked the main door.

"High-tech." She'd made the same comment to Ryder the first time she'd come home with him.

"The barn draws a lot of tourist interest." Once inside, Tim gestured to the gorgeous wooden staircase leading to the second floor. "No one wants to walk in and find strangers gawking in the lobby of where they live."

"How big is the unit?"

"The Barn has two twelve-hundred-square-foot units on each level, along with one six-hundred-square-foot efficiency."

"What size is the one you'll be showing me?"

"Two-bedroom, twelve hundred square feet," Tim informed her. "Main floor."

Once inside, Trinity nodded approval at the nine-foot ceilings and open floor plan. Of the two bedrooms, the smaller one could easily function as an office. Quality workmanship was evident as she inspected the cabinets, trim and windows.

"Notice you have your own laundry area," Tim pointed out as they continued the tour. "There's also a garage, which includes not only space for a vehicle but for additional storage. Though not attached, there's a covered walkway out to it."

Living down the hall from Ryder wasn't a concern. The downside was that the rental price Tim had quoted her was at the top end of what she wanted to spend on housing each month. "Does the rent include the garage?"

"It does. As well as all utilities. That will save you a bundle in the frigid winter months." Tim gestured again toward the laundry area. "The washer and dryer are included."

All those factors made the rent much more palatable. Though she wanted to say yes, Trinity told herself she should look at the other units on the list first. "I'm definitely interested."

"You'd only need to commit to a six-month lease. Then it's month-to-month after that. I brought the paperwork with me, thinking you might like this one." Tim motioned to a folding table and two chairs. He waited until she was seated before pulling papers out of his briefcase. "I realize we have several other units to look at, but, full disclosure, another agent will be showing this unit in an hour. I'm not trying to rush you, but I honestly don't expect it to be available past today."

Trinity tapped a finger on the table. "When could I take possession?"

"As soon as you like. The owner wants someone in here by the first." Tim's expression remained pleasant but businesslike. "We'll prorate the first month's rent depending on your move-in date."

Trinity didn't make snap decisions, but this place was too perfect for her to let it slip through her fingers. "I'll take it. Will I need to fill out an application or—?"

"I have the power to lease the unit on behalf of the owner." Tim smiled. "If you want it, it's yours."

Trinity picked up the pen on the table. "Where do I sign?"

Now that Trinity had her own place, there were a thousand and one things to do. Like telling her brother the good news, having her friends mail the boxes of personal items they were storing for her and buying new furniture. All took second place to letting Ryder know he had a new neighbor.

Trinity wondered if leasing the place without Ryder's input had been a social faux pas. Maybe she should have spoken with him first. Made sure he didn't see her living so close as a problem.

She assumed he'd like the convenience. They'd seen each other every day for weeks. He had to know by now that even if they split up, her being just down the hall wouldn't be an issue, because she wouldn't let it be.

Pushing open the door to the Daily Grind, Trinity smiled at the familiar figure at the counter. "Hey, Raven."

"Trinity." A welcoming smile lifted the girl's lips. "I didn't expect to see you."

She and Raven had bonded in the last couple of weeks over their mutual love of *Gilmore Girls*.

"How are you?" Though there were no customers near enough to overhear, Trinity lowered her voice. "Is Jax still being a pain?"

Jax was Raven's boyfriend and a jerk. Trinity had heard all about the couple's tumultuous relationship when she'd stopped in early one morning. The coffee shop hadn't yet opened, and Ryder was tied up on a call. Trinity wasn't Raven's therapist, but she'd listened to Raven vent.

"He's an ass." Raven's eyes grew hard. "I don't know why he can't be nice."

"It's all any of us wants, to find a nice person to hang out with till we drop dead. Not a lot to ask."

Raven grinned and pointed a finger at Trinity. "You just quoted Lorelai Gilmore."

"She's a wise woman." Trinity returned Raven's smile. "Is Ryder around?"

"He's at the farmers' market," Raven told her. "With our coffee cart."

Our. Raven was taking ownership in her work. And she'd shared sensitive information about her boyfriend. Positive steps for a girl who didn't like to commit or lean on anyone.

"Can I get you a coffee to go?" Raven cocked her head. "Or maybe an iced latte?"

"Sure." Trinity wasn't particularly thirsty, but she appreciated Raven offering.

"Coming right up."

Trinity watched Raven make the drink with quick, well-practiced moves. In a few short weeks, the teenager had mastered her job duties. "School is just around the corner."

"Next week." Trinity saw Raven's shoulders slump as she turned, drink in hand. "I'd like to give Jax the boot, but if I do, he'll make senior year a living hell."

"You deserve better."

Handing the drink to Trinity, Raven shrugged.

"Nobody's stopping you from making whatever you want happen."

Raven inclined her head, the suspicious gleam in her narrowed eyes nearly making Trinity smile. "Is that another Gilmore quote?"

"Logan Huntzberger," she said, referring to one of Rory Gilmore's loves in the popular television series.

"I was Team Logan," Raven admitted, looking embarrassed.

"I was torn between Logan and Jess." Trinity lifted her latte. "How much do I owe you?"

"Take it up with the boss," Raven told her, then greeted a customer who walked in with a smile. "Welcome to the Daily Grind. How may I help you?"

Trinity's heart gave a leap when she spotted Ryder in the town square, his mobile coffee bar surrounded by stands of vegetables, fresh flowers and baked goods. She watched him laugh and chat with three women in their fifties as he made their drinks.

His work ethic was only one of the many things she admired about him. Though he owned a whole chain of coffee shops, he still liked to be hands-on. Trinity stood off to the side until the women strolled off with their iced coffees.

Now that he was free, with no new customers in sight, she stepped to the cart and held up her nearly empty glass. "How much do I owe you for this iced latte?"

"Trinity." He flashed a smile. "I didn't expect to see you this morning."

"I came to pay my debt."

"Raven made that for you?"

"She did, and it's as good as yours."

"Ouch." His lips twitched. "That stings."

She laughed as he pretended to study the drink. "One kiss should do it."

"You're working."

"Not at this moment."

She slipped around the cart, framed his face with her hands and kissed him on the mouth. "Good morning and thanks for the latte."

"Thank you for the kiss." His gaze narrowed. "Weren't you with Tim this morning checking out places to rent?"

"We're done."

"Any of them possibilities?"

"I found the one."

"Congratulations." He grinned and took her hand, giving it a squeeze. "Where is it? Tell me about it."

"Well..." She paused for dramatic effect. "It's really close to your place."

His expression brightened. "Even better."

"You won't mind me living nearby?"

"Mind? Are you kidding? I'd love it." He swung her hand. "How close?"

"Down the hall from you."

His eyes went wide.

"It won't be a problem, I promise," she reassured him.

"This morning, I overslept, then went out and discovered I had a flat. Once I changed the tire, I stopped by the shop to pick up the cart and discovered I'd forgotten to have Raven restock it."

Trinity's heart sank. "Your day sucked. Now you find out I'm moving in down the hall."

"It's like the sun decided to come out from behind the clouds and play."

Confused, Trinity inclined her head.

"This is the best news." Ryder slung an arm around her shoulders. "How soon can I help you move in?"

CHAPTER SIX

"We'd love for you to join us this evening." Wyatt slanted a glance at his fiancée before refocusing on Trinity.

Greer offered her an encouraging smile. "It's really a lot of fun."

Wyatt didn't wait for Trinity to answer, he just started talking. As Trinity listened to her brother, she repeatedly swallowed the *no* that kept wanting to form on her lips.

She didn't feel like dressing up. She'd spent the past three days either shopping for or moving items into her new place. Yesterday, Ryder had been there when some of the furniture she'd purchased had been delivered. They'd worked from early morning, stopping only to grab bites of leftover pizza.

Today, Ryder was working at the Grind. Labor Day weekend was, according to everyone she'd spoken with, a kind of last hurrah for the tourist season. Which meant Good Hope's premier coffee shop was hopping.

Wyatt and Greer had been a great help today, which only made it more difficult to turn down their offer. Though going to a bar on a Friday night wasn't the same as attending a party, she'd still have to clean up and change.

Wyatt's gaze fixed on her. "Greer and I would really like it if you'd join us tonight for karaoke at the Ding-A-Ling."

Trinity went for teasing. "You've got the wrong sister, Wy. It's Sage who loves singing karaoke."

"You can drive separately if you don't want to go with us." Wyatt's tone turned persuasive. "That way, you can leave early if you want."

Greer added her own perspective. "It'll be a good opportunity to mingle and get acquainted."

As far as persuasive arguments went, Greer had hit a home run. Liam had mentioned he thought being visible in the community was an important part of the position at Connections.

That, and not wanting to disappoint her brother and Greer, had Trinity giving in and agreeing to meet them at the bar.

She wasn't sure how late Ryder would be working tonight, or exactly what his plans were once he got off. The thought that he might enjoy a night of karaoke—or maybe it was that misery loved company—had her texting him.

Join me tonight. D-A-L.

Trinity decided if he showed up, spending the evening at a cowboy bar and listening to tone-deaf people sing karaoke might not be so painful.

Trinity had never worn the sleeveless red dress with the flirty hem with cowboy boots before, but when in Rome…

The second she stepped into the Ding-A-Ling, noise engulfed her. Friday night at the bar was a boisterous affair—voices, lots of voices, talking and laughing. Voices arguing about the position of a dart or calling for another round. Voices crooning off-key from the karaoke stage.

If Wyatt hadn't appeared in that moment and pulled her in for a big hug, she might have turned on those boot heels and headed back out the door.

Ryder texted he'd try to make it, which in her experience with men meant *probably not.*

Before she could consider another means of escape, Wyatt took her arm and maneuvered her through the crowd. "Greer got us a great table."

"Why are so many people here?" Trinity had to raise her voice to be heard above the crowd.

"Still tourist season." Wyatt gestured toward the platform. "And all-week karaoke has been drawing a crowd."

Greer sat at a four-top to the left of the stage. Her brother's fiancée looked relaxed in denim and a white shirt that opened at the neck. When the bank executive spotted her, a broad smile lifted her lips.

"I'm glad you could make it." Greer glanced around. "Wyatt and I love it here."

"It's..." Trinity considered what word to use. Noisy? Claustrophobic? Overwhelming? "Busy."

Greer nodded. "The guys have been pleased with the uptick in business."

The guys, Trinity knew from an article in the weekly newspaper, were Greer's brother David, construction company owner Kyle Kendrick and business executive Ethan Shaw.

"They're hoping to develop this entire area," Wyatt told Trinity.

"Not hoping. We're going to make it happen."

Trinity looked up at the handsome man with the black hair and gray eyes standing at the side of the table. In his dark pants and pinstriped cotton shirt, he seemed overdressed for the Ding-A-Ling crowd.

"Ethan." Wyatt rose to shake his hand. "It's good to see you. Have you met my sister?"

"I don't believe I've had the pleasure." Ethan gazed at her with obvious appreciation, while Wyatt performed the introductions. "You're Liam's new business partner."

Trinity wondered how he knew that, then remembered this was a small town. "I'll start seeing clients next week. I'm just waiting for my Wisconsin license to be issued."

Ethan grinned. "Katie Ruth left the waiting-for-license part out of her article in the Open Door."

Ah, yes, the online daily newsletter that kept residents of Good Hope up to date on all the latest news and gossip.

Greer gestured to the empty chair. "Won't you join us?"

Instead of immediately answering, Ethan scanned the bar as if making sure everyone was doing their job. "I can sit for five."

His gaze shifted to Wyatt and Trinity. "If I'm not intruding."

"Not at all," Trinity spoke for both of them. "One of the reasons I'm here is to get better acquainted with people in the community."

He smiled. "You couldn't have a better guide than Greer. She knows everyone."

"Ethan is also well-connected," Greer told Trinity. "The Shaw family were original settlers."

Ethan gave a pained look, as if he'd heard this fact repeated a thousand times. "How are you liking Good Hope?"

"Very well. I—" Trinity started when warm hands closed over her bare shoulders. Then her body recognized those magic fingers. She tilted her head back and smiled up at Ryder.

He'd come after all. Her gaze locked with his for a heartbeat, and she saw he wanted to kiss her. Or maybe that was only the reflection of her own desire in his dark eyes.

Ryder shifted his gaze to Ethan. "Sitting down on the job, are you, Shaw?"

"You know me." Ethan chuckled. "I'm not much of a worker."

Something in his tone told Trinity that these two men were not simply friends, but good friends. She didn't believe for a minute that Ethan was a slacker.

"What are you doing here?" Ethan cocked his head. "I didn't think you liked coming out when we have karaoke."

"Since you decided to have the sing-alongs every night this week as a last blast before Labor Day, my choices were to stay home or brave the noise."

Trinity didn't know what got into her. Truly, she didn't. "I'm in search of a duet partner."

Ethan lifted his hands. "Don't look at me."

"You should give it a try, Ethan," Greer urged. "Take a step outside your comfort zone. I wouldn't have been caught dead on a karaoke stage three months ago. Now I love it."

"Another time." Pushing back his chair, Ethan rose and punched Ryder's arm, then glanced at Trinity. "Nice to meet you. Good luck finding a partner."

Ryder held out his hand to Trinity. "She already has one."

She considered telling him she hadn't meant it. During the drive over, Trinity had vowed that Wyatt and Greer would have to drag her kicking and screaming onto the karaoke stage.

But Ryder had one thing right. He was her partner. When his hand closed over hers, warm and familiar, she rose to her feet.

"Knock 'em dead," Wyatt told her.

"Have fun," Greer urged.

As she and Ryder took their place in line behind a young man in a cowboy hat, Trinity felt a tingle of excitement.

"I didn't know you were into karaoke." Ryder leaned close to be heard. As he spoke, he stroked her palm with his thumb.

"I'm into doing things with you," she blurted.

The words might have been impulsive, but that didn't make them any less true.

She and her ex Miles had shared academic interests, and he'd challenged her intellectually, but looking back, she realized they hadn't engaged in many "couple" activities.

"Thank you for that." Ryder's eyes, dark and soft, settled on her as he trailed a finger down her cheek. "That's one of the nicest things you've said to me."

Trinity's lips tingled. She leaned close. Just when she thought the connection between them couldn't get any stronger, it—

"You're up."

The amused voice was like a splash of cold water. Trinity blinked and saw Oaklee grinning.

"What song do you want?" Oaklee, taking a page from the Ryder Goodhue bible, had gone all black this evening. Black pencil skirt and a black tee, coupled with her platinum and black hair, made for a sophisticated look.

"Oaklee! Nice to see you again. I didn't know you were a DJ."

"*Guest* DJ. It's my first time, but I'm pretty sure I'm awesome at this." Oaklee waved a hand at the karaoke machine. "What song?"

Trinity looked at Ryder, who only lifted his shoulders in a shrug. She realized too late they should have been discussing song choice instead of gazing into each other's eyes.

Oaklee cast a glance at the growing line behind them. "I can pick one for you."

"Perfect." Taking Trinity's hand, Ryder pulled her to the center of the stage.

"What if we don't know the song she chooses?" Trinity spoke in a hushed whisper, conscious of dozens of eyes on them.

Ryder grinned. "I guess everyone will get a good laugh."

Later that evening Oaklee keyed in the code and stepped into the quiet of the Good Hope Living Center. Though it was late, she knew the girls would still be up. And Oaklee knew just where she'd find them.

The fancy dining room was empty save for a round table for eight in the back where Gladys held court with Ruby and Katherine. Dominoes were spread over the table, but the three seemed to be more interested in wine and conversation than rolling the dice.

When Gladys spotted Oaklee weaving her way through the tables, her face brightened. In the months since Oaklee had arrived in Good Hope, she'd come to view Gladys as a mentor.

"There's our girl," Gladys called out and motioned Oaklee over. "She can settle this controversy."

Oaklee took a seat at the linen-clad table and inclined her head. "Controversy?"

Katherine sniffed. "More a difference of opinion."

"Between Katherine and Gladys." Ruby lifted her hands, palms facing Oaklee. "I'm steering clear of this battle."

"A battle. This sounds interesting." Oaklee leaned forward. After manning the karaoke machine all evening, it felt good to relax with friends.

"The issue concerns whether you can go out on a double." Gladys slanted a look at Katherine. "I say you can. Katherine insists you can't."

"We tried to find a list of rules, but came up empty." Ruby shrugged. "It's left us up the creek without a paddle."

A pained look crossed Katherine's face at the idiom.

"Hardly. Not when we can look up the answer online." Oaklee pulled out her phone, her thumbs flying. After reading what popped up, she shot Katherine a sympathetic look. "Sorry, Kate. You lost this battle. It says here you *can* go out on a double in dominoes."

Oaklee passed the phone around, giving each woman the opportunity to read the answer for herself. It shocked Oaklee that Gladys didn't gloat.

"Thank you, Oaklee." Gladys lifted one hand in an imperious gesture. "I don't know what we'd do without you."

The sentiment sent a rush of warmth coursing through Oaklee.

"How did it go tonight at the Ding-A-Ling?" Ruby asked. "Did you have fun?"

"I did." Oaklee expelled a happy breath. "The manager said she'd call me if they need someone to fill in again."

"It was good of you to help them out." Katherine took a sip of wine.

Oaklee quivered, feeling like a racehorse at the starting gate. She knew all three women would be interested in what she had to say and couldn't wait to share. She wished she could think of a way to make the telling more dramatic, but she was tired and it was late, so she gave it to them straight.

"Trinity and Ryder were at the bar tonight." Oaklee's words came out in a rush. "They sang a duet."

"Did they?" Gladys's lips curved, and her pale blue eyes gleamed. "That's very interesting."

Ruby paused from putting the dominoes back into their box and looked up. "What song?"

"Does it matter?" Gladys asked.

"It matters," Ruby insisted.

"*I Got You Babe*," Oaklee said. "Sonny and Cher."

Ruby sighed. "Did he hold her hand while they sang? Sonny always held Cher's hand."

"How would you know that?" Katherine asked.

"I watched their variety show." Ruby placed another domino into the box. "Back in the sixties."

"The seventies," Gladys and Katherine corrected at the same time, then looked at each other and chuckled.

"Ryder held her hand, and they gazed into each other's eyes." Oaklee sighed. "It was incredibly romantic."

"That's quality intel." Gladys nodded her approval.

"Start at the beginning," Ruby urged. "Give us the whole picture, not just a piece of the pie."

At Oaklee's startled look, Gladys smiled. "She's had pie on the brain all evening."

Ruby sighed heavily. "I could really use a piece of peach pie a la mode."

"I could really use a million dollars." Katherine's droll tone had Gladys snorting out a laugh. "The banks and kitchens are closed. Neither of us is getting what we want tonight."

"Start at the—"

"Beginning," Oaklee finished Ruby's sentence, then continued. "Trinity came in with Wyatt and Greer. Ryder arrived minutes later and sat at their table."

"A double date." Gladys's expression brightened even more. She tapped her long nails against the tabletop. "Anything else?"

"They got to the stage, but hadn't picked a song." Oaklee smiled. "I very generously offered to select one for them."

"You chose a romantic ballad." Gladys tapped her temple with an index finger. "Brilliant."

Pleasure coursed through Oaklee at the approval in Gladys's eyes. "Trinity left the bar with him. His arm was around her shoulders."

Gladys patted her arm. "You did fine work tonight, Oaklee. Yes, indeed, things are moving along nicely."

"What's the next step?" Oaklee asked, helping Ruby add the remaining dominoes to the box.

She knew there had to be a next step. Even though things appeared to be on track with Trinity and Ryder, Gladys's philosophy was that everyone could benefit from a little nudge—or shove—down the path to true love.

"I'm taking over from here." Gladys brought a glass of wine to her lips and took a sip.

Oaklee's eyes flew open. A tightness gripped her chest. "I'm off the team?"

"Pishposh. You're stuck with us, Miss Oaklee." Gladys patted her arm. "I'm simply saying that it's time for the master to step up to the plate."

"What are you going to do?" Katherine asked.

"You have a plan." Ruby pointed a finger at Gladys. "You always have a plan."

Setting down her glass, Gladys rested the back of one hand against her forehead in a melodramatic gesture. "Alas, my bosom friends, I believe it's time for me to see a counselor."

Ruby's brows drew together. "Whatever are you talking about?"

"Tomorrow, I'm going to call and make an appointment to see Dr. Trinity McConnell." Gladys's lips lifted in a sly smile. "It'll be a reconnaissance mission. She and I will speak of life and love. Instead of a normal counseling session, she'll be the one doing most of the talking, and I'll be asking the questions."

CHAPTER SEVEN

Wyatt sat across from Trinity at the dinette table he'd helped her unpack that morning. His reward—and hers—was fresh coffee and pastries.

After forking off a piece of kouign amann, her brother looked up. "I'm glad you came with us last night."

"I had fun." She couldn't help smiling, had in fact not quit smiling since she'd left Ryder's bed at the crack of dawn. His, because her bedroom furniture had yet to be delivered.

Picking up his coffee cup, Wyatt shot her a quizzical glance. "How did I not know my sister has such a good singing voice?"

Trinity had heard him utter that same sentiment last night. He wasn't the only one surprised. She curved her fingers around her own steaming cup and smiled at the memory of the startled look in Ryder's eyes. "*I Got You Babe* by Sonny and Cher is an easy song to sing. And it was familiar. Dad was always singing it to Mom."

Their parents had done silly, romantic things like that all the time. They'd not only sung to each other, they'd danced in the living room when a tune came on they both liked. They'd even held hands when out in public. When she'd been a teenager, she'd been mortified and yet touched by the closeness and love between them.

Wyatt chuckled and took a sip of coffee. "I remember neither Mom nor Dad has a particularly good voice."

"It didn't matter."

"No," Wyatt agreed. "Not at all."

"Ryder was no Sonny, but he turned in a respectable performance." Trinity's lips curved, remembering. "The crowd liked it."

The onlookers weren't the only ones. Trinity sighed. Despite the packed audience and the lights, there'd been something intimate about standing onstage and singing with Ryder.

"The words to the song are sweet." Even now, remembering how Ryder had taken her hand as their voices blended on the chorus had Trinity's heart swelling and unexpected tears stinging the backs of her eyes.

The enthusiastic applause had surprised them both. Oaklee had given them a big smile and two thumbs-up.

The evening hadn't ended there. They'd danced, shot pool and joined Wyatt and Greer in a game of darts.

Greer, Trinity discovered, was incredibly competitive and—

"I don't like to get in your business."

Trinity slowly lowered the cheese Danish to her plate. The serious look in her brother's eyes told her they were about to head down a road she didn't want to travel. "Then don't."

Wyatt ignored the warning. "You and Ryder."

She gritted her teeth, said nothing.

"You've been seeing a lot of him. Every day for almost three weeks."

Trinity fortified herself with a gulp of the extra-strong Ethiopian blend and waited for her brother to spit out whatever was chewing at him.

"I like Ryder. Don't get me wrong. He's a good guy. But are you sure it's wise to jump into a relationship so quickly?" Two lines of worry formed between Wyatt's brows. "It reminds me of when you met Miles. You went from acquaintances to married in a matter of months."

Having her actions questioned, even by a concerned brother, didn't sit well. Trinity thought about reminding Wyatt that his own relationship with Greer had gone from new-guy-in-town to engaged-and-planning-a-wedding in a nanosecond.

Trinity stifled the impulse. She didn't want to compare him and Greer to her and Miles. The situation between her brother and his fiancée was much less complicated than Trinity's relationship with her ex. For one thing, no children were involved.

Her reluctance to lash out didn't mean she'd tolerate Wyatt butting into her business.

"I enjoy Ryder's company. He enjoys mine. We have a connection, and we're enjoying getting better acquainted." Trinity heard her clipped tone and deliberately softened it. "I appreciate your concern, but this is my life, and it's up to me how much—or how little—to see him."

"I understand." Wyatt spread his hands out on the table. "I just don't want you to rush into anything and get hurt."

"I don't want to get hurt either, Wy." Trinity fought to keep her irritation under control. "You and I both know relationships don't come with guarantees. But without the willingness to take a chance, we close the door to the possibility of true intimacy."

Wyatt's brows remained drawn together as he considered her words. "Are you saying things are getting serious between you and Ryder?"

"What I'm saying is, for now, I'm leaving the door open."

"Do you think Trinity will stop by today?" Raven asked after they'd served the last person in a line that had seemed like it would never end.

Ryder looked up from where he was replenishing the pastries, surprised by the hopeful edge in the teen's voice. Trinity had mentioned that she and Raven had become friends, but he hadn't seen the connection...until now.

"I don't believe so." Ryder spoke matter-of-factly, hiding his own disappointment. "She's got furniture being delivered today and a party to attend tonight."

"That's a bummer."

The fact he couldn't spend any part of the day—or evening—with Trinity was very much a bummer. He wanted to be there with her, not simply because he enjoyed her company, but to help her with the move.

The living room and bedroom furniture were scheduled to be delivered between eight and five, with a dinette set coming this morning. Tonight, Trinity would celebrate the completion of the move with a "family" dinner at the home of Lynn Chapin and Steve Bloom. He'd been invited to attend as Trinity's date, but had had to decline. There was no way he could get away. Labor Day weekend was crazy, and he was short-staffed.

Ryder refused to leave high schoolers to run the shop, especially when they were all relatively inexperienced. His college student employees had already headed back to their respective universities, and with Cassie Slattery now in Green Bay, he didn't have an assistant manager. He'd find one eventually.

But hiring the right person, then training them, would take time. Being involved in the day-to-day of the Good Hope location allowed Ryder to understand the challenges his franchise owners and their managers faced in other states. This year, based on his experiences on the front lines, he'd upgraded training materials and provided the shops with scheduling software free of charge.

As Ryder placed the last pastry into the glass bake case and slid the door shut, he realized Raven was still standing there, staring at him.

Why wasn't she working? There were tables to bus and counters to wipe, along with a dozen other tasks.

Ryder opened his mouth to assign her a couple of those duties, when it struck him there might be more going on here. "Is everything okay?"

He wasn't prepared for the tears that filled Raven's eyes. She blinked them back, but he'd seen them, and there was a haunted look on her face.

"I dumped Jax." Raven blinked rapidly. "Trinity encouraged me to make the break."

Ryder was aware Raven had a boyfriend, since he'd been in a couple of times—a scruffy-looking boy with a sulky mouth and hard eyes.

He mentally brought up what he knew about Raven's home life. Mom worked full time at the Cherry Acres processing plant and cleaned houses on the side. No dad in the picture.

Now, she'd dumped her loser boyfriend.

She needs to speak with Trinity.

Even as the realization surfaced, Ryder reminded himself Trinity was busy with movers. He could keep Raven busy with work.

The sight of a bus tour pulling into the lot told him they were about to get slammed. There were two other employees on duty, in addition to him and Raven. To handle a bus tour, they needed all hands on deck.

With a heavy sigh, Raven moved to clear a table.

Ryder pulled out his phone and texted Trinity.

Raven needs to talk. Do you have time?

In answer, the phone in his hand rang.

"What's wrong?" Trinity asked without preamble.

Ryder watched the bus door open and the first of the group step out. "She dumped her boyfriend. She nearly started crying. She asked if you'd be by today, and I said no."

"Put her on the phone."

"Thank you. Hold on." With the phone in one hand, Ryder called to Raven, motioned her over. "Trinity wants to speak with you. Take my phone into the office."

"The bus group—"

"We can handle it." Waving her off, Ryder stepped behind the counter to take an order.

Minutes later, Raven returned, muttering something about lots of Chinese food.

Ryder didn't care what she ordered for lunch, he was just glad to see her clear-eyed and solid.

Working together, they tackled the bus tour crowd.

Trinity mulled over her conversation with Raven as she dressed for the upcoming evening. When she'd received Ryder's text, she'd worried Raven might be distraught. After a few minutes of listening, she'd realized Raven simply needed someone to affirm she'd done the right thing in dumping her abusive boyfriend.

She'd even gotten the girl to laugh by quoting Paris Geller from *Gilmore Girls*: "No men. Just lots and lots of Chinese food."

By the time Raven ended the call, alluding to some senior bus tour, the girl had seemed steady. Since it sounded as if things were crazy-busy at the Grind, Trinity hadn't asked to speak with Ryder. But she would thank him for giving Raven those few minutes to talk when she spoke with him next.

Right now, she had a dinner to attend. When she reached the Chapin house, Trinity was prepared for an evening of home cooking and conversation. Instead, she found herself stepping into a scene straight out of a movie.

An Irish linen tablecloth. A chandelier glittering overhead that competed with the warm glow of strategically placed candles. China in a pastoral pattern and crystal glasses glinting in the light.

With Wyatt on one side and Greer's brother Clay on the other, conversation over the meal—roast beef tenderloins with cognac butter and a carrot mash with a hint of tart cream—flowed easily.

"Your mother is a terrific cook," Trinity told Clay as they stood in the living room, enjoying after-dinner cocktails. "The meal was terrific. I'm not fond of oysters, but the appetizer with the bacon and the oyster on the half shell was amazing."

"My mother *coordinated* the meal," Clay clarified, a twinkle in his eye. "She has a cook who takes care of the details. That makes everyone happy."

Stella, Clay's date and the manager of a boutique in Sturgeon Bay, glanced pointedly at the Dresden clock on the mantel. "While this has been enjoyable, when you mentioned a family dinner, I didn't realize we'd be here all evening."

As Trinity had been seated next to Clay, she'd had ample opportunity to observe interactions between the couple. If she had to venture a guess, she'd say that Clay was more into the pretty brunette than Stella was into him.

"Just a few minutes more and we can leave." The principal spoke in a soothing tone, stroking a hand down her arm.

Trinity took a sip of her Autumn Serenade, the cocktail Wyatt's future mother-in-law had urged her to try. Maple syrup, peach brandy and dark rum came together in a sweet drink that packed a punch.

As a designated driver this evening, Wyatt had opted for club soda. Unlike many men, her brother hadn't whined about having to turn down the alcohol.

"You'll have to let me know when you're settled into your practice," Clay told Trinity. "I'd love to have you do an in-service for our staff."

At her questioning look, Clay added, "Liam managed to do one for us when he first arrived, but Connections expanded so rapidly his availability became limited."

"I love high school kids," Trinity told Clay. "Shoot me some dates and times, and we'll get it scheduled."

"I don't know how he does what he does." Stella shot a teasing glance in Clay's direction. "Teenagers drive me crazy."

"They can be a challenge," Trinity agreed.

Stella's brows pulled together. "You're what? Some sort of counselor?"

"I'm a clinical psychologist." Trinity sipped her drink. "I'll be joining Liam Gallagher at Connections."

Noticing Stella's blank expression, Trinity offered, "It's a psychological counseling clinic. I start on Tuesday."

In addition to her furniture arriving, the hard copy of her Wisconsin license had been delivered today via the USPS. Trinity was eager to get started and knew Liam was ready to begin sharing his caseload with her.

They'd agreed she would start as a nonequity partner with the option to buy in down the road. Trinity wanted some history with Liam before she—metaphorically speaking—got fully in bed with him.

Her past had taught her that something could look like a solid deal on the surface, but underneath there could be cracks, ones that didn't show up until later. Her marriage had been one such instance. She'd jumped in with both feet when she should have dipped in a toe.

If she'd spent more time with not only Miles, but also with his daughters, she might have spotted the fissures. But she'd been so confident in her decision-making that she'd ignored everyone's advice and jumped in feet first.

"To be honest, I think people use psychology as an excuse."

Trinity jerked her attention back to Stella.

The brunette, her short red dress showing curves in all the right places, waved a perfectly manicured hand. "They're allowed to be jerks because their mommy didn't love them or something."

Trinity thought of how the therapists she'd seen after her

mother died had helped her work through her abandonment issues. Another time, Trinity might have continued the conversation in the hopes of opening Stella's eyes to the benefits of counseling, but her brother and Greer strolled up.

"Did Trinity tell you she found a place to live?" Wyatt asked Clay.

"No." Clay brightened. "Did you end up going with an apartment or a house?"

"A condo. In the big red barn on the edge of Good Hope."

"A barndo." Clay grinned wide. "Congrats."

"It's only minutes from Connections." Trinity took another sip of her cocktail. "If there were sidewalks alongside the highway, I could walk to work."

"You know Ryder, right?" Clay asked. "He lives there, too."

"Have you been living under a rock?" Greer teased. "Ryder and Trinity have been dating for weeks."

Out of the corner of her eye, Trinity saw Cade and Marigold Rallis stroll up.

"The duet you did at the Ding-A-Ling last night rocked." Marigold, chic in black, with a mass of blond curls tumbled around her shoulders, thumped her hand over her heart. "Your rendition was über-romantic. It helped that Ryder has a decent voice, and yours is absolutely gorgeous."

"I told her the same thing," Wyatt said. "Except for the romantic part."

"Thank you for the kind words." Trinity placed a hand on Marigold's arm. "Sincerely. That was my first time doing any sort of karaoke, and I admit I was intimidated. Onstage, Ryder assured me the worst that could happen was everyone would laugh."

Marigold smiled and shook her head. "There's a comforting thought."

Stella inclined her head. "You're dating Ryder?"

Something in the woman's tone had Trinity hesitating for just a second. "Yes, I am."

"Been there, done that." Stella's narrowed gaze locked on Trinity. "Take my advice and be careful. You can't rely on him. I mean, he isn't even here with you tonight."

"He's working." Trinity kept a smile on her lips. She reminded herself it didn't matter what Stella or anyone else thought. All that mattered was what *she* thought. What *she* knew.

Still, the rest of the evening, the warning rattled around in her head. Even a second Autumn Serenade couldn't completely quell the uneasy feeling in the pit of Trinity's stomach.

CHAPTER EIGHT

By the time the following Saturday night rolled around, Stella's ridiculous warning was a distant memory. On Labor Day, Trinity and Ryder had celebrated the holiday with family and friends at Beck and Ami Cross's backyard barbecue.

Trinity had spent her days at Connections and her nights in her new home. Ryder came by nearly every evening.

He reported Raven seemed happier and appeared to be adjusting to her new school/work schedule.

On Saturday, Ryder treated Trinity to dinner at Sombreros, a Mexican restaurant in Egg Harbor.

He smiled at her as the server cleared away their dinner dishes. "I keep forgetting to thank you for speaking with Raven last Saturday."

"I was happy to do it." With his warm brown eyes on her and a delicious margarita in hand, Trinity couldn't recall the last time she'd been this content.

"You must be one terrific therapist, because when she returned from speaking with you, she didn't seem upset at all." He chuckled. "She was even hungry for Chinese food."

Trinity's burst of laughter had the couple in the next booth turning around.

"*Gilmore Girls*," she told Ryder.

A confused smile hovered on his lips. "You lost me."

"It was a quote from the television series." Trinity went on to explain.

Ryder lifted his hands. "Hey, whatever works, I say…and it obviously worked."

"Raven is a good kid." Trinity moved the ice around in her glass with a stir stick. "She has so much potential. I love it that underneath all the swagger is a kind heart."

"You're good with teens." Ryder lifted his bottle of beer to his lips and studied her. "It's a talent and a gift."

"I don't know about that…" Trinity thought of Miles's daughters.

"No need to be modest." He paused when the server appeared to set down the fried ice cream they'd decided to share.

"I'm not being modest. If I was a talent with teens, I'd have been able to build a healthy relationship with my stepdaughters."

Ryder's spoon, filled with ice cream, stopped halfway to his mouth. "You mentioned something about being divorced that night in Chicago. I didn't realize there were children involved."

"Three girls. They were fourteen, twelve and ten when Miles and I took the plunge."

"Wow. Not little kids." Ryder's eyes sought hers. "How old is Miles?"

"He'd just turned forty-five when we married."

"And you were…"

"I was twenty-three."

Something flickered in Ryder's dark eyes. "How long had he been divorced?"

"He was a widower. And a professor at the university I attended."

"That's quite a gap, both in age and life experience."

"It didn't seem so much at the time." Trinity lifted a shoulder, let it drop. "I thought I was ready, that he was ready. I didn't see he was still grieving, as were the girls. His wife hadn't been dead for even a year. There are many things I'd do differently now. At the time, whatever I tried only seemed to make the situation worse."

"I can't imagine becoming an instant parent to three nearly grown girls." He finished off the ice cream on his spoon, took another spoonful. "Are you still in touch with the girls?"

"Two are in college, and the youngest graduated from high school this spring. I made a few attempts to contact them after their dad and I split." Trinity felt a familiar sense of failure wash over her. "But I'd been a part of their lives for such a short time, and we never really connected."

"You were young." Ryder reached across the table, covered her hand with his. "How you were then, what you knew then, isn't you now."

She turned her hand over and linked her fingers with his. "Anyone ever tell you that you're a great guy?"

His fingers tightened on hers. He opened his mouth just as his phone rang.

"Hold that thought." He flashed a smile as he picked up the phone, his finger poised to decline the call until he appeared to notice the screen. "Hey, what's up?"

After listening for a second, his expression went blank. "Hold on a minute. It's too noisy in here."

Ryder met Trinity's curious look with unreadable eyes. "I need to take this. I'll be back in a minute."

Without waiting for a response, he strode off with the phone pressed against his ear.

By the time he returned, one minute had stretched into fifteen. While she waited, Trinity finished off the fried ice cream. Either that, or let it melt.

She offered an apologetic smile when he returned. "I was forced to eat it all."

"What? Oh." He waved a dismissive hand. "Let's go."

"What's wrong? Bad news?"

He tossed several bills on the table. "I'll tell you once we get to the truck."

Trinity's mind raced. She didn't know much about his parents and brother, only that they lived out of state. She waited until they were settled in the cab of the truck to ask. "Is it one of your parents?"

Ryder leaned forward and rested his head against the steering wheel, seeming to fight for control.

Alarm skittered up Trinity's spine. She placed a light hand on his back. "Take all the time you need."

After several long moments, he drew a shuddering breath and sat up, his face a blank mask. "The call was from an attorney in Portland. He'd been trying to reach me. My phone security must have flagged his calls as spam."

"How did he finally get through?" *Keep him talking,* Trinity thought. *Give him time to steady.*

"He called from Jenna's phone. I told you about her." Ryder closed his eyes for a moment. When he opened them, she saw the pain and sorrow.

Trinity tried to recall the little she knew. "Jenna was an old friend."

"We dated during our freshman year at Stanford." His eyes swarmed with memories. "We were close back then. She'd had a horrible home life and suffered with depression and anxiety because of it. Stanford ended up not being a good fit. She transferred to a smaller school after that first year."

Ryder paused, kept his gaze straight ahead as he steadied himself. "We stayed in touch. Most recently, she's lived and worked in Portland. Whenever I'd go to the West Coast, we'd get together. Have dinner. Catch up."

"Was she in an accident?" Trinity gently probed when he didn't continue, still unsure why an attorney would be calling Ryder.

"Jenna is dead."

Trinity inhaled sharply, bringing a hand to her throat. "I'm so sorry. What happened?"

"An overdose of pills and alcohol."

Reaching over, Trinity took his hand, found it ice-cold. "Suicide?"

Ryder shook his head. "Jenna wouldn't have killed herself."

"You said she suffered from anxiety and depression. Were the drugs found in her system related to that?"

"I didn't ask." Ryder pulled his hand from hers, and it trembled when he ran it through his hair. "The guy, the attorney, simply said the combination of drugs and alcohol killed her."

"I'm so sorry," she said again.

"It can't be suicide." Ryder massaged his forehead. "I just saw her. She was in good spirits. Her life was on track."

Trinity kept her voice low and soothing. "It's not always easy to see or to know what's going on in someone's head."

"Jenna would not have killed herself." His fierce tone brooked no argument.

"Why did the attorney call you?"

"He's the executor of her estate." Ryder blew out a breath. "Apparently, she left everything to me."

"Really?" Surprise had Trinity's voice rising. "Not to her family?"

"She was an only child and had been estranged from her parents as long as I'd known her." Ryder's dark eyes met hers. "The attorney, he said something else, but it can't be. That part has to be some kind of mistake."

"What did he say?"

"He said he was determined to reach me because of the child."

Ryder gulped. "He said with Jenna's death, I became our daughter's sole guardian."

Trinity froze. Was she hallucinating? She blinked. Blinked again.

Ryder still sat before her, a dazed look on his face.

"You-you and Jenna had a child?" she stammered.

He shook his head. "We didn't have a child. That's what is so crazy."

"But there is a child."

His shoulders lifted and dropped. "Apparently."

"Jenna never told you she was pregnant with your baby?"

"No."

At her look of disbelief, he turned strident. "We were friends. I've seen her dozens of times over the years. She never once mentioned having a daughter, much less that child being mine."

"You're right," she soothed. "This isn't making sense. It's as if a big piece of the puzzle is missing."

He slumped back against the seat. "Tell me about it."

"What are you going to do?"

"I'm going to go to Portland. Find the missing puzzle piece and get this mess straightened out." He searched her eyes, but she wasn't sure what he was looking for. "Jenna would never have kept my child from me."

There was a note of pleading in his voice. Trinity wasn't certain who he was trying to convince, himself or her. Wanting to comfort him, she wrapped her arms around him.

"I can't believe she's dead." His voice broke before he buried his face against her neck.

When his body began to shake, Trinity tightened her hold on him and stroked his soft, wavy hair. "It will be okay."

She spoke with confidence, wanting to believe it.

Inside, she wasn't so sure.

~

Monday morning, Ryder strode into the Portland office of Jerome Widby, Esquire. He'd spent fifteen endless minutes waiting for the attorney to finish the call he was on before the receptionist ushered him in.

The office reminded Ryder of a dozen other attorney offices, with rows of built-in bookcases and a massive desk with a polished cherrywood finish.

Jerome, a balding man somewhere in his late forties, rounded the desk, holding out one hand. "Mr. Goodhue, I'm happy you were able to get here so quickly."

"I didn't ask about a funeral or memorial service." Ryder shook the man's hand. "Your call was so unexpected, I—"

"Once the coroner determined the death was a result of an unintentional overdose, Ms. Swanson was cremated per the instructions in her will. I have her ashes and will be providing those to you."

"She's already been cremated." Ryder frowned. "When did she pass away?"

"Two weeks ago." Instead of taking a seat behind his monster desk, Jerome gestured to a sitting area where a love seat and two chairs were arranged for conversation.

Ryder sat on the love seat, and Jerome took the nearest chair.

"It took time to track you down." Jerome leaned forward. "Thankfully, Ryder Goodhue isn't a common name. And then there was the phone snafu."

Ryder waved that away as old news. "You mentioned Jenna died because of an overdose of pills and alcohol."

"That's correct. The coroner has ruled the cause of Ms. Swanson's death as an unintentional overdose."

Ryder expelled a breath he hadn't realized he was holding. "It had to have been unintentional. She'd never have killed herself. I saw Jenna recently, and she was in high spirits. She'd started a new project at work and was super excited about—"

When Jerome's eyes filled with sympathy, Ryder realized he was rambling and stopped.

"Yes, well..." The attorney steepled his fingers. "About the child."

Unease crawled up Ryder's spine. This was the part that had had him grabbing the first flight he could get to Portland. "Yes. Tell me about the child."

"Her mother's death has been, as you can imagine, very difficult on her." Behind his tortoiseshell glasses, sympathy flickered in Jerome's blue eyes.

A child. Jenna had a child. One she never mentioned.

When his thoughts threatened to overwhelm him, Ryder reined them in. He needed to pay attention and listen. There had to be a logical explanation.

"Zoe is eleven. She's in temporary foster care. It's why we were eager to locate you."

Ryder nodded. *Eleven*. He tried to do the math in his head, but found it too difficult to focus.

How many times had he met with Jenna when he was in town? Too many to recall. Not once during the past decade had she mentioned a daughter.

His daughter?

"...birth certificate."

Ryder blinked and pulled his attention back to the conversation. He had questions, and this was his best opportunity to get those questions answered. "You have Zoe's birth certificate?"

"Indeed, I do. As well as her medical, dental and school records."

For the first time, Ryder noticed a folder on the glass-topped coffee table.

Jerome flipped it open and pulled out the certificate.

Ryder scanned the document. Listed on the certificate under father was his name and date of birth. Jenna had even gotten his place of birth—Good Hope, Wisconsin—correct.

Zoe, at eight pounds, five ounces, had been born on—

Ryder's brows pulled together. This math wasn't difficult. Not now that he had the exact date of birth. The last time he and Jenna had been intimate had been well over a year before Zoe's birth.

She isn't mine.

Ryder breathed out a relieved breath at the thought. Even if he was listed on the birth certificate, a simple DNA test would quickly clear up the matter.

Before he could say a word, Jerome spoke. "I realize you haven't been a part of Zoe's life."

"No. I haven't. I—"

"An attorney representing Jenna's father has been in contact with me."

Ryder froze.

Jenna's dad. City councilman. Church elder. Child abuser.

The memory of Jenna's tear-streaked face as she'd confided how that monster had molested her from the age of seven had Ryder's hands clenching into fists.

In his mind, her mother had been equally to blame. Jenna had told Ryder that when she'd gathered the courage to tell her mom what was happening, the woman had accused her of making up stories. With her father being a big deal in their home community, Jenna had seen no way out.

"His interest surprises me." Ryder managed to keep his voice even. "Jenna and her parents were estranged for years."

"I know. It's very sad." Jerome shook his head. "Apparently, Mr. Swanson kept tabs on his daughter, hoping one day they'd be able to reconcile. You know Jenna had mental health issues."

Jerome's hushed tone had Ryder stiffening.

"Jenna's depression and anxiety were under control for years," Ryder said. In his mind, Jenna had done remarkably well, considering she'd been betrayed by adults who were supposed to be her protectors.

"I wouldn't know about that."

"You didn't know her?" Ryder couldn't keep the surprise from his voice.

"I didn't. She worked with one of my associates on her will, but he left the group last month." Jerome glanced back to the papers. "Upon learning of his daughter's death, Mr. Swanson contacted his attorney, who contacted me. Should you not be interested in asserting your parental rights, the Swansons are willing—eager, in fact—to bring Zoe into their home and act as her guardians."

Ryder thought of Jenna. This was her daughter.

Who Zoe's biological father was didn't matter. Ryder's name was the one Jenna had placed on the birth certificate. He was the person Jenna had trusted to take care of her child should anything happen to her.

Any thoughts he'd had of asking for a DNA test disappeared. What was the point? Ryder already knew he couldn't be Zoe's biological father.

For a second, Ryder wondered who *was* Zoe's dad. A college classmate of Jenna? A neighbor? A guy she'd met casually and never seen again?

Why hadn't she told that man she was having a baby? And why hadn't she put *his* name on the birth certificate? It was pointless to speculate. With Jenna gone, there was no way Ryder would ever know.

Why hadn't she discussed this with him? Not once had she mentioned she had a child, nor asked if he'd be willing to step in to care for the child if something happened to her. Ryder wasn't sure how he'd have responded to such a request, but at least he'd have had the opportunity to ask questions and get answers.

He couldn't search for those answers now without putting Zoe's future at risk.

One thing was certain. If Jenna's father took that young girl into his home, another child would be victimized.

Not on my watch.

"Mr. Goodhue." Jerome cleared his throat as the silence lengthened. "What would you like me to tell Mr. Swanson?"

Ryder set his jaw. "Tell him Zoe is going home with her father."

CHAPTER NINE

Trinity was tempted not to answer when her phone rang Monday night and she saw Ryder's name on the screen. Considering she'd been wondering all day what he found out, her hesitation made no sense.

"How are you?" she asked in lieu of a greeting.

"Overwhelmed."

Grief underscored the word. Trinity waited for him to elaborate, but was forced to prompt him. "What did you find out?"

He hesitated for so long she wondered if the call had dropped. Then she heard him clear his throat. "It appears I have a daughter. Zoe is eleven."

Trinity expelled the breath she hadn't realized she'd been holding. Memories of the tears, tantrums, and tension that had been hallmarks of Miles's daughters assaulted her brain. Miles hadn't wanted to admit there was an issue, and no matter what she had tried on her end, nothing worked.

Focus on Ryder, she told herself. "Have you met her?"

"Tomorrow. The social worker felt it best to wait until morning."

Trinity sat back in the overstuffed chair, ignoring the glass of wine she'd just poured. "Where is she now?"

"She's in temporary foster care."

Trinity's heart went out to the child. Losing her mom unexpectedly, then being forced into an unfamiliar setting… She only hoped the home was a good one. "She'll be happy to see you."

Ryder didn't respond for several long seconds. "I'm a stranger. I don't even know what to say when I see her."

She heard the uncertainty in his voice, and her heart swelled with compassion.

"I could, maybe," Trinity hesitated, "give you some tips."

"I'll take any you have to offer." Once again, he cleared his throat. "Like, what do I say if she asks where I've been and why I haven't been involved in her life?"

"You tell her the truth. Answer her questions honestly. Tell her you didn't know about her, that her mom chose not to share that information with you. She must have had a good reason, though you don't know what it was."

"Okay." For a long moment, the only sound was his uneven breathing. "I can do that."

"What else?" she prompted when the silence lengthened once again.

"What if she doesn't want to come with me? Like I said, I'm a stranger."

"You're also her father," Trinity gently reminded him. "While you need to give her choices whenever you can, not coming with you isn't an option. Unless there's someone else—"

"There's no one else." He snapped the words, then expelled a ragged breath. "I'm sorry. This is…difficult."

She tightened her fingers around the phone. "If there's anything else I can do from here to help, all you have to do is ask."

"There is something but…no, I can figure that out once we're back in Good Hope."

"Ryder." Trinity forced a light tone. "I really do want to help. You should take advantage of my willingness. Who knows how long it will last?"

When silence was the only response, she gave an awkward laugh. Her attempt at a joke had clearly fallen flat.

"I've got two bedrooms at my place, but I've been using one as an office," he murmured.

She sensed he was thinking aloud rather than speaking to her.

"Zoe and I will fly back on Friday," he continued. "We'll stay here in a hotel suite until then. That will give us a chance to get acquainted and time to go through Jenna's townhouse."

Trinity pictured the scene. Deciding what to ship, what to discard. The week would be a difficult—and emotional—one for both of them. By the time Ryder returned to Good Hope, the last thing he'd feel like doing would be changing an office into a girl's bedroom.

"I can't guarantee my decorating skills, but I'd be willing to make your office into a bedroom for Zoe."

"You'd do that for me?" Relief washed through his words.

"For you and for...your child." This time, it was Trinity's turn to clear her throat. "A girl that age will need a space that feels like her own."

"Whatever it costs, I'll pay. Just have them send—"

"Don't worry. I know where to find you. And your money."

He laughed.

The lightness of the sound had Trinity smiling. She would help him. She'd do the same for any friend. Perhaps she'd enlist Wyatt to help with the furniture.

"Thank you, Trinity. You don't how much this means to me." The warmth in his voice arrowed straight to her heart. "I wish you were here with me."

"You'll do just fine," she assured him.

Somehow, Trinity made it through the rest of the conversation, which ended with his promise to call her tomorrow.

As soon as they hung up, she dropped the phone to her lap and found herself blinking back tears. This overwhelming sense of sadness made no sense. Then again, how many times had she told clients that feelings don't have to make sense?

It might have been early days for her and Ryder's relationship, yet she'd loved him. Underlying the intense connection had been the flickering promise of more.

Her grief wasn't for a woman she hadn't known. Nor for a little girl left without a mother. It was for a relationship that would never bear fruit.

Trinity admired Ryder for taking responsibility for a child he hadn't known existed. Every one of the men her mother had dated had done everything possible to shirk their responsibilities.

Not Ryder.

No, he was good and decent and committed to doing the right thing. Even if that meant becoming an instant father and raising a child who was a stranger.

Ryder might be panicking, but he had good instincts. With a little encouragement and direction, he and Zoe would soon be on solid footing.

Trinity would follow through with her offer to help. She would be a good friend and neighbor to both him and Zoe.

What she wouldn't be was Ryder's girlfriend. There would be no more dates or lovemaking. No daydreams of a future together. This decision was as much for his and Zoe's benefit as for her own.

Ryder and his daughter needed to grieve for the woman they'd both loved and become a family. And this time, she was smart enough to know they needed to travel the road without an outsider in the middle.

~

"Is this where you want the bed?" Wyatt slanted a glance at his sister.

Hands on hips, Trinity eyed the bed's position in the office-turned-bedroom and smiled. "That's perfect. Being against the wall allows more room for the study area."

Ryder had given her carte blanche in terms of decorating. Though realizing no two tweens were alike, Trinity had taken Hadley Chapin and her ten-year-old daughter with her when shopping for furniture.

The desk they'd chosen, white with sawhorse-type legs, had a shelf underneath with space for books or personal items. At Trinity's direction, Wyatt had pushed the bed against the wall, like a daybed. A vibrant striped rug in black, teal and white added a bright splash of color to the small room.

"I hope she likes it." Trinity would have killed for a room like this when she'd been eleven. She'd been a foster kid then, shuttled from one home to another, her clothes traveling with her in a garbage bag. "It's got a fun vibe without being too young. If she likes frilly, girly stuff, those touches will be easy to add."

Wyatt moved to her side. "Are you thinking what I'm thinking?"

Something in his low voice hit a chord.

"She's lucky." Trinity knew the truth of the words. "If she didn't have Ryder—"

"She'd be dumped in the system."

"It won't be easy for them," Trinity mused.

"No, but Ryder has you." Wyatt clapped a hand on her shoulder. "You'll be a great resource."

"I won't date him anymore."

At Wyatt's astonished look, Trinity quickly added, "I'll be his friend. That's it."

Understanding filled Wyatt's brown eyes. "Because of Zoe."

Trinity leaned over and adjusted a round throw pillow on the bed.

"I could say Ryder isn't Miles." Wyatt's offhand tone mirrored his shrug. "But with you and Ryder's relationship being so new, and if you were considering pulling back anyway, this is a good time."

The ring tone that split the air came as a welcome relief.

"Hey, Ryder." Trinity's voice might be calm, but her heart kicked into overdrive.

"How are you?"

"The room is ready."

"I can't tell you how much I appreciate all you've done."

"That's what friends are for." Trinity kept her tone light. "See you Friday."

"Sounds like you're busy, so I won't keep you, but thanks again. For everything." He lowered his voice as if not wanting to be overheard. "I'm really looking forward to seeing you."

The sentiment, softly spoken, wrapped itself around her heart and wouldn't let go. "Me, too."

Trinity slipped the phone back into her pocket and met her brother's assessing gaze. She lifted her hands. "What?"

"Nothing. I need to get going. Greer will be waiting." He moved to her, his arms sliding around her in a brotherly hug.

Their parents were big on hugs. It had taken both Trinity and Wyatt months before they would accept the comfort they'd offered.

Trinity closed her eyes briefly, then stepped back. "I hope your new fiancée knows how lucky she is to have you."

"I'm the lucky one."

She gave a quick nod, not trusting her voice. By the time they reached the door, Trinity had her emotions under firm control.

"Make sure to tell Greer thanks for lending you out to me for the day."

He smiled. "She'd have been here pitching in, but she had a bunch of stuff she wanted to review with Jeremy."

"Bunch of stuff." She flashed him a teasing smile. "Your vocabulary has definitely taken a nose dive."

"Brat." Wyatt playfully tugged her hair before his expression turned serious. "Remember. You're the one who knows what's best for you."

"Don't worry about me, big brother. I've got this under control."

~

Zoe hopped out of Ryder's truck and turned to him with a startled look. "You live in a barn?"

The question confirmed what Ryder had suspected. She'd tuned him out on the drive from Green Bay to Good Hope. Though Zoe pretended to be listening, the earbuds stuck in her ears had made him wonder. The fact it had been a long day—heck, an endless week—had him cutting her some slack.

"It's a barn that's been renovated into condominiums. The units are called barndominiums. It's a goofy name, but there you go." Ryder grabbed her large suitcase and his travel-size one from the trunk. "Three units on the main floor and three upstairs."

She surveyed the structure with blue eyes that held a profound sadness. She was tall for eleven and rail-thin with teeth that seemed too big for her narrow face. Her resemblance to Jenna had had his heart lurching when he'd first seen her.

Ryder had quickly discovered Zoe was soft-spoken, but not shy, strong-willed but not difficult. Other than that, he didn't know her any better than when they'd first met Tuesday morning.

The meet had been awkward, feeling as if they were two boxers circling in a ring, sizing each other up, both hesitant to make the first move.

He'd been relieved—okay, and a little disappointed—that on

both legs of their flight from Portland, Zoe hadn't wanted to talk. She'd had her nose in a book the entire time they were in the air.

The earbuds had gone in the second they'd picked up his truck in the Green Bay airport's long-term lot. Now, they were home. Their new life together would begin.

Her suitcase felt as if she'd loaded it with rocks, but he reminded himself this bag carried all of Zoe's worldly possessions. He'd arranged for Jenna's personal stuff—items he thought Zoe might one day want—to be shipped back.

Ryder set the bags down outside the front entrance, swiped his card and turned to Zoe. He offered the girl a friendly smile. "If you could hold the door open, I'd appreciate it."

She did as he asked, stepping back to give him—and the suitcases—the space needed to get inside.

Once inside the soaring entryway, Zoe's gaze was drawn upward. She studied the beams, the ornate staircase and the large pendant light with patches of square and rectangular shapes.

"It's like a wrought-iron work of art." Ryder let his own gaze linger. "The patchwork design is perfect for this lobby. Notice how you don't really see the interior lights?"

"Which way?"

For a second, Ryder was confused, thinking she was referring to the light. Until he realized she was asking about his unit. "This floor. First one on the right."

He'd leaned over to retrieve their suitcases when the exterior door opened behind them.

Ryder's breath caught at the sight of Trinity. Even dressed simply in jeans, a sleeveless shirt and hair pulled back in a tail, she was gorgeous. Her arms were wrapped around several grocery sacks, while she kept the door open with one foot.

Just seeing her had a weight lifting from his shoulders. He rushed over and held out his hands. "Let me help."

"I've got them." Despite the protest, Trinity let him lift two of the sacks from her arms.

Ryder turned to Zoe, who studied them with assessing blue eyes. “Zoe, would you mind holding Trinity’s door open for her? She lives just down the hall.”

Zoe frowned. “What about my suitcase?”

“You can leave it,” Ryder instructed. “It’ll be safe.”

Conscious of Zoe’s scrutiny, Ryder resisted telling Trinity how much he’d missed her and how glad he was to see her. Seeing her reminded him just how much he longed for things to get back to some semblance of normalcy.

Obligingly, Zoe made the short trek down the hall in the direction Ryder indicated.

Zoe turned the handle, looked back. “It’s locked.”

Juggling the sacks she still held, Trinity unlocked the door and pushed it slightly ajar with her hip.

Zoe returned Trinity’s smile and held the door open wide.

Trinity placed her sacks on the counter, then slanted a glance at Ryder. “You can put those beside mine.”

“If you ever need help with groceries or anything, don’t be shy about asking.” Ryder gestured to Zoe. “We want to be good neighbors, don’t we, Zoe?”

“I like to help.” Zoe gave a jerky nod. “My mom always said we should be kind and help others.”

Trinity placed a hand on the child’s shoulder. “You mother sounds like a compassionate woman.”

The sudden sheen in Zoe’s eyes had Ryder tensing.

“Well, thanks again for your help.” Trinity extended her hand to Zoe and offered a friendly smile. “I’m Trinity McConnell.”

After several heartbeats, the child took her hand. “Zoe Swanson.”

“Zoe, that’s a pretty name.”

“Thank you.” Zoe’s gaze dropped to her bright red flip-flops. “My mommy chose it for me. She’s dead.”

CHAPTER TEN

Trinity took a long look at Zoe. The girl put up a good front, but the paleness of her skin and the haunted look in her eyes said she was hanging on to control by a fingernail.

"I'm sorry about your mother." Trinity spoke in a low tone designed to comfort and soothe.

"Why are you sorry?" Zoe's head jerked up. "You didn't know her. She was the best, and now she's gone. You don't know anything about her."

Ryder's brows slammed together at the girl's words.

Trinity didn't flinch.

"You're right." Trinity kept her gaze firmly focused on the child and her tone sympathetic. "I didn't know her. I'm still very sorry for your loss. I lost my mother when I was young, and it made me very sad."

Zoe stilled. "What about your father?"

"I never knew who he was."

"I never knew who mine was either." Zoe slanted a glance in Ryder's direction. "He says he didn't know he had a daughter. I'm not sure I believe him."

Trinity hid a smile at the child's almost prim tone.

Ryder opened his mouth, then shut it as if realizing words weren't enough. Trust took time.

"I've only known your dad a short time, but he strikes me as the kind of man who'd have been in your life if he'd known about you."

"Maybe." Zoe lifted a thin shoulder, then let it drop before turning to Ryder. "I'm tired."

"We can get better acquainted another time." Trinity offered Zoe a smile. "It was nice meeting you."

Trinity turned, but Ryder reached out and touched her arm. A simple brush of fingers that sent her heart into overdrive.

"Won't you come with us for a few minutes? It'll be nice for you to show Zoe what you did with her room."

Even as Trinity shook her head, Zoe's blue eyes filled with suspicion.

"While your dad was in Portland, I changed his office into a bedroom for you." Trinity kept her voice light. "I hope you like it, but if you don't, it'll be easy to change."

Those assessing eyes narrowed. "Are you his girlfriend?"

"Your father and I are friends. Now we're neighbors," Trinity added. "I'm new to Good Hope. He's made me feel welcome."

Out of the corner of her eye, Trinity saw Ryder open his mouth, then close it. She could tell he didn't agree with her description of their relationship. In time, he'd see that keeping things at the friend level would be for the best.

"I took a ten-year-old girl, Brynn Chapin, and her mom with me when I went shopping." Trinity chatted with Zoe as Ryder paused to pick up the luggage in the hallway. "Though Brynn is slightly younger than you, she had definite opinions on a couple of my suggestions."

Trinity smiled, recalling how Brynn had made a gagging noise at one of the possibilities.

Ryder's condo was identical to hers. Same open floor plan. Same great room with stone fireplace. A comfortable sofa, two chairs and accessories added to the warm, homey feel. A mission-style table separated the eating area from the great room.

"It's small." Zoe flopped down on the sofa as if her legs were no longer capable of holding her.

"Big enough." Ryder shrugged. "Two bedrooms. Two baths. We'll each have our own."

"Let's check out the bedroom," Trinity said. "Then I'll leave and let the two of you relax and get settled. I'm like you, Zoe. Traveling wipes me out."

Trinity could read the child's body language. This wasn't the life Zoe would have chosen for herself, a new school and an unfamiliar community. Worst of all, a life without her mother.

In time, Zoe would realize she was lucky to have Ryder in her corner, a man willing to raise a child he hadn't known existed. Trinity's own past had shown her that without a responsible parent in your corner, life could be very, very bad.

Ryder was someone who would do the best he could to give his daughter a happy life.

Ryder hefted Zoe's suitcase from where he'd just set it. "I'll put this in your bedroom. I can help you unpack?"

Zoe shook her head, her long blond hair falling forward, screening her face from view. "I want to do it myself."

Ryder glanced at Trinity, who gave a slight nod.

"Sure. There should be everything you need in the bathroom. Towels, washcloths, soap. Even shampoo." Ryder's tone turned hearty. "If you can't find what you need, just ask."

He was babbling, Trinity realized, something she'd never heard him do.

In seconds, Zoe stood wide-eyed in her new room. Her gaze lingered on the desk, moved to the fluffy rug, then to the bed.

"Th-thank you," Zoe stammered, her gaze shifting to Trinity. "This is nice."

"You're very welcome. It was my pleasure." Trinity felt a lump form in her throat. The girl looked so young and forlorn standing there in her striped side-knotted tee and leggings. "You know where I live. I hope you'll stop over."

Zoe nodded, then glanced back at her feet. Tears flooded her blue eyes. "I'll never be able to go home again."

It sounded as if the child had enjoyed a warm and loving relationship with her mother. While that closeness would make this loss more profound, it also meant that Zoe had been given a good foundation that would help her navigate the difficult days ahead.

Going with her gut, Trinity stepped forward, wrapped her arms around the child. "It will be okay."

Zoe leaned into the embrace and spoke through a voice thick with tears. "I miss her so much."

"You loved her, and she loved you." Trinity stroked the girl's silky hair. "I think she'd be happy to know that you're safe with your dad."

"I was scared where they put me," the girl admitted. "I didn't want to stay there, but I had nowhere to go."

"You don't have to worry anymore." Trinity felt the wetness of the girl's tears against her shirt. "Your dad won't let anyone hurt you."

Trinity glanced at Ryder. The fierce protectiveness she saw in those dark depths confirmed she'd spoken the truth.

Anyone who tried to get to Zoe would have to go through Ryder. And seeing the look on his face, she pitied anyone who might try.

Once they heard the shower turn on, Ryder stopped Trinity's exit with a light touch to her arm. "Can you stay for a glass of wine?"

Trinity hesitated for a long moment. "Sure. For a minute."

"I've been looking forward to this." Ryder brought out a bottle, poured two generous glassfuls and sat opposite her.

Being able to share his concerns face-to-face was something

he'd looked forward to all week. When he'd called his parents to inform them they had a granddaughter, all they'd wanted to talk about was him doing a DNA test to make sure Zoe was really his child.

"You've had a rough week." Sympathy filled Trinity's voice.

He reached across the table and took her hand.

She stared at their joined fingers for a long moment. With a wistful smile, she sat back. "Have you thought about what comes next?"

For a second, Ryder thought she was referring to them, to the relationship they'd begun to build. Then he realized she was talking about Zoe.

Ryder blew out a breath. "Sign her up for school. Luckily, the year just started. Hopefully, that will make the transition easier. The attorney handling Jenna's estate gave me all her papers, so registering her shouldn't be a problem."

"Has she spoken much about her mother?"

"She asked why I haven't been around. Why her mom never said anything about me." He took a gulp of wine. "I did as you suggested. I was honest and told Zoe I didn't know she existed. I wasn't sure why her mother hadn't told me, but I'm here now."

Trinity nodded approval.

"Jenna had already been cremated by the time I got there. I have the ashes. I'm hoping down the line, Zoe and I can do something meaningful with them."

"Was there a funeral or memorial service?"

"I don't know." Ryder frowned. "I don't think so."

"Perhaps once Zoe gets settled, you can do your own memorial service." Trinity kept her tone offhand. While he'd asked for her input while in Portland, now he was home. "Including her in the planning could be therapeutic."

"That's a good idea." Ryder sipped his wine. "I'll wait until she's settled, then bring it up."

"What about her personal effects?"

"Zoe's?" Ryder set down his glass. "They're in her suitcase."

"I meant Jenna's personal items." Trinity twisted the stem of her glass back and forth.

"I had them shipped. They should arrive early next week."

"Each child is different. Some find comfort in having pictures and memorabilia around, others don't."

Think of Ryder as a client, Trinity told herself. As a man with a grieving preteen daughter. "Ask Zoe what she'd like to keep out. You can pack the other items away and store them for now. Zoe might want them later."

"What if she won't tell me what's important?"

"You do the best you can. The tendency will be to try to jump in and fix the situation. You can't. Rephrase what she says to you and listen. Use her mom's name, talk about memories you have of her."

Trinity's heart ached for what Ryder was going through. "Jenna would be proud at how you've stepped up."

"She always knew she could count on me."

Then why did she hide the fact that you have a child all these years?

The question, poised on the tip of her tongue, remained unasked. It surprised her that Ryder wasn't angrier with Jenna.

Suddenly, this comfortable back-and-forth seemed far too familiar.

Miles had used her as a sounding board after his wife's death. He was an English professor. For him, psychology was a foreign language. Trinity had been eager to offer the knowledge gained in her classes and practicums to help ease his suffering.

She thought of his daughters. Once they'd figured out that her relationship with their father went beyond simple friendship, they'd turned on her. The girls had focused all the pain and anger over their mother's death on her.

And despite voicing great respect for what she did, Miles hadn't been willing to make his daughters participate in family counseling.

It had been a bitter pill when she'd finally admitted she couldn't fix what was wrong in her relationship with Miles and his daughters.

That was the past. She'd made peace with it.

Now, she faced a similar situation with Ryder. A preteen grieving child. A dead mother.

"I feel like I'm in over my head and sinking fast."

She pulled her thoughts back to this situation, to this man, to this reality.

"Take it a day at a time. Remember that no matter what you do, or how well you do it, there will be rocky patches." Trinity's eyes took on a distant glow. "After my mother gave me up, I went for long periods being furious with her. How could she just walk away from her own child? Then she died, and I was really alone in the world."

Ryder stared into his glass. "It's like being thrown into the bay and not knowing how to swim."

"Are you referring to Zoe? Or yourself?"

He chuckled. "Both, I guess."

"You and Zoe will get through this and be stronger because of it." Her hand rested over his. When he looked up, she offered a reassuring smile. "You have friends in this town, Ryder. Friends with children. They'll be a big help, a wonderful resource. You and Zoe, you'll be on solid footing in no time."

He curled his fingers around hers, met her gaze. "Thank you. For everything."

She pulled her hand back and stood. "The shower is off. I need to get home." Trinity paused. "You may want to make an appointment for her to see Liam. It will be good for Zoe to have an objective person to talk with about her feelings. It could be good for you, too."

Surprise had his voice rising. "I thought she could talk to you."

"We're friends, neighbors." Trinity shook her head. "In her

mind, you and I are connected. She needs someone else. Liam specializes in children's needs."

"What if she won't go?" Ryder remembered seeing that stubborn tilt to her jaw several times in the past few days. She might be quiet, but the girl knew how to dig in her heels.

"You'll persuade her that Liam will help her work through her feelings." Trinity spoke in a matter-of-fact tone. "Trust me. You can be very persuasive when you set your mind to it."

"I'm out of my depth here." He grimaced. "Way out of my depth."

"Take it a day at a time. You don't become a dad just because a piece of paper says you are." She met his gaze. "You'll get there. I believe in you."

"Will I see you tomorrow?"

"Probably." She flashed a smile. "After all, I live right next door."

CHAPTER ELEVEN

Saturday night, Trinity stayed at the bar long enough to indulge her brother's request by stepping onto the karaoke stage and performing one song.

Thinking about the crowd's enthusiastic response had her smiling when her garage door slid open. The smile vanished when her headlights caught the silhouette of a man in the shadows near the row of garages.

Her heart jumped, then steadied when she saw who it was—and the dog on the leash.

Moments later, she stood beside Ryder in the yard. Though she'd gone to the Ding-A-Ling to fill her mind with things other than him, it hadn't worked. "Where's Zoe?"

"In bed." He offered a quiet laugh. "She insisted she wasn't tired, but the second her head hit the pillow, she was out."

"What did you two do today?" Despite it being the weekend, Trinity had been at the clinic at the crack of dawn. She'd stayed there until it was time to meet Wyatt and Greer for dinner.

"Zoe and I met with Clay. We got her registered for school. She starts Monday."

Trinity frowned. "That was fast. Today is Saturday."

Ryder grinned. "I have friends in high places. Though Clay is the principal of the high school, he gave Zoe a personal tour of the middle school and signed her up for classes himself."

Trinity recalled vividly how her stomach had hurt each time she'd had to start over somewhere new. "What does Zoe think of the school?"

"She didn't say much, but I know she's apprehensive. Starting a new school is a big deal at her age."

Trinity gave his shoulder a comforting squeeze. "She'll be fine."

He blew out a breath. "I hope so."

Time to change the subject, Trinity thought. "I didn't realize you were thinking of getting a dog."

He chuckled. "That's a story."

"I'd like to hear it." Trinity studied the puffball, who was sniffing a bush like a wine connoisseur checking out an exceptional vintage. The dog had caramel-colored fur on its body, jet-black fur on its face and a smashed-in snout. "What kind is he? His body reminds me of a Pomeranian, but his face is pure pug."

"On that score, your guess is as good as mine." Instead of telling her the story, Ryder cocked his head. "You look nice. Evening out?"

His tone was pleasant and conversational, but she caught the underlying question.

In the weeks they'd dated—and slept together—they'd never discussed being exclusive. It had simply been understood. Now, she needed to let him know things had changed.

Not that she wanted to date anyone else. She had no desire to be with anyone but Ryder. But right now, what she wanted didn't matter. This was about what was best for him and Zoe.

"Wyatt and Greer asked me to join them for karaoke at the Ding-A-Ling," she heard herself say.

"Did you wipe the floor with your amazing vocals?" He motioned to a nearby bench.

"Yeah." As she sat, the dog moved to another bush. "One song. It went well, so I left on a high note."

He chuckled then sobered. "I wish I could have been there with you."

When Ryder took her hand, she let her fingers curve around his for just an instant.

Trinity understood the wistful quality to his voice. His days of being a carefree bachelor had come to an abrupt end. The fatigue on his face and the lines of stress around his eyes told her he was feeling the full weight of fatherhood.

"I wish you'd been there, too." The fact that she couldn't allow herself to date him didn't mean she didn't care. If only she could wave a magic wand and drive the shadows from his eyes. "Tell me about the dog."

"Raven came to work yesterday with her eyes bloodshot and red-rimmed." Ryder leaned back against the bench, but kept a firm hold on the retractable leash. "She said something about allergies. I didn't buy it. I could tell she'd been crying."

Like a mama bear ready to defend her cub, Trinity went on high alert. "Is Jax bothering her?"

"No. From what I understand, he's kept his distance. He may have said a few nasty things that she flung right back at him. Raven's a spitfire."

Trinity expelled the breath stuck in her throat. "Good. That's good. Now where does the dog fit?"

"Well, apparently, Scully—that's the name Raven gave him." He gestured with his head toward the dog, who'd moved to inspect the wide base of an oak tree. "He was a stray hanging around her house the past couple of weeks. The house is a rental with a strict no-pets policy. Her mom went ballistic when she discovered Raven was hiding the dog in her room. Raven had twenty-four hours to find him a home. None of her friends wanted him, and the clock was ticking. I offered to take him to the shelter."

Trinity grinned. "You saw him and fell instantly in love."

"Not even close." He jerked on the leash, spoke firmly. "No digging."

Scully froze, lifted his head, then trotted away from the flower bed, all nonchalant.

"My mistake," Ryder admitted, "was having Zoe in the car with me when we picked him up."

Trinity glanced at the furry teddy bear of a dog. Her lips curved. "I was right about love at first sight, but that was on her part."

"Both of their parts." Ryder shook his head. "Scully is crazy about Zoe, too. Lots of doggy kisses. By the time we reached the shelter, Zoe was begging me to keep him."

Trinity didn't bother to hide her smile.

"Go ahead and say it." A rueful smile tipped his lips. "I'm a soft touch."

She cupped his cheek with one hand, and her heart gave a *ker-thump*. "You're a good father."

Touching him, she realized, was as much a mistake as sitting so close. She dropped her hand and scooted over, putting some distance between them.

Though appearing puzzled by her sudden coolness, he continued. "I drove to the shelter and had them check for a chip. Nada. The lady there called several area vet clinics. No reports of a missing dog, at least not one that looks like him."

"I'd have thought Raven would have already checked all that out."

"She called, but hadn't taken him in to see if he was microchipped." Ryder expelled a breath. "I'm not sure getting a dog now is smart, but I believed I'd be breaking Zoe's heart—and Raven's as well—if I left him at the shelter."

Such a good man, Trinity thought.

"What do you think?"

She brought her thoughts back to the conversation with a start. "About?"

"Getting a pet now. In the midst of chaos."

As confident as Ryder appeared, he needed reassurance and support. That was something she could offer him freely and willingly. "I think it will be good for both of them."

"Zoe and Raven?"

"Actually, I was referring to Zoe and that little guy over there." She pointed to Scully, who'd returned to the flower bed to dig. Paws in the dirt, he stopped abruptly as if sensing their eyes on him. "Scully has likely suffered a loss. Wherever he made his home previously, that family isn't there for him anymore. From what you've said, he appears to be a loving dog, which means it's unlikely he was abused. He needs Zoe. More importantly, she'll need him during the upcoming months. He'll give her unconditional love and acceptance as she transitions to her new life in Good Hope with you."

Ryder expelled a breath. "It seems so clear when you explain it that way."

"I'd give Zoe as much responsibility for caring for Scully as you believe she can handle. That will give her a purpose and facilitate the bond between them."

His dark eyes searched hers. "Anything else?"

"Maybe let Raven see Scully every now and then." Trinity wasn't surprised to hear that Raven had a softness for a stray. She'd sensed a kind heart under all that bluster. "It'll ease her mind to know the dog is happy in his new home."

"I already told her she's welcome to visit anytime." Ryder scrubbed a hand across his face. "Kids and dogs."

Trinity inclined her head.

He offered a crooked smile. "A couple weeks ago, my biggest concern was where to take you for dinner. Now, I have a daughter and a dog."

Trinity's heart went out to him. It was easy to forget Zoe

wasn't the only one adjusting to a new normal. "I'd say you're rocking this father thing."

"You think so?"

"I wouldn't have said so otherwise."

"You're good for me."

The intensity of emotion in his eyes had Trinity fighting the urge to lean in and kiss him. Oh, how she'd missed him while he was in Portland. Missed talking with him. Missed simply being with him.

He wanted to kiss her, too. She saw that clearly in his eyes. But after searching her face for a long moment, he sat back.

"We've talked enough about my day." He cleared his throat. "How was yours?"

Trinity knew she should go inside before she let the pretty night—and the handsome man—seduce her. Just a few minutes more, she told herself.

She remained seated and let the light breeze caress her face. Scully, tired of roaming and sniffing, sat contentedly on the lawn near them. As the animal glanced around, he reminded Trinity of a king surveying his new kingdom.

"Did you get all settled in at Connections?" he prompted.

"I'm getting there." Telling Ryder about her day was something else she'd missed. She realized there'd been a gaping hole in her life the week he'd been gone. "Liam and I spent time reviewing files of clients who indicated they'd be willing to transition over to me, as well as ones scheduled for neuropsychological testing."

"Sounds like a busy, but productive, week."

"I already had a patient call and specifically ask to see me." Trinity didn't tell him that patient was Gladys Bertholf.

"Word is getting around about the new psychologist in town." Ryder gazed straight into her eyes. "The more you're out in the community, the better people will get to know you. That will help, too."

"Liam suggested I get involved with an upcoming health fair." The way her new partner had explained it, this was a community effort to remind people to stay healthy during the holidays. Restaurants would showcase healthy foods, and the YWCA would be there to sign people up for the Turkey Trot. "Connections is going to hand out stress balls and offer suggestions for easing holiday tensions."

"The Daily Grind will be there. We're one of the sponsors."

Trinity couldn't hide her surprise. "I realize coffee isn't considered *unhealthy*, but—"

"We'll have the coffee station going, offering both regular and decaf." Ryder's dark eyes twinkled. "But I'll really be there to hype our new line of healthy smoothies."

She really was out of the loop. "What kind of smoothies?"

"Three new flavors for fall—a pumpkin pie protein, a winterberry and a maple cinnamon sweet potato. If the response is positive, we'll keep them on the menu through Thanksgiving and consider adding more seasonal favorites."

"They sound amazing."

"Stop by. I'll make you one." He brought their joined hands to his mouth and brushed a kiss across her knuckles before she could stop him. "Can I say again how much I missed you and how glad I am to be back?"

Trinity's heart cracked in two, and she knew she couldn't put off for one moment longer what she had to do.

She wasn't living in a romance novel where people fell in love overnight; she lived in the real world. If she'd made the hard choices—the right choices—with Miles, he and his daughters would have had the time they needed to heal as a family.

Ryder needed time to forge a bond with Zoe and grieve for Jenna without her in the middle.

"There's something I need to say to you."

Concern blanketed his face. He reached for her, but she shook her head.

"This is difficult for me. I can't think clearly when you're touching me."

His gaze, serious now, searched hers. "Just spit it out."

Trinity cleared her throat. "Your life has been turned upside down, Ryder. Not only did you lose a dear friend, you found out you have a daughter. You're learning how to be a dad."

Ryder only continued to stare at her.

"You and Zoe need time to grieve—you for Jenna, Zoe for her mother. You need time to build a strong relationship. What you don't need is a distraction. That's what I would be."

"You—"

"No. Please. Take your heart out of the equation and think about what I'm saying." Trinity fought to keep the emotion clogging her throat from spilling into her voice. "Look at this logically. Don't think with your heart, think with your head and you'll see I'm right. We can be friends. I want to be your friend. But for now, we need to put anything other than friendship on pause."

"For how long?"

"As long as it takes."

Scully came to him then, putting his paws on Ryder's knees and dropping his head. Ryder didn't speak for several long moments. "I see what you're saying. I understand where you're coming from."

She blew out a breath. "You agree."

"I see what you're saying," he repeated, and when he looked at Trinity, the light that had shone so bright earlier had left his eyes. "If the only thing you want from me right now is friendship, you have it."

Ryder thought he'd done a good job of keeping his emotions under control, but when he shut his front door, he noticed his hands trembled. He was angry. With her. With himself. With the situation.

He wanted to throw something, but knew if he did, he'd be the one to clean up the mess.

If he gave a primal roar of anguish, he'd wake up Zoe. Might even scare her. Right now, she was sleeping soundly, her mass of blond hair spread out over the pillow like a halo.

Since options for venting appeared limited, he paced and mentally reviewed his conversation with Trinity.

Scully lay, head on paws, in Ryder's favorite chair. The dog's large, expressive eyes followed his every move. The third time Ryder passed the kitchen, he grabbed a bottle of whiskey from the cupboard, poured two fingers and drank it in a single gulp.

He couldn't deny it. Trinity telling him she just wanted to be friends had been a punch to the gut.

Reeling and not sure how to respond, he'd simply listened. Even as she'd explained the reason their relationship had to change, he still hadn't understood. Now it was clear—at least to him—that this all circled back to what had happened with her ex and his kids.

Trinity worried her presence in his life would mess things up between him and Zoe. Ryder shook his head. She obviously didn't realize she was comparing apples and oranges.

He was tempted to knock on her door and point out her faulty logic. His situation wasn't the same as what she'd faced with Miles and his daughters.

For starters, he didn't have a wife of twenty years who'd recently died. Jenna had been simply an old friend, one he'd see once or twice a year for dinner.

Instead of three girls resenting that their father was moving on too quickly, Zoe didn't feel possessive or believe he was betraying her mother. Heck, the girl barely knew him.

Ryder's hand was on the doorknob and one foot already in

the hall when he came to his senses. He'd forgotten that when emotions were involved, logic didn't mean squat.

Closing the door, Ryder scooped up the dog and deposited him on the floor before dropping into the chair.

It could be worse, he reassured himself. Trinity could have said she didn't want anything to do with him or Zoe. Instead, she'd made it clear she wanted to remain friends.

This was undoubtedly a compromise Trinity had made with herself. She hadn't really wanted to step back from what was building between them, but she was convinced it was the right thing to do.

At least, he hoped that was the case.

He could go along, *would* in fact go along, with her plan. Ryder was all for deepening their friendship and eager to facilitate one between Trinity and Zoe. Taking the time to build a strong foundation of trust between them would only benefit their relationship once they became a family unit.

Deep in thought, Ryder barely noticed Scully jumping onto his lap. Absently, he stroked the animal's soft fur as a plan solidified.

He would be Trinity's friend.

He would spend as much time with her as she'd allow.

He would do whatever he could to encourage a relationship between her and Zoe.

And he would do all this because he believed—he *had* to believe—Trinity would accept eventually that not only couldn't he and Zoe live without her, she couldn't live without them.

CHAPTER TWELVE

All week, Trinity avoided Ryder and Zoe without—hopefully—being obvious. She knew she was doing the right thing in backing off of her relationship with Ryder. She just wished she didn't miss him so much.

Thankfully, it was a busy week for all of them. Greer mentioned Zoe had started school, and Trinity had seen Ryder and his daughter leaving in the morning.

No one had asked how she and Ryder were doing now that he had a daughter. Probably because the only people she'd seen were Liam, Peyton and her clients. Without a doubt, Gladys would have had a lot to say, but the older woman had rescheduled her appointment.

As Connections was one of the sponsors of the upcoming A Healthy Taste of Good Hope, Trinity accepted, at Liam's urging, Hadley's invitation to brief her on the details of the upcoming event.

They settled on Saturday afternoon. Since Hadley and Brynn had helped her furnish Zoe's room, Trinity prepared for the questions.

What's Zoe like? *She's a sweet, smart girl. I really like her.*

What did she think of the room? *The bed and all the accessories, including the sawhorse desk, were hits. She loved everything. Thanks again for your help.*

Trinity cringed, realizing she'd been so focused on her own issues she'd forgotten basic courtesies. She should have reached out and thanked Hadley and Brynn—again—for going with her on that shopping trip. She should have let them know, long before now, that their suggestions had been on target and appreciated.

Today, she'd rectify that faux pas. And if she had to answer a few questions about her relationship with Ryder, she was prepared. *For now, Ryder is focusing on being the best father he can be to Zoe. He and I are still good friends. That hasn't changed.*

Hadley wouldn't press further. That much Trinity knew from the time they'd spent shopping.

The drive out to the Chapin home had Trinity venturing onto an unfamiliar road that offered breathtaking views of Green Bay. Tall and majestic homes sat far back from the winding roadway, leaded-glass windows sparkling in the afternoon sun.

Hadley's house, which appeared to have been built in the early decades of the twentieth century, sat at an angle in a wooded area at the end of a winding drive. The placement of the home offered a stellar view of the bay.

Trinity parked in the back, then rounded the side of the house to the front porch. By the time she climbed the last step, Hadley had stepped out, a welcoming smile on her lips. "I hope you didn't have any trouble finding the house. GPS isn't always accurate."

"Greer gave me excellent directions." Trinity made a broad sweep with one hand. "You have an amazing view and a beautiful home."

"Thank you. David designed the home and supervised the construction."

Trinity couldn't hide her surprise. "I pegged the house for early-twentieth century."

"The style was popular in the 1920s." Hadley opened the screen door and stepped aside. "David designed ours to fit in with the others in the area."

Once inside, Trinity was struck by the classic beauty of the home. The gleaming hardwood floors, the massive stone fireplace and the amazing detail work on the staircase banister.

"I know it's unusually warm today, but hot apple cider and pumpkin cookies sounded good to me." Hadley lifted her hands. "But if you'd like something else, I have cold drinks and several different kinds of cookies."

"I love cider and pumpkin anything." Trinity drew in a breath, not wanting to wait a second longer to say what she should have said last week. "I need to say—"

A fussy cry from the second floor had Hadley casting Trinity an apologetic smile. "Make yourself at home. I'll be right back."

As Hadley flew up the stairs, Trinity took a moment to study the water before wandering to inspect the gorgeous stone fireplace.

A faint scent of yeast, chocolate and sugar hovered in the air, adding to the homey ambience.

Trinity looked up when she heard footsteps coming down the steps.

"Is everything okay?"

"I got him back to sleep."

"This is a lovely room, Hadley." Trinity trailed her fingers along the edge of the mantel. "So warm and welcoming."

"I love it. When there's an applewood log crackling in the hearth and snow is falling outside the window while you're cozied up inside with the ones you love, well, it's magical."

"It's sounds magical." Trinity thought of Ryder and how special it was when they'd been together. "I want to thank you and Brynn again for helping me shop for Zoe's furniture. Zoe loved—"

"Zoe has already thanked us." Hadley's eyes grew soft. "She raved about her bedroom."

Ryder must have had Zoe call Hadley.

A good dad, Trinity thought again.

"Give me a sec to grab the cider and cookies. We can enjoy them in here or in the kitchen."

"The kitchen works for me."

"It works for me as well." Hadley continued to talk as they made their way down the hall to a room that would have made a professional chef weep with envy. Two sinks, what Trinity recognized as a high-output gas range that her mother would have killed for, and double electric ovens. "Since it's a gorgeous day, I'd suggest we sit out on the deck, but with David gone, I want to be close enough to hear Carter."

"Is your husband out of town?" Trinity asked, her eyes drawn to a marble countertop where chocolate chip cookies sat cooling on racks.

"David is playing in some basketball tournament thing at the Y." Hadley grabbed a couple of napkins, scooped up one cookie for Trinity and one for herself. "We'll still celebrate the arrival of fall with apple cider and pumpkin cookies, but who can resist chocolate chip cookies warm from the oven? Not me."

"Not me either." Trinity bit into the one Hadley gave her and groaned when the rich chocolate and butter came together on her tongue. "These are a-ma-zing."

"I agree." Hadley's eyes twinkled as she finished off the last bite of hers. "I find it ironic that we're chowing down on cookies before talking about a health fair."

Trinity laughed. "That's how I roll."

Minutes later, hot apple cider—served in clear glass mugs with a cinnamon stick—and pumpkin cookies topped with cream cheese frosting sat before them on the small table.

If Hadley had any questions about Trinity's relationship with Ryder, she didn't ask.

"We had an excellent committee," Hadley informed her. "Gladys helped initially, but had to bow out when the musical she's directing started rehearsals."

"Gladys Bertholf?"

"There's only one Gladys." Hadley grinned. "She made the switch from acting to directing last year. Her latest production is *Pump Boys and Dinettes*. It sounds really cute."

"I saw it in Chicago once," Trinity recalled. "I loved it."

"Oaklee will be making her main-stage debut." Hadley took a sip of cider. "She's playing Prudie Cupp."

Trinity blinked in surprise. "That's one of the leads."

"I hear she has an exceptional voice." Hadley bit into a cookie, dabbed at the corner of her mouth with a napkin. "Gladys is giving us all passes to the dress rehearsal."

"That's nice of her."

"She's an amazing woman. You know she matchmakes on the side." Hadley studied her for a long moment.

Here it comes, Trinity thought, the questions about her and Ryder. "That's what I hear."

Hadley shrugged. "She doesn't mean any harm."

After several beats of silence, Hadley opened the tablet she'd brought with her to the table. "I suppose we should at least attempt to cover your questions. Just in case Liam requests an update from his partner."

Hadley's impish smile had Trinity grinning.

"All the vendors have been contacted and reconfirmed." Hadley glanced at the screen. "The management of Sombreros expressed their unhappiness with the placement of their booth. I reminded Tomas that they'd been notified months ago that the wide aisles to allow for adequate foot traffic might impact booth placement."

Trinity sipped the cider. "Was he satisfied with that

explanation?"

"He was, once I explained the water and electrical constraints our operations team had to consider."

Trinity thought of the meal she and Ryder had shared at the Mexican restaurant in Egg Harbor. "The event is called A Healthy Taste of Good Hope, but their menu items aren't particularly healthy."

"Tomas assured me that they'll be showcasing foods from the new healthy options section they're adding to the menu this fall." Hadley smiled at Trinity. "Ryder probably told you about the smoothies he's planning to debut."

"They sound yummy."

"I can't wait to try one." Hadley glanced again at her tablet, scrolled. "The staging and scaffolding are set."

Trinity inclined her head. "Is there entertainment?"

"We have a variety of local talent scheduled, all having to do with health and fitness." Hadley took a sip of cider. "We have a YMCA-based clogging group, yoga from Salutations, as well as tai chi and Zumba demonstrations. There will be a little something for everyone."

Trinity's head spun. Wyatt and Greer hadn't been exaggerating. This community was a vibrant one with much to offer all ages.

Hadley moved on to the sponsors and publicity. "Fin Rakes included our event in other Good Hope public relations, marketing and advertising campaigns. Oaklee approached Tim Vandercoy, one of our media sponsors, about extending his sponsorship to roving reporters."

Trinity stirred her cider with the cinnamon stick. "Roving reporters?"

"It's something new we're trying. These media-savvy roving reporters will do live tweets and updates to the town blog during the event." Hadley's smile was rueful. "We're using high school students. We'll see how it goes."

"Did Tim agree to extend his sponsorship to the reporters?"

"He said he'd sponsor T-shirts for them to wear. This will make them easy to identify. They'll be lime green with the event logo on the front." Hadley's lips twitched. "Advertising for Tim's real estate agency will go on the back. The man is a genius when it comes to marketing his business."

"When I was looking for an agent to help me find a place, Steve Bloom told me Tim was the top agent in Door County."

"Did he also tell you his ex-girlfriend—Anita Fishback— used to date Tim?"

"The one who owns Crumb and Cake?"

"That's her. From what I hear, she's fairly serious now about Len Swarts, who used to be the sheriff. Cade Rallis moved to Good Hope and took over that job a couple years ago when Len retired."

Trinity could only stare as Hadley rattled off the names with such ease. The connections in this community boggled Trinity's mind.

"Didn't he help you find your condo?"

For a second, Trinity was confused. Then she realized they'd circled back to Tim. "He got right on it and found me exactly what I wanted."

"That's why he's successful. He—"

The sound of something crashing in another part of the house had Hadley springing to her feet. "That sounds like something I need to check out."

Trinity stood as Hadley sprinted from the kitchen. Taking her cup of cider with her, Trinity finished off the pumpkin cookie before she reached the great room.

Thanks to Hadley, Trinity now had a good understanding of all that went into the health fair. The discussion had spurred a couple thoughts of things Connections might do the next year in terms of promotion. She couldn't wait to talk to Ryder and get his thoughts.

The realization that Ryder was who popped into her head—rather than Liam—had Trinity frowning.

"We didn't mean to break the lamp." The childish voice came from the top of the stairs. "We weren't goofing around or anything. We just bumped it. It was an accident."

"It wasn't your fault, Brynn." This voice had Trinity's breath hitching. "I knocked over the lamp. I'm sorry, Mrs. Chapin. I'll pay for it."

The tears in Zoe's voice brought Trinity to the base of the stairs.

"Zoe." Trinity greeted the girl when the trio reached the landing. "I didn't realize you were here."

Zoe came to an abrupt stop, her eyes widening. "I didn't know you were here."

"I'll pay for the lamp," Trinity volunteered.

"The lamp was an old one that none of us particularly liked." Hadley slipped an arm around Zoe's shoulders and gave a comforting squeeze. "You did us a favor. It'll be a relief not have that ugly old thing around anymore."

Brynn giggled. "Daddy used to throw his shirt over it because he hated it so much."

Though Trinity wondered why they'd kept a lamp everyone hated, she was happy to see that Zoe's stiffened shoulders relaxed.

"Would you girls like to join us for cider and cookies?" Hadley asked.

Brynn looked at Zoe. "You want a cookie?"

Zoe paused. "Do you?"

"I do if they're chocolate chip." Brynn thrust her hands in the air and twirled around, bumping against her mother in the process. "Bring 'em on."

Hadley laughed and planted a kiss on the top of her daughter's head.

Zoe's smile slipped, and shadows filled her eyes.

"The chocolate chip cookies are amazing," Trinity told Zoe, wishing she could give the girl a hug. "The pumpkin ones are fantastic, too."

"I like any kind of cookie." Zoe dropped down on the sofa and patted the spot beside her. "I haven't seen you lately."

Trinity sat, keeping an easy smile on her lips. "We've both been busy."

"I go to school now," Zoe began, "and—"

"We're in the same grade," Brynn interrupted. "Zoe and me and Lia sit together at lunch."

"Is that right?" Trinity wanted to cheer. At Zoe's age, having someone to sit with at lunch was huge.

"Ryder had to work today, so I thought this would be a good chance for the girls to get together." Hadley returned from the kitchen and set down a tray loaded with cookies and cider.

Trinity had no trouble reading between the lines. Ryder would be gone all day and had wanted to keep Zoe busy.

"How's Scully?" Trinity fought the urge to pick up another cookie.

"He's super sweet." Zoe lowered her cup. "My da—ah, Ryder, was going to stop home over lunch and let him out."

The child couldn't quite bring herself to call Ryder her dad. Understandable. That would come in time.

"When I found out Hadley was my birth mom, it took me a while to call her Mom." Brynn spoke matter-of-factly. "If my other mom wasn't in Florida, it might be confusing to call them both Mom. But she's not here, so it isn't."

Brynn must have told Zoe the tale of her two mothers, because Zoe only reached for a cookie and didn't ask any questions.

Trinity's mind, on the other hand, whirled with speculation.

As if Hadley could read her thoughts, she smiled. "I'll tell you about it sometime. It's complicated."

The ringing of the doorbell had Hadley rising and the baby upstairs letting out a wail.

Clearly torn, Hadley glanced at the door, then at the staircase.

Trinity stood. "Let's tag-team this one. You get Carter. I'll get the door."

"And I," Brynn announced, snagging a chocolate chip this time, "get another cookie."

CHAPTER THIRTEEN

Ryder waited for Hadley to open the door. He couldn't believe that at the end of Zoe's first week with him, he'd been placed in this predicament. At her age, Zoe needed more of a companion than a sitter. He didn't like the idea of her spending the whole day alone. If he and Trinity…

He stopped himself before the thought could fully form and reminded himself that Zoe was his responsibility, not Trinity's.

What was taking so long for Hadley to answer the door? Ryder frowned and considered punching the bell again.

The door swung open.

"Thanks again for—" Ryder stopped. Trinity stood before him.

Her dress, awash in autumn hues, complemented her blond prettiness. The color of the lips that curved in welcome reminded him of fresh peaches. "Hello, neighbor."

He glanced around in mock confusion. "Did I take a wrong turn? You're not Hadley Chapin."

She stepped back, laughed. "Aren't you the funny one? Come in."

The foyer wrapped around him, sucking out all the air, pulling them together. "What are you doing here?"

"Hadley gave me an update on A Healthy Taste of Good Hope."

"Who is it?" Brynn called out. "Is it Zoe's dad?"

"It is," Trinity responded.

"Tell him to wait a minute," Brynn yelled back. "We need to get Zoe's stuff from my bedroom."

"He'll wait." Trinity gestured in the direction of the great room. "There's cider and cookies."

"I'll pass. It's nearly time for dinner. Do you have plans?"

Trinity, who'd started to turn, refocused. "Plans?"

"Dinner plans?" Ryder offered an engaging smile. "I ordered a couple of pizzas from Bayside. I'm picking them up on the way home. With two large on order, we'll have plenty."

"I was just going to make a salad—"

"Perfect. You supply the salad. I'll supply the pizza." He held out a hand. "Deal?"

She stared at his hand for a long moment. *Just say no,* Trinity told herself. The hope that glimmered in Ryder's dark eyes had her reconsidering. Sharing pizza and salad with a neighbor was not a date, especially when you added a chatty eleven-year-old and a rambunctious dog to the mix.

"Okay." Even though Trinity took his hand for the briefest of moments, her heart skipped a beat. "If you'd like, I can give Zoe a ride home. She and I could take Scully for a quick walk while you pick up the pizzas."

"You'd do that for me?"

She wasn't doing it for him, she was doing it for Scully. Trinity didn't have a chance to explain, because Zoe appeared.

Her assessing gaze slid from Trinity to Ryder. "What are you two discussing?"

"I'm grabbing a couple of pizzas from Bayside—that's the best pizza joint in town." Ryder jerked a thumb in Trinity's direction. "And our neighbor has agreed to join us and supply the salad."

Trinity searched Zoe's face for any sign of resistance. If the girl objected at all, the deal was off.

Zoe thought for a second, then smiled. "That's cool."

"I told your dad, if you're okay with it, he could get the pizzas and you could ride home with me. That way, we could take Scully for a quick walk before dinner."

Before Zoe could answer, Hadley appeared with Carter, who sported a Chicago Cubs onesie. "Ryder. I didn't expect you this early."

Ryder simply smiled, gestured with his head toward Carter. "He's bigger than the last time I saw him."

"Growing like a weed."

"Thanks for inviting Zoe over." Ryder appeared to struggle for words. "It was—"

"She's welcome anytime." Hadley put a hand on Zoe's shoulder. "Did you get your suit?"

Zoe exchanged a glance with Brynn. "It's hanging on the line."

"I'll go with you." Brynn looped her arm through Zoe's.

Trinity pulled her brows together. "I didn't realize you had a pool."

"Just an above-ground one. We put it up for the summer." Hadley gave a shrug. "It's usually down by Labor Day. This year, the temps have been so warm we left it up. But it's coming down tomorrow."

"I'm glad Zoe had a chance to enjoy it."

Hadley smiled. "She's a lovely girl."

Barking filled the air. When the girls stepped into the room, a huge shepherd was with them.

Without realizing what she was doing, Trinity stepped closer to Ryder. Years ago, she'd been attacked by a dog like this one.

"Ruckus. Sit." Hadley's no-nonsense tone had the animal's rump hitting the hardwood. "He's gentle, but loud."

"A friend of my mom's," Trinity waved a hand, realizing there was no need to overexplain, "had one like him. That dog was mean."

"Ruckus is a baby," Brynn crooned, crouching down to kiss the top of the shepherd's head.

The dog licked her cheek, making her giggle.

"Since Ryder is picking up pizza, I told him I'd give Zoe a ride home," Trinity told Hadley, though she wasn't sure why she felt the need to explain.

For a second, Hadley looked confused, then understanding dawned on her pretty face.

"We both live in a barn," Zoe told her.

A pained look crossed Ryder's face.

"An extremely nice barn." Hadley chuckled, then gave Trinity a hug. "Thanks for coming over."

"I appreciate the invitation and all the information." Trinity inclined her head as a thought struck. "I realize everything is pretty much done, but is there anything I can do to help, anything at all?"

Hadley jiggled the baby, then pointed to a side table by the entrance. "Gladys was going to distribute flyers around town. But she's tied up with her work at the playhouse."

Trinity strode over and grabbed the box before shifting her gaze to Zoe. "Are you okay riding home with me?"

"She's got this really cool red car." Brynn's voice took on a hushed reverence. "The top goes down."

"In that case," Zoe flashed a smile, "you've got a rider."

Despite the warm temperatures, the scent of fall was in the air. Trinity put the top of the convertible down and felt herself relax as she drove.

Zoe closed her eyes, leaned her head back and let her hair flutter in the breeze.

They covered the short distance to the barn in comfortable silence. There were many questions Trinity could have asked, but she remembered her first days at the McConnells. Her new parents had given her the space she'd so desperately needed. Neighbors and family friends, on the other hand, hadn't always been that considerate.

Recalling that transition time, Trinity let Zoe simply *be*.

Scully burst through the door the minute Zoe unlocked it. Once outside, he visited his favorite bushes. He followed happily along when Trinity showed Zoe a shortcut to a nearby walking trail.

"We can't go far." Trinity glanced back at the barn. "Your dad will be home soon with the pizza."

For most of the walk, Zoe talked about her friends and school, and Trinity listened. It wasn't until they'd turned back toward the barn that she brought up her father.

"It's hard to think of Ryder as my dad," Zoe confided. "I mean, I know he is, but I don't understand why my mom never told me about him. He said they were friends and used to have dinner whenever he was in Portland."

Trinity saw the bafflement and hurt on the girl's face.

"Her not telling you about him is puzzling," Trinity admitted. "Your dad doesn't understand either. She must have had her reasons, but it's difficult to know what those reasons could be."

Zoe heaved a resigned sigh. "Now, I'll never know."

"Probably not." Trinity wondered if Ryder had mentioned having her see Liam. If he hadn't yet, she might be able to grease the way. "Do you know what I do for a living?"

Zoe shook her head.

"I'm a clinical psychologist," Trinity explained. "People come to me to discuss their problems."

Zoe cocked her head. "Do you tell them what to do?"

"What they do is always their choice. What I do is help them learn the skills that help them deal with troubling issues and feelings." Trinity slanted a glance at Zoe. "The man I work with, Dr. Gallagher, works with a lot of kids your age."

Zoe's shoulders stiffened. "I'm doing okay."

"My parents—they were my foster parents before they adopted me—had me talk with a psychologist. Her name was Leona Eveleigh." Trinity's lips curved as she recalled those sessions. "I didn't want to go, but I ended up loving it."

"Why?"

"I was angry with my mother for dumping me into foster care. Then I was angry with her for dying." Trinity expelled a long breath. "Dr. Eveleigh helped me see things in a different way. I learned skills that helped me not stay angry and stuck in the past."

"I'm not stupid. I get what you're doing." Zoe met Trinity's gaze. "You think I should talk to Dr. Gallagher."

"Yes, I do. But what I think doesn't really matter. That's something for you and your dad to discuss." Just as they reached the edge of the yard, Trinity saw Ryder's truck pull into the garage. "Right now, it's time for pizza."

Trinity saw immediately that something had happened between the time Ryder left Hadley's house and when he arrived home with the pizzas. Oh, he hid it well, laughing and joking with her and Zoe. He listened intently as his daughter told him some funny anecdotes about her first week in middle school.

But an undercurrent of tension he couldn't quite hide told Trinity he was worried.

During dinner and the cleanup afterward, Trinity didn't ask if anything was wrong. She already knew something was and that it involved Zoe.

He kept stealing furtive glances at the child, and his brow would furrow.

"Would you like to play a game?" Ryder asked them after everything was put away. "I've got Pictionary, Scrabble or cards."

"No, thanks." Zoe waved away all suggestions. "If it's okay, I'd like to go to my room and read."

"Of course it's okay." Ryder smiled. "If that's what you want."

"Sounds like a relaxing way to end a busy day." Trinity impulsively gave the girl a hug.

To her surprise, Zoe hugged her back.

"Thanks for the ride in the cool car," Zoe told her before turning to Ryder. "The pizza was fantabulous. Especially the pepperoni."

"I'm glad you liked it." Ryder's gaze softened. "Good night."

Zoe wiggled her fingers and disappeared down the hall. Seconds later, her door clicked shut.

"It sounds as if her school year is off to a fantabulous start." Her use of Zoe's word didn't even make him smile.

"I need a drink." Ryder surged up and strode to the kitchen, where he pulled a bottle of whiskey out of a cupboard.

She reached his side just as he splashed amber liquid into a glass and downed it.

When he reached again for the bottle, Trinity put a staying hand on his forearm.

"Tell me what's wrong."

He turned, and his gaze met hers for a long moment. Then he gestured with his head toward Zoe's room.

Obviously, whatever it was, he didn't want to risk Zoe overhearing.

Trinity held up a finger. "Zoe," she called out. "I need to borrow your dad for a few minutes to help me move something."

"Okay," came a distant voice that told her Ryder's fears had been justified.

What had her mother always said? *Little pitchers have big ears.*

"He won't be gone long, but if you need him, just come down. My door will be unlocked."

"I won't, but okay."

Trinity smiled at the response.

Neither she nor Ryder spoke until they were in her condo. As promised, she made sure her front door was unlocked, then plopped down on the sofa and patted the spot next to her.

Ryder took the chair instead. He leaned forward, resting his forearms on his thighs.

"I can see that whatever is troubling you has to do with Zoe." She kept her voice steady, her gaze never wavering from his face. "What is it?"

"Jerome, the attorney I dealt with in Portland, contacted me again." Ryder straightened and let out an exasperated breath. "I said no the first time he asked. It pisses me off he's asked again."

"You're going to have to back this train up, mister." Though the look in his eyes had red flags popping up, Trinity kept her tone easy. "What was it he already asked you?"

"When I was in Portland, he mentioned Jenna's father wanted custody of Zoe. I said absolutely not. No contact." Ryder pressed his lips together. The fierce expression returned. "Now, he tells me the grandparents want to come to Good Hope and visit Zoe. She's their only grandchild, their only link to Jenna, blah, blah, blah. The answer is still no. In fact, it's not just no, it's hell no."

The intensity of his emotion took Trinity by surprise. From all she'd observed, Ryder was an even-keeled kind of guy.

Something more going on here.

"You don't want them to visit." Trinity carefully kept all emotion from her voice.

"I don't want either of them anywhere near her." He spoke between gritted teeth. "Ever."

The reason behind that refusal was one issue, Trinity thought. Him getting so riled over them simply asking about visitation was another.

Trinity stopped herself from pointing out the value of having loving grandparents in a child's life. She didn't have enough information on Jenna's parents. Many unsavory relatives were best kept as far away as possible. "Why don't you want them to visit her?"

Ryder hesitated. She could almost see the wheels turning in his head as he tried to decide how much to divulge. He heaved a heavy breath.

"Jenna and I got close the year we were together." His eyes took on a distant glow. "She trusted me, and trust didn't come easy for her."

That, Trinity knew, usually meant someone had let her down. "She learned she could trust you."

"One night, I went to pick her up for a date, and she was crying. I asked what was wrong." A muscle in his jaw jumped. "Apparently, her father was in town and surprised her by stopping by the dorm. He planned to take her out to dinner."

"That upset her."

"She hated him. And her mother."

Something told Trinity there was more than teenage rebellion at play.

"That's when she said…that's when she—" Ryder took a second to compose himself. "She told me her father started raping her when she was seven."

"Oh no." Trinity wasn't sure why she was so shocked. She'd counseled many abuse victims. For many of them, the abuse started at a young age.

Ryder's hands clenched into fists. "The assaults didn't stop until she left for college. He threatened to hurt her or her mother when she tried to fight back. After a while, she gave up fighting. She felt guilty she'd been submissive and let it go on for so long."

Trinity closed her eyes as sympathy rushed through her. Sympathy for a young girl who'd seen no way out of the horror of her life. Outrage at the monster who'd done that to a child.

Sensing Ryder's eyes on her, Trinity reined in her emotions. "Guilt and self-blame are common in such cases."

"I told her none of it was her fault. Anything that happened was totally on him." Ryder expelled an unsteady breath. "I said a bunch of other stuff I can't remember. Whatever I said seemed to steady her."

"We all want to be heard." Trinity met his gaze. "And believed."

"We talked about it, what that monster did, several other times." Ryder's right hand clenched and unclenched. "She said her father was a big deal in her hometown. City council president. Active in the church. I think he was an elder or deacon or something. Mr. Wonderful, or so everyone thought."

Trinity's heart hurt for Jenna. She knew what it was like to feel scared and vulnerable. "Did she tell anyone before you? A friend? A family member? A school counselor?"

"As if that did any good." Ryder gave a derisive snort. "Six months after it started, Jenna finally gathered up her courage and told her mother. She told her what he was doing to her, what he made her do to him."

By the look in his eyes, that hadn't stopped the abuse. She spoke quietly. "What happened?"

A muscle in his jaw jumped. "Her mother told her she was imagining things. When Jenna insisted it was the truth, she was told only bad girls told lies and she should feel ashamed of herself for making up such terrible stories about her own father. As she grew older, she started having panic attacks. She tried to talk to her mother again and was told no one would believe her because she was mentally unstable. Once again, that woman, the one who was supposed to love and protect her, berated her, telling her she should be ashamed of trying to ruin her father's reputation."

Trinity closed her eyes. She'd never been sexually abused, but had come close a couple of times. Her biological mother hadn't been known for picking the best guys. "Jenna must have felt so alone, as if there was no way out. No one to protect her."

"She told me she thought off and on about killing herself, but couldn't bring herself to do it." Ryder rushed on, as if worried she'd think the event that had taken Jenna's life might have been a suicide. "Once she left home, she cut all ties."

"The damage had been done," Trinity murmured, almost to herself.

"Yes, but she got help. Went to a women's center and got involved with a group." Ryder's voice took on a hard edge. "That man is never coming near Zoe. Never."

"I wouldn't let her near him either."

He expelled another breath. "You agree with me?"

Trinity frowned. "Did you think I'd be on his side?"

"I thought you might support supervised visits."

Trinity cleared her throat. "Early in my career, I counseled a client who was molested by her uncle, a known pedophile, while they sat in the backseat on a road trip. This happened with her parents in the front seat. A predator finds ways to get to their victim."

"I can't believe Jerome would even forward the request."

"Did you tell him what Jenna's father did to her?"

"I have no firsthand knowledge, so what would be the point?" Ryder lifted a shoulder, let it drop. Then his jaw set in a tight line. "I don't have to explain anything to him. All he needs to know is I won't allow Jenna's father to see Zoe."

"Where does Wisconsin stand in terms of grandparent visitation?"

Ryder's eyes narrowed. "Are you saying the law could compel me to let that monster see Zoe?"

"I'm saying it's something to check out." Trinity reached forward. "Can I give you a little more advice?"

He nodded.

"Tell Zoe that her grandfather wants to see her and tell her why you won't allow it. If you decide to have Zoe see Liam, tell him everything."

"We already have an appointment scheduled. Liam wants to see us together for the first session."

Trinity offered an approving nod.

"I don't understand why Zoe needs to know." He frowned. "If I keep him from her—and by God, I will—none of this will affect her."

"Don't you see that it does? Or it will eventually. If she hasn't already, she'll begin to wonder about her mother's parents. Especially once she meets yours. Be open and honest with her, Ryder. Secrets destroy a relationship."

Some look, some emotion she couldn't quite identify flickered across his face.

"I'll think about it." He raked a hand through his hair. "And I'll consult with Beck."

"Beckett Cross?" Trinity had spoken with Beck briefly at the Chapin family dinner. She liked his easy manner and smooth Georgia drawl.

"Beck is a family law attorney. He's someone I trust to give it to me straight."

"You're smart to have surrounded yourself with people you trust and whose opinions you respect."

"You're one of those people." Ryder reached out as if to take her hand, but let it drop when she sat back. "I should go home. Zoe is probably wondering what's keeping me."

"Yes, you don't want her to worry." Trinity stood, and her gaze met his. "Zoe needs to know that she's your first priority."

CHAPTER FOURTEEN

Gladys exchanged a glance with Oaklee when Ryder pushed open the door of the Daily Grind early Sunday. This morning, Gladys had experienced a momentary twinge of conscience when her desire for coffeecake had led her to play hooky from church.

Now it appeared something good was about to come out of being bad.

"Did you see him?" Oaklee asked.

"I'm old. Not blind." Gladys spoke in a terse whisper, her eyes following Ryder as he strode to the back, a man on a mission.

"Why do you think he's here?"

"The more important question is where is Zoe and Trinity." Thankfully, the table Gladys had commandeered when they arrived sat at the front of the dining area and afforded her a perfect view of the counter.

"Maybe they're at—"

Gladys hushed the girl silent when she saw Ryder exit his office, headed straight for the front door.

"Yoo-hoo, Ryder." She motioned to him with an imperious hand when he turned. "Over here."

"Gladys. Oaklee." Ryder offered a polite smile. "What can I do for you ladies?"

Lines of tension bracketed his mouth, and his expression gave nothing away. Was being a father more than he could handle? Or was something more at play here? Only one way to find out. "How is Zoe doing?"

Surprise flickered in his dark eyes. "She's fine."

"It must be difficult for her." The sympathy in Gladys's voice came from the heart. "Being without a mother, I mean."

"She's adjusting." Ryder rocked back on his heels and shot a glance toward the door.

Gladys could see him planning his escape. She smiled brightly. "Well, before long perhaps Zoe will have a new mother. What a wonderful mother Trinity will make."

Because her eyes were fixed on his face, Gladys saw the muscle in his jaw jump. The polite smile that lifted his lips didn't come close to reaching his eyes. "Trinity is a friend, that's all. I'm the only family Zoe needs. Now, if you'll excuse me, she's waiting for me out in the truck."

Gladys exchanged a glance with Oaklee as Ryder disappeared out the front door.

"That didn't sound good." Oaklee frowned. "Do you think he and Trinity broke up?"

Gladys tapped a nail against the tabletop, processing the brief, but troubling, conversation.

"What happened during your session?" Oaklee leaned forward, her forearms resting on the table. "Did Trinity give any indication there was trouble in paradise?"

"I had to postpone it." Gladys recalled the look on Ryder's face when she'd mentioned Trinity. "I believe it's time to reschedule."

~

Trinity spent Sunday with Wyatt and Greer in Cave Point County Park. The kayak trip was every bit as fun as they'd promised. Being with a couple so much in love had been bittersweet. She was happy for her brother and Greer, but watching them hold hands, hearing their good-natured banter and seeing the love in their eyes had her missing what she'd shared with Ryder even more fiercely.

When she'd returned home late that evening and seen the light shining in Ryder's window, it had taken all of Trinity's self-control not to knock on his door just to "say hello."

Monday morning, she awoke with a clear head and a firm resolve. There was even a bounce in her step as, coffee mug in hand, she headed for her car.

"Trinity."

Zoe's voice had her turning.

The child, backpack strap over one shoulder, stood several feet behind her on the walkway leading to the garage. Her father was at her side.

"Good morning." Ryder gestured with one hand toward her cup. "Indonesian blend?"

"Ethiopian." Trinity lifted her lips in a rueful smile. "Call me weak, but I need the extra-strong kick to get going this morning."

Ryder cast a glance at his daughter. "You're not the only one moving slowly this morning."

"My hair looked really weird when I got up, so I had to wash it and then, well, dry it. I couldn't go to school with wet hair, could I?"

Ryder opened his mouth, then shut it.

Trinity studied him. "I take it you were hoping to get to the Grind a little earlier?"

She didn't know why she bothered to ask. The tight lines around his mouth told her as much.

"I have a new employee starting this morning, along with a relatively new one opening." He let out an impatient breath when his daughter stopped to bend over a rosebush. “No time to smell the roses, Zoe.”

Zoe straightened, and her blue eyes flashed. “You’re spending more time talking than I spent smelling.”

Ryder took a breath, then another.

“I’ve an idea. Why don’t I drop Zoe off at school? That’ll save you a few minutes.” Trinity smiled at the child. “It will give you a chance to catch me up on Scully’s latest adventures.”

“Her school isn’t on your way,” Ryder protested, but she could see it was only for form.

“It’s not on your way either.” She offered a friendly smile. “I was going in early to review some testing and dictate the reports. A few minutes won’t make a difference.”

“Can we put the top down?” Zoe asked.

“Zoe.” Ryder’s tone held a warning.

Trinity’s gaze returned to Ryder. “Is it okay with you?”

“Your decision.” His head tipped back, and he studied the clouds. “Doesn’t look like rain.”

For a second, Trinity was confused, then she laughed.

Their garage doors opened simultaneously, and Zoe gave Ryder a quick wave. “See you at three fifteen.”

“I’ll be there.” He squeezed his daughter’s shoulder. “Make it a good day.”

Zoe rolled her eyes.

Trinity waited until Ryder was down the road before backing her own car out, then lowering the top.

“I hope the wind doesn’t mess too much with your hair,” she told Zoe.

“It won’t.” Zoe leaned her head back, seeming to revel in the warm breeze against her face.

“How is Scully?”

“He’s good.” Zoe shifted in her seat toward Trinity. “Ryder and I took him with us on all our errands yesterday.”

"I bet he loved being with you." Asking about the dog was one thing, but she would not pump the child for other information.

Zoe smiled. "We went to that little park down by the docks to watch the boats in the harbor. Then we drove around the peninsula. Did you know there's a dog park in Sister Bay?"

"I didn't."

"Scully had a blast." Zoe turned quiet. "Did you know my grandfather isn't a nice man?"

So, Trinity thought, Ryder had taken the plunge and told Zoe about Jenna's father. He'd obviously broached the topic during one of yesterday's excursions.

Smart. Much more natural than sitting her down to address the issue. Trinity didn't want to lie to the girl about not knowing—or admit she did know—so she simply said, "He isn't a nice man."

"No. What he did to my mom..." Zoe expelled a shuddering breath. "It was gross. My grandmother didn't help my mom get away from him. That wasn't right."

"A parent's job is to protect their child." Trinity kept her voice even. "It sounds like that's what your mother did. She made sure your grandfather couldn't harm you."

"My grandparents want to see me, but I don't want to see them. Not ever." Zoe's chin jutted out.

Trinity saw Ryder in her profile, and her heart sighed.

"Your dad won't let anyone hurt you either."

"That's what he said." Zoe bit her lower lip. "I wasn't sure I wanted to come here. I didn't know him, and it was scary to go far away with a stranger."

"He's not a stranger now."

"No, he isn't." Zoe flashed a smile. "I'm glad he came for me and that I'm here. Even if he is a growly bear before he gets his coffee."

Trinity laughed. "Aren't we all?"

The school, a single-story brick building, came into view, and

Zoe sat up straighter. The child's gaze scanned the groups of boys and girls who were apparently in no rush to get inside.

"I see Lia and Brynn." Zoe's voice held an excited quiver. "Stop right here and let me out."

Trinity pulled up behind a minivan unloading two kids. "Make it a good day."

Zoe chuckled as she pushed open the door and called out, waving wildly, "Brynn. Lia."

Trinity expected her to dash off, like a racehorse hearing the starting bell. Instead, Zoe turned back. "Thanks for the ride. You're the best."

As Trinity watched her race across the schoolyard to join her new friends, her heart stuttered.

You're the best.

As she put the car in gear and pulled away from the curb, she thought of Miles's daughters. They'd never said such a thing to her, would never have even thought it.

Some of that was on them, sure. But had she done all she could to build a relationship?

She'd been so young. So in love with Miles. And so overwhelmed by her studies that there hadn't been a lot left of her to give. Still, she'd tried.

When guilt threatened to swamp her, she reminded herself she *had* tried. They hadn't given her a chance. They hadn't wanted to give her a chance.

They saw Miles's marriage as an act of disrespect toward their mother. Their ages hadn't helped the situation. Neither had the fact that Miles refused to address the issue of their rudeness to his new wife.

She shoved the memories aside. That was then. This was now.

Helping Ryder felt good. She liked Zoe. If she could help ease their transition into becoming a strong family unit, that's what she'd do.

Only when she reached Connections did it hit Trinity that she wouldn't be just dealing with numbers and reports this morning. She had a session with a client on the schedule.

When Trinity walked through the front door, she spotted Gladys Bertholf sitting in one of the chairs, a full thirty minutes before her session.

Gladys immediately stood. "I hoped we could start a little early. My Wii bowling team made it to the finals of the tournament. I'd like to be back in time to help my teammates win."

Trinity paused. She *could* refuse to move up the start time of their visit. But why would she do that when she had the time and the woman's reason for this visit intrigued her?

"I can make that work." Trinity turned to Peyton, who'd been watching the interaction with curious eyes. "Peyton, would you please show Mrs. Bertholf to my office? I'll be there in a few minutes."

When Trinity strolled into her office, she found Gladys perusing the framed diplomas on the wall.

Gladys turned, the silver threads in her caftan catching the overhead light. "Summa cum laude. Impressive."

"Thank you." Trinity smiled and gestured to the seating area. "Now, if—"

"Especially impressive considering your background."

Trinity cocked her head. "My background?"

"Sit. Sit." Gladys motioned to one of the chairs. "These old bones need to rest, but I make it a point not to sit while someone else is standing."

Trinity knew immediately what Gladys was doing, and it didn't have a thing to do with *old bones*. It had to do with control.

Instead of Trinity requesting Gladys have a seat, Gladys was the one ordering Trinity to sit. Trinity found herself even more intrigued.

Once they were both seated, Gladys waved an imperious hand, as if giving her the nod to speak. "I know you were once in foster care, like your brother. I don't know the particulars."

Gladys paused and the silence stretched.

Trinity had to hand it to her. Gladys knew that silence was a mighty weapon. Most people became uncomfortable after a handful of seconds and rushed to fill it.

"Why don't we start by you telling me about yourself and what brought you in today?" Trinity might have broken that silence first, but not in the way Gladys had obviously hoped.

Those pale blue eyes narrowed. "I thought we'd get better acquainted first."

"Isn't that what we're doing?" Trinity asked innocently.

"We have all the time in the world to talk about me." Gladys's husky voice lowered, and she leaned slightly forward. "I need to know more about the person with whom I'm sharing my secrets."

Though a bit unusual, this wasn't the first time a client had inquired about her background. Usually to make sure she had credentials they felt were appropriate. More often because it diverted the focus from their issues.

In Gladys's case, Trinity would assume the former, though she suspected the latter.

"As you saw, I received my PhD in clinical psychology from the University of Minnesota in the Twin Cities. It's one of the top-ranked programs in the country. I've been practicing for the past three years in Omaha."

"Impressive." Gladys studied her for a long moment. "Now tell me about your personal life."

Trinity didn't know Gladys well, but the woman was clearly a boundaries-pusher. If Trinity didn't set firm limits now, she'd be answering all sorts of questions about her personal life in each session.

It was time to make it clear that such questions were inappropriate.

Trinity inclined her head as the silence once again lengthened. "The focus of this session is to help you with your issue. Why don't you tell me what brought you here today?"

Gladys blinked and straightened in her seat. Clearly, she hadn't expected any pushback. "I'm surprised you're refusing to answer my question."

Trinity liked women with spunk, and this one had it in spades. "As I said, the focus in this session is you and your needs. If you're wondering if I have the necessary skills to help with your issues, I've offered you my credentials. You've inspected my diplomas and licenses. A counseling session is not a chat with a friend."

"Well." Gladys adjusted the fabric of her lime-green caftan, a style she seemed to favor. "I have another question for you. Your answer is very relevant to this session, so I must have an answer."

Trinity kept a polite smile on her face. "What's the question?"

"Do you believe in love at first sight?"

"Do you?"

Gladys surprised Trinity by leaning over and patting her hand. "I see what's happening here. It's easy to forget you're new to Good Hope and I'm a stranger. Of course you wouldn't feel comfortable confiding your thoughts and feelings to me."

Trinity blinked. The woman was a master. She could shift the discussion so quickly that even Trinity was caught off guard —*almost*. But Trinity knew this game. She'd wait to see where Gladys was headed before redirecting.

"I've lived in this community my entire life. I was married to a wonderful man for more years than you've been alive. Henry passed twenty years ago this month, and I miss him every day." A shadow passed over Gladys's face. "We had one son, Frank. He's retired now and lives in Gills Rock. He's a wonderful man, just like his father. I've been active in a number of civic organizations, but community theater is my passion. I have many good friends, and my life has been blessed beyond measure."

She had a voice that mesmerized as she offered details of her life, details that gave no explanation as to why she was here today. Other than the question about love at first sight.

Gladys flashed an expectant smile. "Now—"

"I hear you're a bit of a matchmaker."

Startled surprise skittered across Gladys's face. "Is that what you heard?"

Trinity found it interesting that Gladys neither confirmed nor denied the assertion. "You've been instrumental in bringing lots of couples happily together."

The older woman's lips curved. A softness filled her pale blue eyes. "As I said, I was happy in my marriage. I want the same for others. Like you and—"

"What about for yourself?"

"What about me?"

"You asked about love at first sight. Is romantic love in the cards for Gladys Bertholf?" Trinity settled back in her chair, getting comfortable.

"I'm too old."

Trinity chuckled. "C'mon. You're an attractive, vibrant woman."

"I'm also ninety-seven."

"All the more reason to go after what you want." Trinity kept her voice offhand. "Has someone caught your eye?"

Trinity had been in Good Hope long enough to hear the stories of Gladys and her matchmaking friends. Hadley had teased that Gladys had her and Ryder in her cross hairs.

She didn't doubt that for a minute. Perhaps that was part of the reason Gladys had made this appointment, to try to suss out the progress of her and Ryder's relationship. But Trinity knew in her gut that wasn't the only reason.

"There's a man at the Living Center, Albert August. His wife died several years ago. He used to be a principal at the high school. Fascinating gentleman."

"He caught your eye."

"He's caught the eye of every woman at the Living Center. Once you get past eighty, good men are nearly impossible to find."

The flippant tone didn't fool Trinity.

Trinity offered an encouraging smile. "Tell me about Albert."

"He's eighty-eight." Gladys twisted a large emerald ring back and forth. "I enjoy his company, the conversations we have, our debates on issues that matter. He makes me laugh."

Just like Ryder and me, Trinity thought.

"When we spend time together, my friends tease that I'm robbing the cradle."

"I happen to think when two people are both over twenty-one, there's no cradle to rob."

Gladys's eyes widened ever so slightly. "You don't think he's too young for me?"

"No." Despite what Gladys might claim, Trinity was now confident her relationship with Albert was the reason Gladys was here today. "Why have you been holding back?"

Gladys sniffed. "Who says I am?"

Trinity simply offered an encouraging smile.

Gladys hesitated for a long moment. "His children hate me. They told Albert point-blank they don't want him spending so much time with me." Emotion swarmed her eyes. "I don't know why. They only come by to see him every couple of weeks and on holidays. It isn't as if I'm taking time away from them."

For some reason, the comment brought back memories of a concert Trinity had been looking forward to attending with Miles. The tickets had been bought and dinner reservations made. Trinity had sensed her marriage slipping away and hoped this would be a step in the right direction.

"You never spend any time with us," the girls had wailed, asserting they'd planned a movie night especially for him, with popcorn and Jujyfruits. It was to be an evening at home like the ones they'd enjoyed as a family before their mom got sick.

Touched and overcome with guilt, Miles had told Trinity he needed to stay home. She hadn't argued, had merely called a friend and spent the evening with her, smiling on the outside while inwardly contemplating the demise of her marriage.

"This likely isn't personal. They would probably feel this way about any woman he showed a special interest in."

Gladys inclined her head and motioned for Trinity to continue.

"Their reaction could be fear or jealousy. Or they could simply be protective of their father and worried he'll get hurt."

"You're saying it's a lost cause."

"Not at all." Trinity leaned forward, resting her forearms on her thighs. "Charles Swindoll once said that great opportunities are often brilliantly disguised as impossible situations."

Gladys's lips curved in a slow smile. "A challenge fires my determination on all burners. If Albert's children don't like me being with him, so be it. He likes me. I like him. Do you know what else?"

Trinity arched a brow.

"I like you." Gladys reached over and gave Trinity's hand a squeeze. "Mark my words, Trinity McConnell. You and I are destined to be bosom friends."

CHAPTER FIFTEEN

"When I met with *Dr. McConnell* yesterday," Gladys lowered her voice for their ears only, "she was not forthcoming with any personal information."

The breakfast crowd at the Living Center had cleared out, leaving Gladys and her three friends alone in the cavernous dining room. The early lunch crowd wouldn't start arriving for another thirty minutes, and the staff was busy getting ready.

"Today is a red-letter day. Gladys is finally ready to share information about her session." Ruby leaned forward and rested her forearms on the table. "Katherine and I have been champing at the bit for the news."

"You kept the details to yourself until now." Disapproval rang heavy in Katherine's voice. "Even though you had many opportunities last night and this morning, even though we repeatedly asked. I don't understand the radio silence."

Oaklee, on tap to run errands for Gladys this afternoon, shared Katherine's frustration. The reticence hadn't been like Gladys. Normally, their fearless leader overshared. Of course, there was power in having information others wanted and keeping it to yourself. "I thought we were a team."

"If you must know, I was extremely frustrated by the session." Gladys tapped a finger on the table, her lips pressed together.

Had that really been a tremble in the older woman's voice? Oaklee dismissed the thought almost immediately. Knowing Gladys, if it was there, she'd included it for theatrical effect.

"Tell us now." Ruby gave Gladys's hand a squeeze. "We acknowledge your great sacrifice in stepping into the lion's den alone."

"I did." Gladys brought a cup of coffee to her lips, seeming to steady at the admiration in Ruby's voice.

Oaklee wasn't sure seeing a counselor—oh, excuse me, a *psychologist*—was such a big deal. Her ultraconservative parents had insisted she see one after she'd come home with her first tat, convinced she was in the fast lane to hell.

"Enough already. You've kept us waiting long enough. What happened?"

Katherine's blunt tone had heat flashing in Gladys's eyes, but she regained control almost immediately.

"Although I pressed, the good doctor refused to say much about her personal life. I went at her from all different angles and came in hard."

"Give no quarter," Oaklee murmured, pouring herself a cup of coffee from the carafe on the table.

"Exactly." Gladys nodded approvingly. "She's a tough nut to crack. All she wanted to do was talk about me and my issues."

"Understandable, considering that's why most people see a psychologist." Ruby appeared to be hiding a smile.

"There is that," Gladys agreed.

"What did you do?" Katherine, never one for long, drawn-out stories, pinned Gladys with a steely-eyed look.

Gladys bestowed a lofty glance on her friend and responded in an imperious manner. "Since the purpose of my appointment was to find out the status of her relationship with Ryder, and she was playing hardball, I saw only one option."

"You lost me." Oaklee might have been the one to voice the thought, but from the looks on the faces of the other two women, she wasn't the only one confused.

Gladys's lips lifted in a sly smile. "Why, I made up my own relationship problem."

"With a man?" Oaklee blurted.

"No. With a donkey." Gladys rolled her eyes. "Of course with a man."

"Did you make the guy up? Or does he really exist?"

Oaklee wasn't sure if it was Ruby or Katherine who asked, because she was too focused on watching Gladys's face. Which was why she didn't miss her heightened color.

"I used Albert." Gladys picked up the luncheon menu. "Shrimp scampi sounds good. I haven't—"

"Albert August?" Katherine pressed. "You told her you were in a relationship with Albert?"

Ruby brought a hand to her throat, her eyes as wide as saucers. "Our Albert?"

With an exaggerated sigh, Gladys set down her menu. "Could there be two?"

Oaklee had met Albert. A widower and retired principal, he was what some of the women at the Living Center called a "flutter bun."

Handsome, intelligent with a dry wit, he excelled at magic tricks. Oaklee had caught one of his performances when she'd stopped by the Living Center during Open Stage Night.

Come to think of it, most of the women in the audience had appeared mesmerized by the man.

"You're saying you told Trinity you and Albert are involved and having relationship issues?" Disapproval ran through Katherine's tone.

"I had to say something." Gladys lifted her chin. "I thought of her and Ryder and came up with a story of how I like Albert but worry about his children's reaction."

"They took their mother's death hard," Ruby mused. "Even though they don't come around often, they seem to resent it if he doesn't give them his full attention when they want it."

Gladys nodded. "I brought up the situation with Albert and his kids, hoping Trinity might see a parallel in her relationship with Ryder and his daughter."

Ruby's blond brows pulled together. "Do you really think Trinity broke up with Ryder because he has a daughter now? I can't believe that. She has such nice teeth."

"Nice teeth? Ruby, what on earth are you talking about?" Katherine dropped her menu to stare fully at her friend.

"I'm talking about her smile. It's nice. People with nice smiles don't dislike children. Everyone knows that," Rudy responded.

"That is not true," Katherine snapped. "Well, Trinity does have a nice smile, that part is true. But as for the other bit—"

"Enough!" Gladys snapped. "I have no idea how—or if—Zoe has impacted Trinity and Ryder's relationship. I simply had to come up with something that would merit an appointment." Gladys straightened her spine and affected her most regal air. "So sorry my scenario doesn't meet with your approval."

"Gladys tried. That's what matters." Katherine smiled as she returned her attention to her menu.

Oaklee looked up from her own menu. Gladys was right. The scampi appeared to be the best option. "I bet you're relieved you don't have to go back for more counseling."

"I made another appointment." Gladys waved a careless hand in the air. "It's simply another way for me to get to know Trinity better and for her to trust me."

"Better be careful," Oaklee warned.

Gladys raised a penciled brow.

Oaklee chuckled. "You're going to talk to her so much about Albert, you'll end up believing you *are* in love with the guy."

The others laughed.

A half smile lifted Gladys's lip. "Stranger things."

~

On Wednesday, Trinity left the clinic early to distribute the Healthy Taste of Good Hope flyers. Though it seemed late to be putting them up—only three days before the event—Liam told her those who lived in Good Hope read the Open Door, which had been hyping the event. Tourists, on the other hand, often arrived mid to late week and stayed through the weekend. In her partner's estimation, this was the perfect time to let them know about the event.

She stepped out of Swoon and had to side-step to avoid running into Raven.

"Excuse me," Raven began, then stopped and smiled. "Trinity. Hi. Where have you been keeping yourself? I haven't seen you at the Grind lately."

Trinity shifted the flyers from one hand to the other. "I've been making my morning coffee at home, then heading straight to the clinic."

Raven glanced curiously at the papers in her hands. "What are those?"

"Flyers advertising A Healthy Taste of Good Hope." Though she'd had the box of them in her car, she hadn't thought to give any to Ryder. "Would you mind taking a few and putting them up at the Grind?"

"Sure." Raven's eyes turned watchful. "Don't you want to stop by and give them to Ryder yourself?"

"I do." Truer words, Trinity thought. She longed to see him. But running into him around the Barn was hard enough. No need to deliberately put herself in the path of temptation. "But I've got a boatload of these still to distribute."

"Is everything okay between you two?"

The girl was nobody's fool.

Trinity smiled. "His priority right now is Zoe. Mine is my

new position. Doesn't leave much time for anything else, I'm afraid."

Raven studied her for a long moment, then took the flyers Trinity held out. "It's like being almost there, but nowhere near it."

Before Trinity could respond to the butchered Lorelai Gilmore quote, Raven headed down the sidewalk in the direction of the Daily Grind.

"All that matters is we're going," she murmured, finishing the quote. But Trinity wasn't going. Not in the direction of Ryder Goodhue.

The thought took some of the shine off of a day that spoke of fall in a crisp whisper.

Several more strides down the sidewalk brought Trinity to Blooms Bake Shop. Pushing the door open, she paused to inhale the delicious aroma of fresh-baked bread and the sweet scent of sugar mixed with cinnamon.

Ami smiled a quick welcome, then returned her attention to two customers who couldn't seem to decide on which pastry to buy.

Trinity hung back, not wanting to rush the women. Though she could have simply left the flyer, she'd learned in her short time in Good Hope that this wasn't a community where you hurried. Fostering connections was as important as completing a task.

As Trinity hadn't spent much time in the shop, this gave her a chance to look around. She loved everything about the boho-chic vibe. The trim around the windows and doors was a soft mint green, one of Trinity's favorite colors.

She stood next to a three-tiered round table that held prepackaged bags of treats. Chalkboards scattered around the shop listed prices. Ami looked more like a college girl than a mother of two, with her hair pulled back in a bouncy tail and wearing a pink tee emblazoned with the shop's logo and the words "Baking Up Some Love."

"You've been so helpful," one of the women gushed.

Trinity shifted her gaze in time to see Ami hand each of the women a white bakery sack. "I have no doubt you're going to love the kouign amann and the cherry Danish."

The other woman, with hair the color of pewter, chuckled. "We're meeting our husbands for an early dinner at Muddy Boots, but I'd almost rather eat these than a meal."

"You'll love the food at Muddy Boots," Ami told the women. "I make the desserts. You really have to try tonight's special dessert, cherry and plum crumble with real whipped cream."

The two women exchanged smiles.

"No need to tell the men about these treats." The one with salt-and-pepper hair lifted her sack. "Otherwise, they'll grumble about us ordering dessert."

The other woman offered her friend a conspiratorial smile. "Agreed."

After another minute of conversation, they left, their happy chatter seeming to linger in the air even after the door jingled shut behind them.

Trinity stepped forward. "Looks like you got yourself two satisfied customers."

Ami smiled. "Meeting new people is the best part of what I do here. I'm sorry I kept you waiting."

Gesturing with one hand, Trinity let her gaze travel around the bakery once again. "It gave me a chance to check out your lovely shop."

"It keeps me busy, but I love it." Ami cocked her head and looked at the flyers in Trinity's hands. "What's that?"

For a second, Trinity had forgotten there was a reason for her visit. "Flyers for the Healthy Taste of Good Hope. We're asking businesses to put one up to remind customers of Saturday's event."

"I'm happy to post one. Both Muddy Boots and the bake shop will be participating—"

The door slammed opened, the bells jingling wildly as Zoe and Brynn rushed in.

Zoe pulled the door shut so hard it rattled.

Alarm skittered up Trinity's spine as Zoe rushed to her.

Ami rounded the counter. "Brynn, honey. What's wrong?"

"A man, he was following us." Brynn's breath came in short puffs.

"I didn't notice him at first," Zoe told Trinity, her eyes wide. "Brynn said he'd been watching us since we left school."

Ami moved to the door and locked it. Her gaze searched the sidewalk, then narrowed. "Is the man tall and really skinny, wearing a green shirt and sunglasses?"

Brynn's eyes widened.

"He's out there?" Zoe's voice was a high-pitched squeak.

Ami pressed her lips together and pulled a phone from her pocket. "I'm calling the sheriff."

CHAPTER SIXTEEN

While Ami dialed Cade Rallis, Trinity looped an arm around Zoe's shoulders. "You did the right thing in coming here."

"The sheriff is on his way," Ami assured the girls. "You're safe now."

Zoe turned to Trinity. "What are you doing here?"

Trinity gestured to the flyers she'd left on the counter. "Handing out the flyers Brynn's mom gave me to distribute."

She wanted to pump the girls for details about the stranger, but knew it was best to let them give their statement to the sheriff first. There was one question that couldn't wait. "Did this guy get close enough to touch either of you?"

Brynn and Zoe shook their heads at the same time.

"We walked really fast." Palms down, Brynn made quick up-and-down movements with her hands.

"We ran the last block," Zoe added.

Two tiny lines appeared between Ami's brows, though she kept her tone conversational. "I called your mom, Brynn, but it went straight to voice mail."

"She had a doctor's appointment today. You have to have them after having a baby. She may have turned the ringer off during the visit. Dad is in Chicago at a meeting." Brynn's nervous chatter told Trinity the girl wasn't as calm as she tried to appear. "That's why I was walking with Zoe to the Daily Grind after school. Mom was going to pick me up there after the appointment."

Ami lifted her phone. "I'll text her."

"I'll call Ryder."

"Don't." Zoe put a hand on Trinity's arm. "He's busy, and nothing happened."

Trinity had already pressed his number. "He'll want to know."

"Trinity," Ryder said. "It's good to hear from you."

In the background, Trinity heard the hiss of the coffee machine and the sound of voices. Lots of voices. What did it mean that instead of letting the call go to voice mail, he'd answered?

"Zoe is with me at Blooms Bake Shop." She quickly explained what she knew, then added, "The sheriff is on his way to speak with the girls. I'll be here, and she can come home with me if—"

"I'll be right there."

The call disconnected.

"Your dad is on his way," she told Zoe.

Ami was now speaking with Hadley, who'd called as soon as she'd received the text "I promise. I won't let her out of my sight."

The second Ami turned to Brynn, a knock sounded at the door.

Trinity's heart gave a solid thump against her chest.

Ami inhaled sharply, then her breath came out in a whoosh. "It's Cade."

He rattled the door handle.

"Ohmigosh, it's still locked." Instead of hurrying to the door, Ami just stood there.

"I'll get it." Trinity flipped the dead bolt and opened the door.

She didn't know much about Cade, other than he was married to Marigold and used to work for Detroit PD. Tall with a square jaw, muscular body and dark hair cut military short, he looked as if he could hold his own against any criminal.

His badge was hooked to his belt, and he wore his weapon in a hip holster. He wasn't wearing the brown uniform Trinity had seen his deputies wear, but managed to look daunting even in a polo shirt and khakis.

He smiled and gestured to a table painted bright pink. "Let's sit down. I need the girls to tell me what happened."

His sharp-eyed gaze shifted to the two girls, who dropped into two adjacent chairs and held hands. Trinity took a seat next to Zoe, while Ami chose the one on the other side of Brynn.

"Did you notify their parents?" Cade asked.

At that moment, Hadley rushed through the door with Ryder on her heels.

Ami rose to give her friend a quick hug, then flipped the Open sign to Closed and relocked the door.

"Looks like that question has been answered. From what Ami tells me, the girls weren't assaulted."

Hadley blanched. "Assaulted?"

A muscle jumped in Ryder's jaw as he crouched beside his daughter. "Are you okay?"

"We were scared," Brynn said before Zoe could answer.

"Really scared." Zoe nodded. "For a minute or two."

Cade's gaze shifted between Zoe and Brynn. "Who wants to tell me what happened?"

"We were walking to the Grind after school because Mom had a doctor's appointment." Brynn frowned as if realizing her brother was nowhere in sight. "Where's Carter?"

"Prim was watching him for me while I had my appointment. I called her on the way here." Hadley kept her eyes on her daughter. "Your brother is fine. It's you I'm worried about."

"We didn't do anything wrong." Zoe glanced at her father.

Ryder took her hand, gave it a squeeze. "I know you didn't. Why don't you tell Sheriff Rallis what happened?"

Zoe and Brynn exchanged a glance.

After a heartbeat of silence, Zoe raised her hand. "I'll tell it."

Brynn nodded. "'Kay."

"I didn't notice the guy until Brynn whispered that we were being followed. I thought she was pranking, but she wasn't."

Cade shifted his gaze. "When did you first notice the man, Brynn?"

"I saw him this morning before school."

"You did?" Zoe turned to her friend. "You didn't say."

"I thought maybe he was a parent, but I didn't recognize him. He was across the street from the school, just…staring."

"At you?" Cade asked.

"I don't know." Brynn lifted one shoulder, let it drop. "The bell rang, and I forgot all about him. After school, Zoe and I talked with Hannah and Sabine for a while, then we started walking. About a block or so from the school grounds, I got this weird feeling—you know how I get them sometimes." Brynn looked at her mother for confirmation.

Hadley nodded.

"Well, I got this feeling, so I glanced over my shoulder." Brynn hesitated. "I didn't say anything to Zoe right away, because, hey, it was just a guy walking."

"Was he alone or with someone?" Cade asked.

"Alone," Brynn said immediately.

Zoe nodded.

"He was still there after another block. There weren't a lot of people in the area, just us and him. When I looked again, he was closer."

"How close?"

"Half a block, maybe less." Brynn glanced at Zoe. "I said something to Zoe about being followed. I could tell she thought I was kidding."

"Then he talked." Zoe wrinkled her nose.

"He spoke to you?" Ryder's voice snapped like a whip.

Trinity put a hand on his arm and shot him a look. She understood he was worried, but he needed to dial it down.

When he blew out a breath and nodded, she knew he'd gotten the message.

"Not exactly to us, but yeah, to us." Zoe considered. "He called out, said he was looking for the Daily Grind and could we give him directions."

Cade's eyes narrowed. "He mentioned your dad's business specifically?"

"Yeah. For a second, I thought about telling him that's where we were headed." Zoe's eyes darkened. "But the request was bogus. I mean, he could find out where it is just by looking on his phone."

"I said run," Brynn told them. "And Zoe and me took off."

Cade cocked his head. "Did he chase you?"

"I don't know, 'cause we didn't look back. At least I didn't." Brynn shot another glance at Zoe.

"I didn't either," Zoe told the sheriff. "Once we reached downtown, we ran in here."

"I looked out the window and saw—" Ami began, but Cade held up a hand, stopping her.

"Can you girls describe the man?"

"He was old, about my dad's age." Zoe glanced at Ryder, who offered a reassuring smile. "His hair was brown and short, and he wore a green shirt."

"His sunglasses were like mirrors," Brynn added. "He was super skinny."

"As I was locking the door, I looked out the window and saw a man fitting that description walk by the shop," Ami explained. "I didn't recognize him, and he made no move to come in."

Cade turned to the girls. "Did he say anything else to you other than to ask for directions?"

"That's all," Brynn said. "Other than he was whistling some dorky tune."

"Yeah." Zoe smiled. "You're right. It was really dorky."

The girls giggled.

"You young ladies did the right thing by not speaking with him and finding a safe place with adults." Cade pushed back his chair and stood. "If you see him again, steer clear and tell an adult. Do you understand?"

Zoe nodded, her face suddenly pale and oh-so-young.

Trinity's heart swelled with love when Zoe leaned close to her. She wrapped a supportive arm around the child's shoulders.

"What's going to happen to him?" Brynn asked.

"My deputies and I will speak with him," Cade advised her. "We'll see what's going on. His behavior wasn't criminal, but it bumps my radar."

"Brynn and Zoe, I went crazy baking brownies this morning and made way more than I can sell. There are two boxes on the bottom shelf of the refrigerator." Ami gestured toward the back of the shop. "Why don't you get them? Each of you can take a box home for you and your family to enjoy this evening."

Zoe's eyes lit up. "Thank you."

"Superduper thank you." Brynn popped up from her seat. "I've been begging my mom for brownies."

Once the girls disappeared from sight, Ryder turned to Cade. "Any idea who this man is? Do you think he targeted the girls specifically?"

"That was my question, too." Hadley's worried look had Ami giving her friend's hand a supportive squeeze.

"I'll know more once we locate him and have a chat." Cade rubbed his chin. "I'd encourage the girls to always be with a buddy and to continue to be aware of their surroundings and 'weird feelings.' Praise them for their quick thinking and smart choices. They paid attention."

"If he'd grabbed—" Hadley brought a hand to her mouth and shuddered.

"He didn't." Ami rubbed her friend's shoulder.

"It may have been nothing." Cade's gaze grew thoughtful. "The fact that Brynn noticed him outside of the school this morning makes it a whole lot less innocent. I'm going to mention this to Clay. See if any of the teachers have seen a guy matching this description hanging around the schoolyard."

"Thank you," Hadley said.

"Yes." Ryder blew out a breath. "Thank you."

"If the girls recall anything else, contact me," Cade instructed. "If I have more questions, I know where to find you."

"We have brownies," Brynn announced, holding her bakery box high.

"Lots of yummy brownies." Zoe lifted hers with a flourish. "With sprinkles."

"I think I'm more traumatized by this whole event than they are," Ryder said under his breath to Trinity.

"You and me both." Trinity flashed a smile in Zoe's direction. "I sure hope you plan on sharing those with your next-door neighbor."

That night, while Zoe was in her room doing homework, Ryder sat with Trinity on the back patio. After setting down a plate with two brownies, he poured them each a glass of wine from the bottle he'd brought outside.

Ryder stared into his glass for a long moment before looking up. "You know, I almost mentioned Geoffrey Swanson to Cade, but when the girls said he looked to be about my age I decided it couldn't be him."

Trinity nodded agreement and took a sip of wine. "Zoe appears to be handling this afternoon's crisis well."

"She is now," Ryder acknowledged. "She cried when we first got home."

"She did?" Concern furrowed Trinity's brow. "Was she worried or—"

"I have no idea." Ryder bit into a brownie and chewed thoughtfully. "We got here, went inside, and she started shaking and crying."

"What did you do?"

"I put my arms around her. I held her until she quit crying." In that moment, he'd silently cursed the man who'd scared his daughter. The overwhelming surge of protectiveness and love he'd felt for Zoe had shocked him with its intensity.

"It's good she feels like she can be vulnerable in front of you."

"I don't know about that." Ryder chased the brownie down with wine. "But she seemed better after she cried."

"I hope you understand why I turned down your dinner invitation." Trinity's gaze searched his face. "I thought the two of you needed the time alone."

"Do you know what she said to me?" Ryder couldn't keep the shock from his voice.

Trinity shook her head.

"She thanked me for believing her. Can you believe that?"

Trinity reached over, covered his hand with hers and gave it a squeeze.

"Why wouldn't I believe her?" Ryder blew out a breath.

"Look at Jenna's mother." Trinity's voice hardened. "She didn't believe her daughter."

"I don't even want to think about her." Ryder made a dismissive motion with his hand, done talking about crying and bad mothers. "Cade called. They located the guy and have already spoken with him."

"That's wonderful news. Who is he? What did he want?" Trinity reached over and gripped Ryder's arm. "Is he in jail?"

"They can't charge him since he didn't do anything illegal." Ryder pressed his lips together. "The guy is a private investigator."

"What's a PI doing following two middle-school girls?"

"He wouldn't divulge the name of his client, and the police can't make him say, but I'm betting he's working for Geoffrey Swanson."

"Why would he have Zoe followed?"

"My guess is he's looking for some signs of abuse or neglect." Ryder tried to tamp down the spike of anger. "It pisses me off that his PI scared two little girls for no reason."

"Maybe in the long run it will be a good thing. Nothing happened, and they'll be more watchful, more careful."

Raising the glass to his lips, Ryder supposed that was one way to look at the situation. But talking about the incident only made him angry all over again.

Trinity rubbed the dog with the side of her foot. "I've been wanting to ask how the session with Liam went."

Her super-casual tone didn't fool him. Ryder hoped she knew just how much he appreciated her willingness to change the subject.

"I'm not asking for a blow-by-blow. That's confidential," Trinity hastened to clarify when the silence lengthened. "I just wondered if you think Zoe and Liam will work well together."

"He put us both at ease. Zoe regaled him with stories about her mother and all the things they used to do together." Ryder smiled. As he'd listened, he'd realized that Jenna had been a terrific mom. "Lots of happy memories. Toward the end of the session, Liam must have sensed it was becoming more difficult for her, you know, to speak about her mom, so he redirected the discussion to school and her new friends."

"I imagine the session could have gone on forever once he got her talking about Brynn and Lia."

"You know her well." Ryder chuckled. "I like Liam's style. More importantly, Zoe likes him. She'll see him again, alone next time."

Relief washed over Trinity. "That makes me happy."

The obvious affection in her voice touched Ryder. It appeared his heart wasn't the only one that Zoe had captured in the last four weeks.

"Being a father feels right," he told her. "I knew I wanted kids someday, but it was difficult to imagine myself as a dad. I'm glad Zoe came into my life."

It might be an odd way to phrase the sentiment, but she appeared to understand. "You two seem to be getting along well."

He reached over and gently touched her hand. "Thanks for talking with her about the counseling. When Liam called and said he had a cancellation today, she was open to meeting with him."

"She's a terrific kid."

"Zoe likes you, too." Ryder gestured with his glass. "Enough about my household. Tell me about your day."

This was one of the things Trinity liked most about Ryder. It wasn't all about him. He appeared to genuinely care what was going on in other people's lives. Or at least he had an interest in hers.

She also understood he was done with this afternoon's incident. Until they had more information—like confirmation of the investigator's client—there was nothing else to say, and speculation served no purpose.

"I wrote up some reports and saw a couple of clients. One Liam had transitioned to me, the other was new."

Ryder arched a questioning brow. "How'd the session with the new person go?"

She understood he wasn't probing for specifics. "Good. When you meet someone for the first time, it's like a puzzle. You get some pieces right away, but not all. Often, a client holds back some of the pieces you need to see to fully understand."

"It's a question of trust."

"It is, and trust takes time to build."

"Zoe is starting to trust me." Pride filled Ryder's voice. "I hope eventually she'll realize she can put her faith in me."

"You're being honest and up front with her. That means a lot to kids that age." Trinity gave a little laugh. "Heck, it means a lot no matter how old or young you are."

"Yes, well, right now my primary concern is keeping her safe." His tone held a terse edge.

Trinity wondered at this change in mood. Was Ryder concerned that trusting fully would never come? She wished she could reassure him, but she knew trust—like most things of value—took time and could be hard to win.

CHAPTER SEVENTEEN

"Is it bad that I feel happy Zoe is under lock and key tonight?" Ryder spoke the words in Trinity's ear.

He had to lean close. The clogging group onstage had Irish music blasting.

Trinity chuckled and took his hand, pulling him farther away from the bandstand.

Though the music wasn't her favorite, they'd drawn a good crowd, and the dancers illustrated how you could get a great cardio workout while doing something you love.

"I still don't understand why Dan and Katie Ruth scheduled a church lock-in for tonight." Trinity made a sweep with her hand. "This is a once-a-year event."

"It doesn't make sense to me either." Ryder shrugged. "I asked Dan, and he said this was the only Saturday they didn't have a wedding scheduled at the church."

"You confirmed, no boys, right?"

"Absolutely. That was my first question." Ryder rubbed his chin. "He assured me that Katie Ruth would be with the girls at all times."

"She seemed excited." The lock-in hadn't started until six.

That had given Zoe time to wander around the health fair with them before they'd dropped her off at the church.

"It'll be interesting to hear what she thinks of it."

"I can't wait to hear all about her experience." Trinity stopped beside the Sombreros booth and inhaled. "The smell of those freshly made tortillas sure brings back pleasant memories."

Ryder's face went blank for a moment. When he smiled, her heart flip-flopped. "That was a wonderful evening. Then again, anytime I'm with you is wonderful."

A warmth flowed through Trinity's body. She considered reminding him—and herself—they were just friends. He didn't feel like a friend. Despite her best efforts, her feelings for Ryder had only continued to deepen.

Zoe, too, was someone Trinity was growing to love. What was even more amazing, Trinity felt like Zoe cared for her as well. It was so very different from her situation with Miles and his daughters, despite the fact that both involved loss.

"I didn't want to ask with Zoe around, but was the private investigator still being in town part of the reason you were okay with the lock-in?"

"His client has to be Geoffrey Swanson." Ryder blew out a breath. "The fact that there's nothing legally that can be done only makes me angrier."

"The PI knows Cade and the deputies will be keeping a close watch on him." Trinity's tone turned soothing, even though she found herself equally frustrated. "He won't be hanging around here much longer now that his cover is blown."

Ryder studied her for a long moment. "Have I told you lately just how amazing you are?"

He looked at her, Trinity thought, as if she was the most beautiful woman in the world. She'd never had anyone look at her the way he did.

"No," she kept her tone light, "but feel free to compliment me that way as often as you like."

He met her gaze. "Another benefit of the lock-in is we can spend as much time together tonight as we want without worrying about cutting the night short."

Trinity's heart began to thud, and heat raced through her body with a force that left her off-balance. Was Ryder asking her to sleep with him?

She told herself that if he *were* asking, the answer would be no. Friends didn't sleep with each other.

Though Trinity was fighting to keep her feelings at the buddy level, if the success of her efforts was measured by the intensity of her regard for him, she'd failed miserably.

She loved him. She could no longer deny that fact. He was a wonderful man, hardworking and kind. Instead of shying away from responsibility, he embraced fatherhood with admirable ease.

But now was not the time to consider a different course. There was no way she could make a rational decision tonight. Not with the moon overhead casting a golden glow and the intoxicating scent of his cologne mingling with all the other delicious aromas. Not when Ryder was looking at her with heat in his dark eyes.

"No pressure." Ryder put a gentle hand on hers, then slid it up her arm, leaving a trail of fire in its wake.

"I know we already ate, but I'm still hungry." Looping her arm through his, she smiled brightly. "What healthy option do you want to try next?"

The rest of the night passed quickly, and when they returned to the Barn, Trinity went to bed alone. As much as she wanted Ryder, before she acted, she had to be certain she was doing the right thing.

For her. For him. For Zoe.

~

Trinity planned to sit with Wyatt and Greer at church on Sunday. Her alarm went off on schedule, but she hit snooze two times before casting a bleary eye at the hour.

By the time she reached the full parking lot of First Christian, strains of the opening hymn wafted through the open front doors. She sent a quick text to Wyatt to tell him she'd be in the back.

Stepping into the sanctuary, Trinity saw with dismay that the back pews were filled with teenagers from the lock-in. She recognized one of the blond heads at the end of a pew as Zoe's. Beside her stood Brynn and Lia. The three shared the hymnal held by Zoe.

Three Musketeers.

Trinity's lips curved. It hadn't taken Zoe long to find her tribe. She hoped Jenna knew her daughter was happy and flourishing in her new environment.

Without warning, Zoe shoved the hymnal into Brynn's hands and slipped into the aisle to talk to Trinity while the congregation launched enthusiastically into the third verse of the opening hymn.

"My dad is halfway down on the right." Zoe's voice remained low as she pointed. "There's room for you."

"Thanks." Trinity remained where she was while Zoe returned to her friends.

She was still standing there when Zoe turned back and made a pushing motion with her hand.

Heaving a resigned sigh, Trinity made her way down the center aisle to where Ryder sat.

When she tapped him on the shoulder, he turned, and his warm smile of welcome had her knees turning to mush.

"Do you have space?" The pew actually looked pretty crowded to her. "I can find another seat if—"

He scooted over. "Plenty of room."

The hymn ended.

When she sat, Trinity realized that while there was room, *plenty* was stretching credulity. One of her thighs pressed tight against the side of the pew, while the other squeezed tight against Ryder's leg.

It wasn't totally unpleasant. Truth was, it wasn't unpleasant at all. Distracting, yes. Unpleasant, no.

He smelled terrific, an intoxicating scent that was spicy and musky at the same time. So faint it tempted her to lean close simply to get a better whiff.

"This will give us more room," Ryder whispered as he rested his arm on the back of the pew behind her.

Giving the nod to autumn, Trinity's burgundy beaded minidress had long sleeves. Despite her arms being completely covered, the warmth of his body pressed against her arm brought memories flooding back.

She thought of the nights they'd spent together. Oh, how she'd loved the feel of those clever fingers on—

Trinity stopped the thought before it could fully form. She made herself focus on the service. If there was ever an inappropriate place for reminiscing about lovemaking, it was here.

Concentrating on anything but Ryder proved difficult due to his nearness. Breathing in his cologne. The warmth of his arm against her shoulders. His fingers absently toying with her hair…

She couldn't sneak a glance in his direction without remembering what it had been like to kiss him. She loved the way his mouth had melded to hers and the way his fingers had tangled in her hair as he pulled her close. It had been as if he'd never wanted to let her go.

Her breath quickened, and her knees wobbled when they stood for the sermon hymn. She'd never have believed it, but there was something oddly intimate about sharing a hymnal with a man.

Well, maybe not just any man. She knew she wouldn't feel this way if it was Liam or Ethan at her side. There was just something about Ryder…

They settled back into their seats, and Pastor Dan launched into his sermon.

Trinity tensed when Dan asked the congregation to think about the worst day of their life. She had plenty of bad memories vying for that "honor."

It wasn't her own memories that worried her, but those of the child in the back pew. Zoe didn't have to look far for the worst day in her life. Losing her mom was a wound that still seeped pain and sorrow.

Ryder's arm tensed behind her shoulders, and she knew she wasn't the only one concerned.

It took everything in Trinity not to jump up and rush to Zoe's side. That, she knew, would only embarrass the girl.

"Bad things are a part of life. God never promises that bad things won't happen." Dan's gaze swept the congregation. "Live long enough, and they will happen to you."

Unable to resist any longer, Trinity shifted in her seat and glanced back.

Zoe's head rested on Brynn's shoulder.

"Brynn is stroking Zoe's hair," Trinity whispered to Ryder. "Giving her comfort."

"Why did Dan have to pick this as the sermon of the week?" Ryder's tone stopped just short of a growl.

"What we discover about ourselves and others in these horrible times can result in good coming out of the bad," Dan continued.

Trinity considered the minister's words. Her times with her mother and in foster care had led her to the McConnells' doorstep. There, she'd experienced a different life, one where people respected each other and education mattered.

Her new parents had helped mold her into the woman she was today. If it hadn't been for that last incident that had led her mother to "give her up," Trinity wouldn't have received the proper care and guidance she'd desperately needed.

"Often, it takes years before we have the wisdom to look back and see God at work in the aftermath of such tragedy."

Dan's words triggered a thought. Jenna's death had brought Ryder into his daughter's life.

The rest of the service passed in a blur. Stand up. Sit down. Sing. Pray.

Then it was over.

Trinity's emotions wrapped around her like a snake, squeezing her heart and making her feel weepy. A feeling she didn't like at all.

Old memories bubbled up, like dirty street water through a rusty grate. She reminded herself that ruminating on her mother's failings served no purpose. Taking a deep breath, Trinity rose and pasted a smile on her face.

She slanted a glance at Ryder as they strolled down the aisle. He was so handsome and so dear. The love rising inside her chased away the shadows. When he looked at her like he was looking at her now, with that knowing gleam in his dark eyes, her breath quickened and a deep yearning filled her body.

Get yourself under control, she thought sternly as they reached the back of the church, his hand on her arm.

It didn't help that the first person Trinity saw when she stepped into the foyer was Gladys. The older woman's pale blue eyes turned sharp and assessing.

After a second, her smile became a light source all its own beaming in their direction.

With her hands outstretched, Gladys barreled toward them, forcing several couples to step to the side to avoid being mowed down. "Just the two I was hoping to see."

Gladys captured Trinity's hands and gave them a tight squeeze. When her gaze swept over Ryder, then settled on Trinity, she had the feeling Gladys knew exactly what thoughts had been going through her head during the sermon.

"I'm so happy," Gladys said cryptically. "Thrilled, in fact."

Trinity didn't ask why. She had a feeling she already knew and worried that if she asked, Gladys might tell her.

"I'm happy you're happy," Trinity said, returning her smile.

"I have tickets for you." Gladys spoke quickly, as if noticing for the first time they were blocking foot traffic. "Friday is the dress rehearsal. I want you to be my guests."

Digging through her huge bag, Gladys pulled out a pair of tickets. "I look forward to seeing you there."

Ryder hesitated. "I'd love to see the show, but Zoe—"

"Don't worry about her and Brynn. I have plans." Gladys took a step back and motioned to her friends, including Oaklee, who'd shown remarkable restraint by remaining back. "See you Friday."

Once Gladys was out of earshot, Trinity touched a hand to her head. "What did she mean she has plans for Zoe?"

"I don't think I want to know." Ryder grinned and leaned close. "Though I got the feeling she knew exactly the path your mind—and mine-went down during the sermon. When you put your hand on my thigh—"

She swatted his arm and spoke in a controlled whisper. "I did not put my hand on your thigh."

"You wanted to."

Trinity chuckled and resisted—barely—the urge to swat him again. They were, after all, in a church. Maintaining some semblance of decorum seemed necessary.

Trinity dropped her gaze to the tickets. "I think I have a busier social life here than I did in Chicago or Omaha."

"That's the beauty of Good Hope. You get all the benefits of small-town life with big-city amenities." He lowered his voice and leaned close. "Not to mention you have me right next door."

This time, she did swat him. Still, she couldn't help but smile.

Getting to know Ryder and having him close was turning out to be the biggest bonus of all of living in Good Hope.

~

Although Wyatt had mentioned that everyone went to Muddy Boots for breakfast while their children were in Sunday school, the last thing Trinity wanted was to sit around rehashing the sermon.

"I believe Dan meant the message to be uplifting, but it was a downer."

Before Trinity could respond to Ryder, Wyatt hurried into the church foyer.

"You made it farther than the back row," he said, then cast a glance at Ryder. "Hey, Ryder."

"Those pews were filled with teenagers." Trinity kept her tone light. "Something told me they wouldn't appreciate an adult in their midst."

"An adult?" Wyatt widened his eyes in mock surprise. "Is that what we are?"

Her spirits lifted at Wyatt's teasing tone. "Difficult to believe, but true."

Greer appeared at her fiancé's side. "Will you be joining us at Muddy Boots?"

The glimmer of hope in her eyes made an outright no impossible.

"I'm not sure," Trinity demurred. "It's been a long, busy week."

"It's very informal," Greer told her. "Some people come every week. Others, like Ryder, show up sporadically. It's all good."

"Your mother and Steve are waving to us," Wyatt told his fiancée.

Greer surprised Trinity by giving her a quick hug, then a direct look. "Please come. We'd love for you to join us."

No pressure. Trinity smiled. She loved Greer's directness. Her parents were going to like her, too.

A few people spoke to Trinity on the short distance toward the exit, but the greetings weren't enough to slow her steady progress. She was nearly out the front door when Ryder fell back into step beside her.

"Where's Zoe?" Trinity glanced around, but the girl was nowhere in sight.

"She went to youth group with Brynn and Lia." Ryder lifted his shoulders in a shrug. "When I asked if she'd rather go home, she looked at me as if I'd lost my mind."

"Is she still upset over the sermon?" Trinity remembered how sad Zoe had looked with her head on Brynn's shoulder.

"Didn't seem to be." Ryder chuckled and shook his head. "If I didn't want to sound so much like my dad, I'd say I can't figure kids out nowadays."

"You're wise to avoid those words." Trinity elbowed him. "Makes you sound ancient."

"Sometimes I feel ancient."

Trinity realized they were headed down an unfamiliar path. "Whoa. This isn't the way to the parking lot."

Surprise crossed his face. "I thought we were going to Muddy Boots."

"You may be going there. Not me." Trinity stepped off the sidewalk to let a couple she didn't recognize pass. "Enjoy a cherry Danish for me."

"You're not coming?" Disappointment filled his warm brown eyes.

"I don't think so." What kind of response was that?

"Sunday morning isn't Sunday morning without a cherry Danish, coffee and conversation."

"It's the conversation part that has me hesitating," Trinity admitted.

Thankfully, he didn't go into the spiel about her being so outgoing and at ease with people.

"I know what you mean." He offered a rueful smile. "That sermon hit way too close to home."

Just like that, Trinity found herself falling into step beside Ryder as they strode toward the business district.

"I thought of my mother." Trinity offered a humorless laugh. "If you want to talk disappointments in life, she figures into ninety-nine percent of mine."

"I couldn't help thinking of Jenna. She was so full of life... until she wasn't. Then there's Zoe."

"Fatherhood was foisted on you. No warning."

The gaze that shot to her was sharp-eyed and assessing. "What do you mean?"

"Isn't it self-evident? You didn't know you had a child. Now, you're not only a father, you have full custody."

His eyes took on a distant glow. "Fatherhood was always one of those far-in-the-distance kind of things. Now, I can't imagine my life without Zoe in it."

"When the minister mentioned finding the positives in the negative, I thought of you and Zoe."

"We're doing well." His lips curved, then tightened. "As long as Geoffrey Swanson leaves us alone."

"I wondered what was going on with that."

"Why didn't you ask me?"

She could have said it had slipped her mind, but Ryder had been honest with her. "I figured if you wanted me to know, you'd tell me."

"Beck is supposed to give me an update in the next couple of days. Not mentioning that to you was my error." Ryder's gaze searched hers. "If you want to know something—anything—please ask. There are no secrets between us."

CHAPTER EIGHTEEN

There are no secrets between us.

Such a noble-sounding sentiment. One Ryder wished were true. He hated keeping things from Trinity.

Still, as they sat in Muddy Boots and he saw how easily information passed around the large table, Ryder knew he couldn't put Zoe's entire future at risk. Not that he thought that Trinity had loose lips, quite the contrary. Because of her background, she, more than most, knew the importance of keeping confidences.

Still, Ryder knew if you absolutely, positively didn't want information to get out, there was only one full-proof course of action. You kept the information to yourself.

Ryder didn't need Gladys's crystal ball to know what would happen if word got out that he wasn't Zoe's biological father.

Jenna's father would swoop in and try to assume custody. Even if Ryder protested and relayed what Jenna had told him, he had no proof.

Zoe would be the man's next victim.

There was no way Ryder would let that monster get anywhere near his girl.

"You two make such a cute couple." Hadley beamed at him and Trinity. "I was just telling David that last night, wasn't I, honey?"

David simply smiled and forked off a bite of pancake.

"Neighbors helping neighbors," Ryder said.

Trinity shot him a thankful look. "Right after he moved here, Wyatt told me that's how it is in Good Hope. I'm getting into the spirit."

The looks exchanged around the table told Ryder no one believed that nonsense. Everyone thought they were a couple, or at least actively exploring the option. Other than Greer and her brother, no one else seemed to grasp that her relationship with Ryder was just friendship.

This seemed as good a time as any to toss that out there. But Greer spoke before Trinity could open her mouth.

"Oh, there's something I've been meaning to pass on." Greer reached into her purse and pulled out a deck of cards.

Chatter around the table instantly ceased.

"Don't send those my way, Greer," David said with a laugh.

Cade Rallis, the sheriff, shook his head. "Once was enough for me."

His wife, Marigold, punched him in the arm. "The questions weren't that bad."

"We liked a few of the racy ones." Eliza winked at her husband.

"Yeah." Kyle grinned. "We definitely had favorites."

Greer shot them all a withering look and handed the cards to Trinity.

Trinity turned the cards over in her hands, then slipped one from the deck. Silently, she read what it said, and puzzlement blanketed her face. "Are these relationship cards?"

"They're meant to help couples get closer. You know, dig deep." Hadley rested her head against David's shoulder, and he leaned down and kissed her.

"I think the deck has been making the rounds since Ami and Beck got together," Marigold informed Trinity. "Cade and I got them from Prim and Max."

Max glanced at his brother-in-law. "No need to say thanks."

"Never crossed my mind," Cade bantered back.

"They're interesting questions." Marigold elbowed her husband when he snorted out a laugh. "Hadley's right. They make you dig deep."

"I appreciate you thinking of me." Trinity smiled at Greer. "I'd love to take a look at the questions. They're perfect for someone like me."

"Someone like you?" Obviously puzzled, Greer glanced at Wyatt, then at Ryder.

"Relationships are a big part of psychology." Trinity dropped the deck into her bag. "I can't wait to study these."

Trinity had planned to retrieve her car and head straight home once she left Muddy Boots. A panicked call from the Daily Grind had come in for Ryder just as they'd reached their vehicles, something to do with the computer system. Trinity offered to pick Zoe up at the church and drop her off at the coffee shop.

Ryder was still busy dealing with the computer glitch when they arrived. Instead of dropping Zoe off, Trinity waited with the girl. She ordered a coffee for herself and hot cocoa for Zoe, then they grabbed a table out front.

"The activities at the lock-in sounded like fun." Trinity lifted a cup of the very strong Indonesian blend and took a long sip. "I only went to one or two, and that was when I was older, close to sixteen. I remember there were lots of discussions on all sorts of issues."

Zoe rolled her eyes and brought the cup of steaming cocoa to her lips. "This one had that, too."

Trinity cocked her head. "Anything interesting?"

"Not really." Zoe paused. "Mostly, it was a lot of stuff on dating and relationships."

That surprised Trinity. "Do many girls your age date?"

"Nobody I know." Zoe thought for a moment, then shook her head. "I think Katie Ruth and Pastor Dan are trying to head off trouble in the future."

Trinity hid a smile as Zoe popped a bite of coffeecake into her mouth.

"When did you start dating?" Zoe asked, catching Trinity off guard.

"Not until I was sixteen. I was more focused on school."

"Was schoolwork the only reason you didn't date?"

"My birth mom…I guess you could say she dated a lot. The men she…dated…weren't that great of guys. They were always running around on her, or she was doing the same to get back at them. Watching all her drama made me cautious."

"You just have to choose the right guy." Zoe's tone was matter-of-fact and supremely confident.

"Who is the right guy?"

Zoe's gaze shifted to Ryder, working behind the counter. As they watched, he said something to Raven, eliciting a rare smile from the girl.

"Someone you can trust. Someone who's honorable and kind and good with kids." Zoe rattled off the traits without a second's hesitation.

"Do you think," Trinity said, just for the sake of argument, "that the guy needs to always be good with kids? What if you don't want children?"

Shock blanketed Zoe's face. "You don't want kids?"

"I wasn't speaking of myself. I happen to love kids. But let's say someone doesn't. Is being good with children really a fair standard?"

"Yes." Zoe punctuated the word with a decisive nod.

"Why?"

"I'm also adding being good with pets." Zoe's expression darkened. "How someone treats kids and dogs tells you a lot about them. They don't have to want a kid or a pet, but they should be kind to both."

Sensing Zoe had more to say, Trinity didn't immediately respond.

"There was this guy my mom hung around with when I was little."

Trinity inclined her head. "A boyfriend?"

"Maybe." Zoe shrugged. "I guess. He didn't like me. I could see it in his eyes. I was always glad when he wasn't around. I don't know why she put up with him as long as she did. They dated off and on until I was seven or so."

"Did she date anyone else?"

Zoe popped the last bite of coffeecake into her mouth. "Sometimes."

Something prickled at Trinity. She wondered if any of these partners had overlapped with Ryder. Something about Zoe being eleven nagged at her. How long had Jenna and Ryder truly been involved? He'd made it sound like it had been only that first year of college. Could it have been longer?

"Once my mom got a new job and we moved to Portland, we didn't see Brad anymore." Zoe smiled. "I was glad. I don't think my mom missed him. She was happier when it was just her and me. Now it's just my dad and me."

"You enjoy that one-to-one." Trinity kept her tone free of judgment.

Instead of immediately answering, Zoe cocked her head. "You think I don't want you around."

Trinity gave a little laugh. The child was perceptive beyond her years. "I didn't say that."

"I like it when it's the three of us, because I like you." Zoe met her gaze, those intense blue eyes boring into hers for a long second, before she shoved back her chair. "I'm going to get another hot chocolate. Do you want anything?"

~

Ryder's heart gave a solid thump when Beck strolled into the Daily Grind the next day. If it had been anyone else, Ryder might have believed that Beck was there to pick up coffee and pastries.

But Ryder knew if Beck needed either of those items, he could easily get them at either Muddy Boots or Blooms Bake Shop. There was only one reason for him to stop by.

"Raven, can you handle the front for fifteen minutes?" Ryder gestured toward Beck. "Mr. Cross and I have business to discuss in my office."

The girl's gaze shifted from Ryder to Beck. "I'm solid."

Ryder smiled. "I won't be long. If you need me—"

"I know where to find you."

Ryder had to chuckle. What did it say about him that he found the girl's brashness more amusing than irritating?

"I didn't mean to interrupt your work." Beck glanced around the crowded coffee shop. "I took a chance you'd have a free minute so I could personally let you know what I discovered."

"I have that minute now," Ryder assured him. "I have as many minutes as it takes. We won't be disturbed in my office."

Or overheard, Ryder thought.

"Can I get you a cup of coffee first?" Ryder asked.

"I left home without grabbing a cup, so sure." Beck cocked his head. "Do you have any of that Indonesian blend kicking around?"

"Good choice. In fact, I think I'll have a cup with you."

Once they were settled in the back office, steaming coffee in hand, Ryder made a come-ahead motion with one hand. "What did you find out?"

"Although nothing has been formally filed, I reviewed the law and any pertinent cases." Beck lifted his cup in a mock salute before setting it on the desk. "This is good, by the way. There was a recent case in Wisconsin where maternal grandparents sought custody of a grandchild after the child's mother died. The father had not been involved previously in the child's life."

Everything in Ryder froze. He'd been worried about visitation. Never once had he thought that Jenna's parents could win custody of her.

"What was the outcome of that case?" Ryder forced the coffee past numb lips.

"The father was awarded custody. The court said a natural parent's rights should outweigh a grandparent's rights, as long as the parent isn't unfit."

Ryder closed his eyes for a second as relief, strong and cleansing, surged.

"In terms of visitation—"

"No. Absolutely no visitation. Supervised or not. I will not allow it."

"I understand and agree." Beck held up a hand. "I need you to answer one question for me."

"Okay." Ryder gave a jerky nod.

"Do you know if Mr. or Mrs. Swanson had any type of relationship with Zoe before?"

"No relationship."

"In the letter from the lawyer, it states that they sent her cards on special holidays as well as birthday and Christmas gifts every year."

"I can't say whether they did or not." Ryder thought for a moment. "Zoe said she didn't know she had grandparents, so if they did, Jenna either sent the gifts back, tossed them in the trash or disposed of them some other way. Is this important?"

"Wisconsin courts require several factors to be met for a judge to grant grandparent visitation. The one that most concerned me is the one that reads," Beck pulled out his phone and opened a document, "'The grandparent has maintained a relationship with the child, or has attempted to maintain a relationship but was prevented by the parent.'"

"There never was a relationship to maintain."

"My thoughts exactly. It was reassuring to see that in most of the cases where visitation was granted, the grandparents had a strong relationship with the child prior to death or divorce." Beck set his phone on the table. "Another factor that must be met is that visitation is in the child's best interests."

"We know for sure visitation isn't in Zoe's best interests."

Beck rubbed his jaw. "Did Jenna have a journal or a diary maybe, where she could have chronicled the abuse?"

"I didn't see anything like that in any of the personal items I packed." Ryder sat back in his chair. "There were some boxes in her storage unit, but they were already taped. I had them sent here, but haven't had a chance to go through them."

"I suggest you make going through those boxes a priority," Beck advised. "I'll respond to their attorney. They may let it drop when you say no."

"Or—"

Beck met Ryder's gaze. "We may have a fight on our hands."

CHAPTER NINETEEN

When Trinity arrived home on Wednesday, she planned to head straight inside, but it was such a beautiful day she found herself changing clothes and going for a run instead. She was just crossing the lawn from the walking trail when Ryder and Zoe drove up.

"Where are you headed?" Ryder asked, not seeming to notice the perspiration on her face.

"Inside." She brushed a strand of hair back from her face. "To shower."

"Why don't you stay out here for a few minutes and keep us company? Zoe is headed inside to get Scully."

"Stay right there." Zoe pointed at her. "I won't be long."

"I should—" Trinity began.

"I have something to ask you," Zoe called out over her shoulder, the door slamming shut behind her.

"Do you know what it is?" Trinity asked Ryder.

"Not a clue." He grinned. "Bet she knew the curiosity would keep you here."

"Probably." Trinity gave a little laugh. "Speaking of curiosity, what did you find out from Beck?"

He updated her on his conversation with Beck, then told her he was still wading through Jenna's boxes, but so far had come up empty.

"If you need help, let me know."

"I appreciate the offer." Ryder started to touch her just as Zoe burst outside, Scully jumping around beside her.

"Someone is excited to be outdoors." Trinity reached down to give the dog a pat before he bolted for the nearest bush.

"You've got me curious, Zoe." Trinity's tone was teasing. "What did you want to ask me?"

Zoe turned. "Do you know Gladys Bertholf?"

"I've met her," Trinity told Zoe.

"I know her very well." Ryder smiled. "Why the question?"

"Brynn and I ran into her after school when we were with Brynn's mom. Mrs. Bertholf—she said to call her Gladys—asked if either of us wanted to help out backstage at the playhouse. Apparently, she's super involved with that kind of thing."

Zoe's eyes narrowed when she saw Scully sniff the ground by the bush, then start to dig. "No. Scully. No."

"Gladys is a big deal in the local arts scene," Ryder said to his daughter. "She's performed, usually in a lead role, at the community theater her entire life. Recently, she moved into directing."

"She's old." Zoe tugged on Scully's leash. "Superduper old."

"She's smart, talented and active in all sorts of community ventures." Ryder placed a hand on his daughter's shoulder. "Age is only a number."

"Do either you or Brynn have an interest in theater?" Trinity returned the conversation to the point of the question.

"Maybe." Zoe shrugged. "Brynn and I thought it might be fun, especially since we could do it together."

"That was kind of Gladys to think of you," Ryder said.

Zoe made a face. "It was a ploy."

Trinity tried not to smile. "What kind of ploy?"

Zoe gave Scully's leash a don't-do-that tug when the dog

started digging. "Okay. First, she asks about the theater stuff. Then she asks how I like living down the hall from you. That was what she really wanted to know."

Ryder glanced at Trinity and grinned. "Why doesn't that surprise me?"

Small-town living at its finest, Trinity thought, resisting the urge to ask how Zoe had replied.

"I said you're okay. That I like having you as a neighbor." Zoe's smile turned impish. "I told her my dad *really* likes having you so close. She was super interested in hearing more about that."

Trinity gaped. "You're kidding."

Zoe lifted her shoulders in a slight shrug.

"Gladys is a matchmaker." Ryder appeared to be trying hard to keep his tone casual, rather than irritated.

"Seriously?" Zoe giggled. "That's very frosty."

"It isn't when she has you in her cross hairs," Ryder grumbled.

"You think she wants to match you and Trinity." Zoe's gaze grew thoughtful. "You think that's why she was pumping me for information."

"It might be best in the future," Trinity began, "if you keep your responses very general should Gladys ask you again about—"

"Just kidding. I didn't say anything." Zoe grinned. "I knew right away what she was after. My mom's neighbors were always asking me about her 'social life.'" She rolled her eyes. "As if."

"Did your mother date much?" Ryder asked.

"Not really. If she wasn't working, she was usually with me." Zoe's tone was matter-of-fact, her gaze focused on Scully, who was chasing his tail. "Like I told Trinity, there was this guy, Brad. He didn't like kids, or at least not me. Once we moved to Portland, I never saw him again. Happy days."

"He never came to see your mom after you moved?" Ryder asked in a too-casual tone that had Trinity's antennas quivering.

"Nope." Zoe shook her head. "He wasn't nice, so I was glad."

Trinity saw the speculative look on Ryder's face. Was he wondering if Brad had come back recently and contributed to Jenna drinking while taking her meds? It seemed a long shot, but stranger things had been known to happen.

As they got better acquainted, Trinity was developing an ability to sense his moods, even sometimes to have an idea what he was thinking.

The next time they were alone, she would ask if she'd been on target this time...or missed the mark by a mile.

Even after Zoe rushed inside with Ryder's phone to text Brynn, Trinity remained outside with Ryder and the dog. Thoughts of everything Zoe had said about Brad continued to circle in her brain. "Something Zoe said got me wondering."

Ryder's gaze shot to her.

"Remember when she was telling us about her mom and that guy Brad?"

His gaze sharpened, and she saw she had his total interest.

"She said this guy was in their lives off and on until she and her mom moved to Portland."

He said nothing for a long moment. "Where are you going with this?"

"She said he never liked her. She didn't know why her mom hung out with him. But Jenna must have liked him enough for him to be around so long. I mean, for Zoe to remember him."

Ryder nodded. "A logical assumption."

"Do you—" she paused, chewing on the words she wanted to say. "Do you, well, I was wondering..."

His eyes flashed like black lightning. "You don't have to beat around the bush with me. I can handle it.."

"Do you think Brad could have come back into her life? Could he have been the reason she was drinking that night?"

The tension seemed to ease from Ryder's shoulders as he shook his head. "There was no indication from any of Jenna's neighbors or friends in Portland that there was a man in her life."

Trinity expelled a breath. "I'm glad. He doesn't sound like a nice man. I mean, what kind of person doesn't like Zoe?"

Ryder chuckled. "Got me."

Love rushed through Trinity. She lifted a hand, cupped his face and kissed him gently on the lips.

He went to pull her in closer when a howling in the distance had Scully jerking on the leash and scrambling toward the back door.

"Looks like someone is ready to go inside." Ryder pulled her to him and closed his mouth over hers, hot and hungry. "Too bad I'm not."

Friday night, Ryder dropped off Zoe backstage before he and Trinity walked into the community theater to find their seats.

He wasn't surprised to see Dan and Katie Ruth front-row center. Dan's parents were there as well, which meant they'd come from Chicago for this performance. Ryder had heard rumblings that Oaklee and her parents weren't close, so he was happy to see them here. Especially with Oaklee having a lead role.

Ryder still had no idea why Gladys had given him and Trinity the tickets, but he was grateful. Not because he had a burning desire to see this particular musical, but because it made for a fun date.

Their seats were center left. While there were lots of people Ryder knew, some he considered friends, tonight he had eyes only for Trinity.

"I saw this show in Chicago," Trinity told him. "You're going to love it."

He took her hand when the lights dimmed, and satisfaction surged when her fingers curved around his.

Ryder had to admit the songs were catchy. Oaklee had an amazing voice and presence onstage. He wondered if others felt as if they were seeing Gladys in the early days of her career.

As much as he enjoyed the performance, he couldn't keep his mind on the stage. Trinity was wearing the same perfume she'd worn the night they'd met in Chicago. The fresh, enticing fragrance had a sultry edge, the scent so faint as to be barely noticeable.

But he noticed, and his body remembered. She looked beautiful tonight in a dress that buttoned up the front. It was unfastened at her throat just enough to grab his interest. Her face as she watched the production was so expressive.

Her eyes widened when the lights came on to signal intermission, and it took everything Ryder had in him not to kiss her then and there.

The cast onstage continued to repair a car, cook food and put up pictures as if they really were at a filling station or the Double Cupp diner.

"This is every bit as good as productions I've seen in big cities." Trinity smiled. "I'm so glad we came tonight."

"Would you like something to drink?" He gave her hand a squeeze. "Or do you want to walk around for a few minutes?"

"If you want to walk, that's fine with me." Her thumb caressed his palm. "Otherwise, I'm content just sitting here with you."

"I feel the same." What was happening to him? Ryder wondered. It had been years since any woman had affected him this way.

Well, he was going to enjoy every minute.

"How are things going at Connections?"

"Really well." Even as her thumb continued the erotic circular motion on his palm, her tone turned serious. "Liam has several more patients he thinks I would work well with, so I'll sit in on the sessions—with the client's agreement, of course—and we'll see how it goes."

"You're doing great. Transitions aren't easy, but they can lead to bigger and better things."

"My sentiments exactly." Her eyes met his. "There's something I'd like to ask you."

The thumb stopped, and her expression was too serious for his liking.

"What is it?"

Just then, the houselights flickered, and everyone who'd gotten up scurried back to their seats.

Ryder stifled a curse. Now he was going to have to wait until the show was over and they were alone to find out what she wanted to ask him.

Nestled in her seat in a community theater that was as fine as any in the Chicago or Omaha areas, Trinity let herself relax and simply enjoy the performance. The music and lyrics tugged at her heart, and seeing the Cupp sisters onstage made her miss her own sisters with a fierceness that took her by surprise.

She needed to call Amber and Sage and make sure all was right in their worlds. There was so much she wanted to share with them about her life in Good Hope. But now wasn't the time. Returning her attention to the stage, Trinity quickly lost herself in the performance. Forty-five minutes later, she rose for a standing ovation, clapping wildly.

They were standing out front when Trinity's breath hitched.

"What's wrong?" Ryder's brow furrowed as his gaze swept the crowd.

She shook her head. "Is the man, the one with Gladys, is his name Albert August?"

Based on Liam's description of the man when Trinity asked

about him after Gladys's appointment, Trinity was almost positive it was him.

Ryder cocked his head. "The former principal?"

Since Trinity wasn't sure, she gestured with her head to where a tall man—she'd place his age somewhere in his eighties-stood beside a concrete bench. Attractive, with gray hair and silver wire-rimmed glasses, he held a large bouquet of flowers.

It was the bow tie that had captured her interest. Liam had told her Albert was rarely seen without a bow tie.

"That's Dr. August." Ryder smiled. "He retired from Good Hope High when I was a freshman. The kids and staff loved him."

"He looks like a nice guy," Trinity said when he smiled warmly at a family walking by.

"Let's go say hello."

Before Trinity realized what was happening, Ryder had taken her hand, and they were weaving their way toward the man.

The family he'd been talking to was walking away as they strode up.

"Dr. August." Ryder held out his hand. "I don't know if you remember me. Ryder Goodhue. I—"

"Of course I remember you." For someone who looked to be in his mid to late eighties, Albert had a hearty voice, and his gaze was sharp and direct as he shook Ryder's hand. "However, I don't believe I've met the lovely young lady with you."

Trinity didn't wait for introductions. She smiled. "I'm Trinity McConnell. I recently joined Connections as a psychotherapist. Wyatt McConnell is my brother."

"It's a pleasure to meet you, Dr. McConnell." The twinkle in his eyes disappeared for a moment. "I was sorry your brother never had the chance to know his grandfather. Roy might have been a bit of a curmudgeon, but he had many redeeming qualities."

Trinity didn't get a chance to respond, because Gladys hurried up.

"Someone said you were looking for me, Albert." Instead of her normal caftans, Gladys wore a purple dress so dark it almost looked black. A string of brightly colored stones hanging from her earlobes saved the outfit from boredom. "I—"

Gladys paused as she caught sight of the large bouquet in his arms. A bouquet he now held out to her. "Another fantastic job, little lady. Your talent never ceases to awe."

"Why…why…thank you."

Trinity could honestly say she'd never seen Gladys flustered. *Acting* flustered, yes. But truly caught off guard? Not until this moment.

"These are so lovely." Gladys rubbed one of the soft petals between her fingers. "I'd say you didn't have to, but I'm happy you did."

If Trinity could have thought of a way to step away graciously without making the situation awkward, she'd have done it. Though they were standing outside in a public area, the exchange she was witnessing seemed private and intimate.

"It was a pleasure seeing you again, Dr. August," Ryder said suddenly. "We need to head off. We're picking up my daughter."

Gladys blinked and turned to them. "Zoe was an immense help tonight. She's a delightful girl."

"Thank you." Ryder took Trinity's arm. "We appreciate the compliment."

We, Trinity thought. *We?* Had he been speaking about him and Zoe? Or her?

"A perfect couple." Ryder sighed as they positioned themselves in an open spot so there was no chance Zoe would miss them.

"Gladys and Albert?" Trinity asked cautiously.

"Actually," his gaze met hers, and he smiled, "I was speaking of you and me."

CHAPTER TWENTY

Zoe chose that moment to breeze out of the theater, a broad smile on her face.

"Tonight was a blast," she told Ryder and Trinity. "Gladys and the backstage manager said I can help anytime."

The girl continued to chatter happily on the drive home. "Hannah and Sabine are going to be so jealous that Brynn and I got to do this."

Trinity turned to look back at Zoe. "Do they have an interest in theater?"

"Nope." Zoe shook her head. "I offered to see if they could help tonight, but they weren't interested."

"Then why would they be jealous?"

"Be-cause it ended up being amazing and so much fun." Zoe flung her arms up in the air, all youthful exuberance. "I didn't think it would be either."

"That's why it's good to try new things." Ryder wheeled the car into the long lane leading to the Barn.

Trinity's heart swelled. Zoe's transition to Good Hope had been a smooth one. Though there would likely be rough times ahead when the loss of her mother would rise up and knock her back, she now had friends and a supportive father.

In so many ways, Zoe was a lucky little girl.

"I have a question for you," Zoe told Ryder, unbuckling her seat belt the instant the car came to a stop.

He smiled. "Ask away."

She leaned between the front seats. "Kids have been asking why I don't have your last name."

Because she was watching, Trinity saw surprise flicker in Ryder's eyes. "What do you tell them?"

"It's simple. When I lived with my mom, I went by her last name. Now that I live with you, I'm changing my last name to Goodhue." For a split second, the child's confident façade slipped. "That's okay with you, right? I mean, we can change my name?"

"I'd like for you to have my name." Ryder cleared his throat. "Perhaps you could be Zoe Swanson Goodhue. That way, you'd carry both my name and your mom's."

Zoe's eyes widened. "Can I do that? Keep my old name and add yours?"

Ryder nodded.

"Let's do that." Zoe's smile was back in full force. "I can't wait to talk to Brynn."

"Didn't you just see her?" Ryder asked as they piled out of the truck. "Like, five minutes ago?"

Zoe laughed as if he'd made a huge joke. "She doesn't know that I've changed my name. Or that I'm calling you Dad now."

The child danced up to him, brushed a kiss across his cheek. "I love my dad."

Before he could respond, Zoe raced up the walkway to the back door, leaving them standing in stunned silence.

~

Ryder turned to Trinity, the tightness in his chest making speech difficult. "What...what just happened?"

She looped her arm through his. "I'd say your daughter has accepted that you're her father and a permanent part of her life."

"I love her." His voice broke, and he pressed his lips together. When he spoke again, his voice was steady. "I won't let anything happen to her."

"I'm sure you'll do your best."

He gripped her arm. "I won't let anyone harm her."

"Ryder." She glanced pointedly at his fingers digging into her forearm.

"I'm sorry." He released his hold and blew out a breath. "It's just that Zoe has been through so much. I feel so protective."

"You're thinking of her grandfather."

"He doesn't deserve that title after what he did to Jenna. The man is nothing to Zoe." Ryder's jaw jutted out. "I won't let him ever be anything to her."

In that moment, Ryder realized it wasn't only Zoe who'd made the transition, he'd turned that corner, too. She was his daughter and would be his for the rest of their lives. They might not share the same blood, but Zoe was his.

"Why don't we grab Scully and take him for a short walk?" Trinity suggested. "Unless you'd rather be alone and—"

He smiled and tugged her to him, a playful smile on his lips. "I always want to be with you."

He loved her. It was just that simple. As his arms folded her close, he realized that's what he was saying to her just now without actually saying the words.

He was in love with Trinity.

The only question now was, did she feel the same? He knew part of the problem with her ex had been his kids. She seemed to like Zoe well enough, but *well enough* would never be good enough.

If they were ever to be a family, she would have to love Zoe, too.

Love me, love my daughter.

It might be a hard line, but his child deserved nothing less.

"We're taking Scully for a walk," he called out to Zoe once he and Trinity stepped inside. "Want to come with us?"

"I'm talking to Brynn," came the reply.

Trinity smiled. "I guess that's a no."

Once outside, they stayed close to the building, in the glow of the yard light.

Trinity inhaled deeply. "In a way, living here is like living in the country. You know, I once considered myself a big-city gal."

"How do you feel now?"

"I love it here." She lifted her face to catch the breeze, and the moon bathed her face with a golden glow.

His heart lurched in his chest. His heart was so full tonight. Full of emotions. Full of unanswered questions. About his future. With Zoe. With Trinity.

Her earlier cryptic comment returned. "You mentioned you had something to tell me."

Turning toward him, she inclined her head. "When did I say that?"

"At the theater," he reminded her. "Right before the lights dimmed at the end of intermission."

Her brows pulled together. "Oh. It was something I wanted to ask, not tell you."

Ryder circled one hand, suddenly impatient. "What was it?"

"I'm finding it difficult to just be your friend." She blew out a breath. "I know it was me who wanted to ratchet back our relationship. I thought I could do it, but—"

When she hesitated, his heart dropped. Had he somehow read all the signs wrong? He'd thought they were getting closer. Now she was saying even being friends was too much?

"Is it because I kissed you?" Even though she seemed to want him to kiss her, perhaps even that had been too much.

"That's part of it."

"I'm sorry. I—"

Her fingers on his lips stopped the words. "The kiss was just one of the things that made me realize we—or at least I—can't go back. I don't want to go back. I want to move forward."

"You're sure?" When he brushed a strand of hair back from her face, his fingers trembled.

"I'm positive." Taking a step closer, she slid her arms around his neck. "Being with you makes me happy."

With relief and love coursing through him, Ryder put his hands on her hips and pulled her tight against him. "I want to kiss you."

"I want you to—"

His mouth closed over hers before she could finish the thought. Ryder knew in that moment he was with the woman he was meant to be with, and that was right where he wanted to be.

Monday morning, Ryder dropped Zoe off at school, ran a few errands, then returned home to go through more of Jenna's storage boxes. Jenna had never spoken of keeping a journal, but it seemed like something she might have done.

If he could find written evidence that there had been no contact between her and her parents after Zoe's birth, that information would add weight to his reluctance to have the Swansons involved in Zoe's life.

Perhaps Jenna had even documented her thoughts on the abuse she'd suffered. Though Ryder knew that would be difficult for him to read, he would force himself if it would help Zoe.

The first few boxes he unpacked were filled with mementos of Zoe's childhood. There was a mold of baby handprints, a rubber giraffe that squeaked, a knitted blanket, a newspaper from the day Zoe was born, tiny teeth in a wooden tooth box and a folder with…letters. Ryder immediately recognized Jenna's handwriting.

Setting aside the tooth box, Ryder sat on the sofa with the folder. He barely noticed Scully hopping up to stretch out beside him.

The letters were in chronological order starting on the day of Zoe's birth. Letters from a mother to her beloved daughter. For the first couple of years, they were monthly, then every year on Zoe's birthday.

He read them all, grateful he had the time since he wasn't planning to go into the shop until noon.

In the monthly ones, Jenna gave a brief history of Zoe's accomplishments. Rolling over. Sitting up. First tooth. First word. As Zoe grew, Jenna wrote of her pride in her daughter and her love.

Zoe would treasure these letters from her mother now and in the years to come. Ryder set them aside for her.

More household items took up most of the space in the next few boxes. Ryder opened the last one thirty minutes before he had to leave, convinced the contents would be more of the same.

At the bottom of the box, he hit pay dirt. A dozen journals and smaller diaries with little locks and keys.

His heart pounded against his rib cage.

Gathering them up, he took them into his bedroom and placed the books carefully in the bottom drawer of the dresser. He kept a handful out.

It would take time to make his way through all of these, especially because he needed to go slowly so he didn't miss anything of importance.

He called the shop and told the clerk she could reach him on his cell if she needed anything. Then he called Beck.

"I found Jenna's diaries and journals," he said without preamble.

"What's in them?"

"I haven't had a chance yet to read them. As soon as I get off this call, I'm going to start going through them.."

"I was going to call you. Swanson's attorney called. They're going to push for visitation. There were thinly veiled threats about pursuing full custody if you don't agree to visitation."

"I meant what I said, Beck. No contact."

"I hear you, and I agree." Beck's soft Southern drawl held a steely edge. "They haven't filed any petitions yet, so we have time. Go through the journals and let me know what you find. Even if it's nothing."

"Will do." Ryder clicked off and pulled out one of the books.

He spent hours reading the diaries. The small books with the flimsy locks and tiny keys, written during the years she was at home, had chunks of pages torn out.

Had she regretted baring her soul, even in a diary she considered private? None of the remaining pages had any mention of abuse. But what came through was a profound sadness, mixed with lots of references to drinking and partying with friends.

Had drinking been Jenna's way of coping with the pain?

When they'd been together, she'd drunk, too. But didn't most freshmen in college drink a lot?

Not finding anything in the diaries that would help his case, Ryder pulled out the journals, stopping in the early afternoon to run errands before picking Zoe up from school.

When Zoe started on her homework after dinner, he returned to his room to continue reading.

Ryder smiled when Jenna first mentioned his name and relived memories of their times together as he read through the pages.

It was a relief to see that, while Jenna had obviously cared about him as a friend, she'd been no more in love with him than he'd been with her. Perhaps, he thought, that was why they'd been able to remain friends.

"What are you reading?"

Zoe's voice had him jerking his head up and shutting the book.

"Some of your mother's old journals." He forced a smile. "I thought you were on the phone with Brynn."

"She had to get ready for bed."

"What time is it?" Ryder glanced at the clock and stifled a curse. After ten on a school night, and the thought of telling Zoe it was bedtime hadn't even occurred to him.

"Don't worry." She dropped down beside him on the sofa, and Scully, her constant companion, jumped up on her lap. "I know when to hit my bed and crash." Curiosity filled her blue eyes. "Why are you reading my mom's journals? I thought things like that were private."

The reproach in her tone came through loud and clear.

"It's necessary." After marking his place with a piece of paper, he set the book down and shifted to face Zoe. "Remember when I told you your grandfather abused your mother?"

She nodded slowly, and her gaze turned watchful. "Does you reading her journals have something to do with that?"

"It does." Ryder carefully considered his next words. "Your mom's parents are asking for visitation."

"With me?" Zoe's voice rose, then broke.

"Yes. But don't worry." He placed his hand over hers when he saw the panicked look in her eyes. "It's not going to happen. I won't let them anywhere near you."

"Then why read her journals?" She pulled back so suddenly Scully gave a yelp and jumped off her lap. "Why not just say no?"

"The only way your grandparents have even the slightest chance of being granted visitation is if they prove they were a part of your life before your mother's death."

"They weren't." Zoe shook her head vigorously. "I don't even know what they look like. I thought they were dead."

She jerked to her feet, and his heart ached as he saw her rising worry. Despite his reassurances, he'd upset her.

"That fact means," he kept his voice even and under tight control, "that their attorney will find it impossible to prove a relationship, and the petition for visitation will be denied."

"That doesn't explain why you're reading my mom's private stuff." The accusatory tone normally would have had him reacting negatively, but he understood where she was coming from.

"I cared about your mom. I was her friend." He puffed out his cheeks, blew out the air. "If there's anything in these pages that will help me better shield you from her parents or help me to be a better father to you, I want to find it."

"Okay." Zoe nodded, and her shoulders slumped. The warrior ready to do battle vanished, leaving behind a young girl up past her bedtime.

He slung an arm around her shoulders, gave a little squeeze. "I do have some good news."

She inclined her head.

"I checked, and it's really easy for us to get your name changed."

"It is?" Zoe's eyes grew wide. "How easy?"

"All I had to do was fill out an online form. Then I took it to the bank and had to sign it in front of Greer."

Zoe frowned in puzzlement.

"Greer is a notary public. That means she verifies it was me signing the form." He walked her to her room. "I went to the courthouse in Sturgeon Bay and dropped it off. There's a couple more hoops we have to jump through, but you should be Zoe Swanson Goodhue by the time the snow falls."

"You did all that today?"

"I can barely believe it myself." Ryder chuckled and shook his head.

The bank hadn't taken long, and neither had the quick trip to Sturgeon Bay.

"Thank you for doing that for me."

He placed a kiss on the top of her head. "I'm doing it for me, too. You're my daughter. I want everyone to know it."

~

Ryder read late into the night, determined to get through all the journals. He discovered his worry that Brad might be Zoe's father was unfounded. According to one of the entries, Jenna was already three months pregnant when she first met Brad Kosmicki.

She mentioned running into him again when Zoe was one. It appeared they'd begun dating, and he'd been in and out of her life until Jenna had moved with Zoe to Portland. Reading some of Jenna's comments about the man's behavior had Ryder wondering why she'd put up with the guy.

It must have had something to do with the loneliness that permeated most of her entries. Jenna had a great job, a promising career and a daughter she adored. She was never without friends.

But what had happened with her father had left her with an inability to fully trust.

Ryder learned a lot about Jenna from reading the pages. By the time he finished, he concluded that Zoe's father was destined to forever remain a mystery man.

In a single entry, written nine months before Zoe's birth, Jenna talked about engaging in some heavy-duty partying with friends. She met someone at a bar, and they'd clicked, but the next morning, he was gone, and she couldn't remember his name. She wrote she doubted their paths would cross again.

Her one-night stand was never mentioned again.

The sense of relief that Ryder felt in knowing that he'd never have to worry about Zoe's birth father showing up to demand *his* daughter was immense. That relief was matched only by the knowledge that the man wasn't Brad.

CHAPTER TWENTY-ONE

"Are you sure neither of you have seen the PI hanging around?"

Trinity resisted the urge to roll her eyes, a childish gesture, but one that seemed appropriate under the circumstances.

"Da-ad, you've asked us that three times."

Though Trinity didn't turn around, she sensed Zoe was doing enough eye-rolling in the backseat for both of them.

"I don't want anything to happen to either of you." Ryder kept his eyes on the road that skirted the bay.

When he reached over and took Trinity's hand, her irritation melted, along with her heart. "I've told Liam and Peyton to keep an eye out for him."

"I go straight into school when you drop me off." Zoe heaved an impatient breath. "Are we almost there yet?"

"Nearly." As Trinity glanced out the window and gazed at trees turning red and gold, she felt the same eagerness.

Last year, heck, six months ago, she'd never have believed she'd be looking forward to a party where baking pies was part of the agenda.

The get-together was originally conceived as a football party. Saturday at noon, the NFL team coached by Krew Slattery—

former Good Hope standout and NFL MVP—would be playing. Trinity knew Ryder was especially interested in watching, since he'd played football in high school, and Cassie, Krew's wife, used to work for him.

"I wonder who all is going to be there." Trinity slanted a glance at Ryder. "I spoke with Wyatt, and he and Greer were planning on it."

Ryder smiled. "The Chapin family is a tight-knit group. I bet they'll all be there."

The number of cars in David and Hadley's driveway and along the lane leading toward the house told Trinity it wasn't just the Chapin brood who were here, but the Bloom family as well.

According to Ryder, the two families had merged last year when Steve Bloom, a longtime widower, had married Lynn Chapin, a longtime widow.

"Zoe."

Something in Trinity's voice had Zoe stopping her trek toward the front door and turning back. "What is it?"

"Callum and Connor will likely be here."

Ryder shifted his gaze from Trinity to his daughter, appearing mildly interested.

"That's okay. I can handle them." Zoe's lips turned up. "Brynn and I talked about them. The twins are like mosquitoes. Irritating, but no big deal."

Trinity smiled. "I like the analogy."

"I'm going to run. Brynn's on the porch waiting." Without waiting for a response, Zoe took off.

"I wish I had that energy." Ryder covered a yawn.

"You look tired." She studied him. "Were you up late?"

He nodded and took her arm. "Reading."

"I'm like that, too, when I get engrossed in a good book." She opened her mouth to ask him what he'd been reading when she spotted Hadley and Ami on the porch. The two women waved.

Ryder shot her an impish smile. "You can run, too. If you want. I don't mind."

She jabbed him with her elbow, then laughed. "I don't know when I've been so excited to bake pies."

While the football game was the original reason for today's party, the side project was baking pies for a soup supper fundraiser First Christian was holding tomorrow. Money raised would go toward replenishing the Giving Tree coffers. The Giving Tree, a neighbor-helping-neighbor fund for residents who'd fallen on hard times, was unique to Good Hope.

Just another thing to love about this community, Trinity thought.

"Do you know how to make a pie?" Ryder asked when they were nearly to the house.

"I didn't until I went to live with the McConnells." Trinity's years with the family had changed her in so many ways, just as Zoe's years with Ryder would change her. "Before they took me in, I thought pies were only made in stores."

He laughed.

Trinity was on the verge of giving him another poke, when he kissed her on the temple.

"I'm glad we came together." His hand tightened on hers. "Being with you makes any party merrier."

"I feel the same."

"I'm so glad you came, Trinity." Hadley glanced at Ami. "See, I told you she was coming."

The two women stepped off the porch to give Trinity a hug.

"Are we late?" Trinity was sure Hadley had said the festivities started two hours before the game.

"You're not late," Hadley said with a wry smile. "Everyone else is early. Including the one person we wished would be late."

Puzzled, Trinity cocked her head. "Who is that?"

"I'm heading around back." Ryder leaned over and kissed Trinity on the mouth. Then he flashed that heart-stopping smile at her new friends. "Nice to see you both. Appreciate the invitation, Hadley."

The two women looked at each other and smiled.

"Once we answer your question, you're going to have to answer ours." Ami's eyes twinkled.

Hadley grinned. "More of a comment. Things are definitely sizzling between you and Ryder."

Trinity laughed. "My question first."

"Stella." Ami wrinkled her nose as if she'd smelled something rotten. "Clay brought her."

"Oh, that's nice." Trinity didn't know what else to say.

Hadley laughed. "No, it's not. We'll be nice because we adore Clay."

"He must really like her." Trinity pulled her brows together. "I mean, to bring her to another family event."

"Let's just say Clay likes her a whole lot more than she likes him. My brother-in-law tends to choose emotionally unavailable women." Hadley lifted her hands. "I don't know why, because he's a great guy with a lot to offer the right gal. He just has bad taste in women."

The two women strolled around the house with Trinity, pointing out the grill with hot dogs, brats and burgers, a huge tub with sodas and water and a basket with individual bags of chips. A table held all the condiments. "It's nothing fancy, but we'll have game food inside," Hadley said.

Trinity eyed the hot dogs on the grill. "Those look really good."

"Help yourself." Hadley glanced around the spacious yard. "I'm going to play hostess out here before the pregame has everyone swarming inside."

"I'm going to find my husband." Ami shot Trinity a wink. "We're without kids for the day."

Trinity saw Ryder speaking with Greer and Wyatt. Seeing how well he got along with her brother made her happy.

It was a beautiful mid-October day with everyone comfortable in their NFL team sweatshirts and jackets.

Everyone was familiar and friendly. Time passed quickly as Trinity mingled and ate, then mingled and ate some more.

~

"I can't believe you can eat two." Ryder stared as he watched Trinity down the last bite of her second hot dog.

It wasn't as if it was that much food, but when combined with what she'd already eaten, it was impressive.

"I didn't eat breakfast." She smiled and dabbed at the corners of her lips with the edge of a paper napkin. "These dogs are delicious."

"Trinity."

Ryder turned to see Ami and Beck crossing to them. Ami almost immediately began talking pies and explaining to Trinity that thimbleberries grew wild in this area.

After a few minutes, Beck motioned Ryder off to the side.

"Any response?" Ryder kept the question general, conscious of being surrounded by other people.

"Not a word." Beck spoke in an equally low tone.

"Are you sure they got the letter?"

Beck nodded.

"Does this mean he's letting it drop?"

"More likely, he's stewing and trying to figure out his next step." Beck shrugged. "He could let it drop."

"But you don't think so."

"Not someone like him. He's used to winning."

"He's not going to win this one."

"What are you two looking so serious about?" Ami turned to her husband, lifted up on her tiptoes and kissed his cheek. "Let me just tell you once again how incredible you smell today."

Beck's quick flash of a grin and the way he pulled Ami against his side had her emitting a little shriek.

"You'll have to excuse us." Beck chuckled. "My wife and I have forgotten how to behave when we don't have children with us."

"Behave?" Ami shot him a provocative look through lowered lashes, a tiny smile teasing the corners of her lips. "What's the fun in that?"

Moments later, they strolled off, holding hands, two married people madly in love.

"Happily ever after can come true," Trinity mused, watching the couple.

"My parents and grandparents are happily married." Ryder took Trinity's hand and gave it a swing. "Anyone can see your brother and Greer are happy together."

She nodded, her gaze turning thoughtful. "Once you find someone you can love and trust, you should never let go."

"You sound like a greeting card," he teased.

"Or a relationship card." Trinity smiled and swung their joined fingers. "I read through a few of them the other night. They're interesting. Eliza was right. A few are quite racy."

"Tell me about those."

She laughed, her eyes sparkling. "Ah, not here."

"You have to promise me that one of these days we'll answer those questions."

"Only in private and over a glass of wine." Trinity studied him for several heartbeats. "To make it fair, we should just pick three at random and not go for the racy."

He laughed and pulled her to him. "What's the fun in fair?"

She gave him a playful push. "Time to socialize."

Ryder took that as her blessing to talk more football with the guys. A half hour later, when he realized it was getting close to the time to go inside, he looked for Trinity and Zoe.

He spotted them across the yard.

The rush of emotion he felt was tempered immediately by

concern. Studying them, it appeared they'd stepped away from the party for an intense, private conversation.

As he drew close, the tear streaks on Zoe's cheeks told him something had upset his daughter. Ryder quickened his steps, determined to comfort her. "Zoe."

Zoe hastily swiped away the signs of tears and asked, "Is everything okay?"

It struck Ryder that she was asking him the question he wanted to ask her.

"I'll be better once I grab a burger and a beer." He gestured with one hand toward the house, where music and laughter flowed. "How's the party going for you?"

Zoe's ever-so-slight hesitation had him tensing. "Did something happen?"

"Not really."

"Tell him," Trinity urged in a low tone.

"I did something bad." Tears suddenly filled Zoe's eyes. "You're going to be so disappointed in me. You're going to want to send me back to…well, somewhere."

"Ah, sweet girl." Without thinking, Ryder stepped forward and wrapped his arms around her. "You're my daughter. I'm not sending you anywhere."

"Except maybe off to college when she's eighteen," Trinity said in a light tone.

"Not even then."

His comment had Zoe giggling.

She stepped back and swiped at her eyes. "I read my mom's letters to me last night. They made me happy, but kinda sad, too. Then I saw Hadley with her mom, and I thought, why can't my mom be here? It's not fair."

"It isn't fair," Ryder agreed.

"I woke up feeling sad. And mad. I wanted to scream at someone." Zoe shrugged. "But you'd already left for the shop."

"Whew." Ryder pretended to wipe sweat from his brow. "Dodged that bullet."

Ryder had done some reading on girls in this age group. The wild swing of emotions due to hormonal changes had made his insides quake.

"You weren't here and—"

"Zoe." Trinity's voice held a warning.

"You're right." Zoe dropped her gaze. "I can't blame my behavior on the fact that my dad ran into work for a few minutes."

My dad.

Ryder liked the sound of those two words coming from her lips.

"Anyway, Brynn and I were playing badminton…" Zoe slanted a look in Trinity's direction and received a reassuring smile.

"We were playing against Callum and Connor Brody." Zoe's blue eyes glinted. "They're twins."

He nodded. "Max and Prim's boys."

"I guess." Zoe expelled a breath. "Connor is nice. Callum is a butt."

Ryder stiffened. "What did he do?"

"He called me names, told me Sarah Rose plays better than me."

Puzzled, Ryder frowned. "Sarah Rose is two."

"I knew that. Well, I didn't, but Brynn told me." Zoe swallowed. "Callum kept dogging me even after we finished playing. His mom motioned for him to come to her. It's not fair someone like him has a mom, and I don't. Before he left, he smirked and said, 'See you around, skinny girl.' I lost it. I threw a cup of water on him."

Ryder could easily picture the scene. He nearly chuckled, but choked it down. What was the proper fatherly response? "What did he do?"

"He laughed, then headed over to his mom." Worry furrowed

Zoe's brow. "She's probably going to talk to you about what a horrible daughter you have."

"Prim isn't like that." Ryder had known Prim Bloom—now Prim Brody—his entire life. Not much got her riled. He had the feeling she'd be more upset about her son harassing a girl than a little tossed water.

Still, Zoe's response to the teasing needed to be addressed. Ryder shot a glance at Trinity, but she remained silent. Obviously, this was one of those situations that was up to him to handle.

If only children came with a how-to guide...

"What do you think you should do?" he asked Zoe.

She sighed. "I should apologize. But he should apologize, too. He was being a brat."

"His actions aren't being addressed here." Trinity's tone was calm and matter-of-fact. "If you want, we can problem-solve later how you could have handled the situation differently."

"I should probably get this over with." Zoe shifted her gaze to the condiment table, where Callum slathered a hot dog with ketchup, mustard and relish.

His brother stood beside him, and even though they looked identical, Ryder could tell them apart. Callum was the one with a wet shirt. Prim supervised the boys, their younger sister propped on one of her hips.

Ryder and Trinity trailed behind Zoe as she made her way to where Prim stood, but they hung back when she drew close. This was Zoe's apology.

Zoe tapped Callum on the shoulder. "I'm sorry I threw water on you. You made me angry, but that wasn't how I should have responded."

Pride surged. His child sounded so grown up in that moment.

Prim glanced at her son. Her eyes narrowed. "You told me you dumped water on yourself."

Ryder wondered how Prim could have believed that story.

Then he recalled other stories of the twins' antics and knew almost anything was possible with those two.

"I didn't want to get her in trouble." Callum jerked a head in Zoe's direction even as his lips curved. "She's got spunk."

A look of pure astonishment blanketed Zoe's face at the compliment.

"I'm thinking it was more you didn't want to get in trouble for what you did or said." Prim shifted her focus from her son to cast an apologetic glance in Zoe's direction before returning her attention to Callum. "What do you have to say to Zoe?"

"Sorry for saying those things." Callum's tone was offhand. "You're a good player."

"Better than you," his twin taunted, before going silent at his mother's sharp look.

"I forgive you," Zoe said after a second's hesitation. "If you forgive me about the water."

Callum shrugged. "Cooled me off."

Ryder caught Prim's amused expression. Raising boys couldn't be easy.

"Well, okay," Zoe said.

She turned to go, but Callum called out, "Next time, you can be my partner. We'll beat everyone."

The look Zoe shot him only had Callum grinning and turning back to his hot dog.

CHAPTER TWENTY-TWO

"Now I really wish I hadn't eaten that second hot dog," Trinity moaned, taking in the game-day buffet that included classic hot wings, meatball-stuffed football bread and a cheese boat. Along with veggies and dip.

"It's pregame now." Hadley waved a hand. "We'll continue to mingle and eat until kickoff. Then, whoever wants to head into the kitchen to make pies, can. Or stay and watch the game."

"What about the children?" Trinity asked, seeing no sign of Brynn.

"Upstairs with the nanny." Hadley shot Trinity a reassuring smile. "Trust me, they're being well-supervised."

"There's a television in the kitchen, too," Ami reminded Hadley. "For those who, like me, want to both bake and watch."

Ami's sister Fin strolled up. "Thanks for distributing those flyers, Trinity. I don't know if you heard, but we ended up with a record crowd."

Fin and her sister looked so much alike that they might be mistaken for twins. The main difference was that Fin retained some of the big-city polish she'd acquired from living in Los Angeles for so many years.

Trinity liked her. Liked her directness, but also the way her eyes softened when she looked at her husband or placed a hand on her growing baby mound.

"I was happy to help," Trinity said. "If my efforts made even the slightest difference, that makes me even happier."

"I don't know how you do it," a woman said behind her. "I can never find the time to volunteer."

Trinity turned, and there was Stella, looking lovely as ever, if overdressed for the occasion, in a short black dress and heeled sandals. Though, Trinity admitted, if she'd had such fabulous legs, she might use every opportunity to show them off, too.

"Hi, Stella." Trinity shot her a bright smile, surprised when the woman looked at her as if she was a stranger. "We met at Steve and Lynn's home."

Recognition flashed in eyes that still managed to look bored. "That's right. You were dating Ryder."

Her gaze shifted to where Ryder stood in one corner, speaking with Beck. Stella let her gaze linger. "He's a hottie, that's for sure."

Before Trinity could process the comment, Stella's gaze swung back to her.

"Are you two still dating?"

"We—"

"Trinity." Zoe called out her name from the top of the stairs. "I swatted a mosquito."

The girl giggled, then disappeared down the upstairs hall.

Stella's nose wrinkled. "There are mosquitoes in the house?"

Trinity could have explained. Anyone else and she would have likely let them in on the inside joke. But she didn't much care for this woman.

Trinity wanted to swat at Ami and Hadley as they mumbled excuses and stepped away, leaving her alone with Stella. "Have you and Clay done anything fun lately?"

"Not really." Stella narrowed her gaze. "You played your cards right."

"Pardon me?"

"Ryder's kid." Stella gestured with her head toward the stairs. "I heard he had one, but at least there's no ex hanging around. Acting as if you like the kid is a smart move."

The admiration in Stella's eyes brought a sick feeling to the pit of Trinity's stomach. This woman actually thought she was using her love for Zoe to get in good with Ryder?

"First off, I genuinely like Zoe." Trinity knew she could have made an excuse and walked away like Ami and Hadley had, leaving Stella to think whatever she wanted. That would have seemed disloyal to Zoe and to Ryder. "I would never try to get in good with a man by sucking up to his child."

"That's only one reason I love you."

Trinity jolted. She hadn't realized Ryder had come over to where they stood.

From the look on Stella's face, she hadn't realized it either. "I didn't mean to imply—"

"Sure, you did." Ryder's pleasant tone belied the steely look in his eyes.

With a toss of her head, Stella walked over to Clay.

A smile blossomed on his face as Stella slipped her arm through his and rose on tiptoes to kiss him lightly on the mouth.

"Are you going to say anything to him?" Trinity asked Ryder.

He shook his head. "Clay's a smart guy. If he's not seeing the truth about Stella right now, it's because he doesn't want to."

Before she could say anything more, the voice on the television announced Krew's team had won the coin toss and would receive the ball.

"Come and sit beside me." Ryder linked his fingers with hers and gave a tug.

"I was going to help in the kitchen." But when she turned in that direction, she saw her fellow pie-makers were sitting with their husbands, their gazes focused on the big screen.

"Unless you don't like watching football…" Concern filled his eyes. "Please tell me you like football."

"I moved here from Nebraska, remember?" She chuckled. "You don't live in that state and not root for the Huskers."

When they reached the sofa, there was room for only one of them, so he sat and pulled her onto his lap. "One more thing to love about you."

Love? Her heart stumbled. This was the second time he'd used the L-word.

Once could be a slip of the tongue, but twice…

As his arms slipped around her and the ball sailed through the air, Trinity knew she was right where she belonged.

With the exception of Stella, the women headed for the kitchen at the end of the first quarter. Ryder hated to see Trinity leave, but liked that she'd found friends in Good Hope. It was the same with Zoe.

"Dad."

Ryder was so focused on the pass interception that it took him a second to realize he was being spoken to.

He looked up from the chair and saw Zoe.

Dad. Such a wonderful word.

"Hi, Zoe. Did you come down to watch the game?"

She shook her head. "It's on upstairs, but Brynn and I are busy doing each other's hair."

"I like the braids." He gave one a tug, making her squeal and earning amused glances from the men.

"Thanks." She touched her hair self-consciously. "I like them, too."

"Why is she in here?"

Ryder slanted a glance at Stella cuddled up on Clay's lap. He shrugged. "She's not into baking pies."

"Oh." Zoe frowned..

"If you didn't come to watch football," he prompted Zoe, "I assume there's something you need?"

"Brynn asked if I could spend the night." Zoe's words came more quickly now, almost as if she saw the refusal forming on Ryder's lips. "I know I've spent the night recently, but her mom and dad are okay with it."

He cocked his head. "She asked her dad?"

Ryder didn't want to doubt her word, but he couldn't recall seeing Brynn speaking with David since the game began.

Zoe shook her head, sending her braids whipping around her face. "She texted him."

"Texted?"

"Her mom, too. She knew they were busy and didn't want to disturb them." Zoe looked at him balefully. "I don't have a phone, or I'd have texted you."

A phone. Ryder closed his eyes for a second. The child was eleven.

Although, he had to admit, her having a phone would be convenient. And a safety thing.

"You and Trinity would be able to spend some quality time without me around," she said in a persuasive tone.

He wondered where this was coming from. "You know I like having you around. You're not an inconvenience to either me or Trinity."

"I know." Her tone was matter-of-fact. "But can I stay the night? Please?"

Ryder blew out a breath. "I suppose so."

Zoe flung her arms around his neck. "Thank you."

When she scampered happily up the stairs, he was still trying to figure out how she'd maneuvered him so easily into agreeing.

Perhaps this would be a good night to pull out the relationship cards with Trinity, the ones with the racy suggestions. He smiled as he picked up his beer.

The game ended up being a close one, with the lead changing hands several times. Ryder wondered how many pies were actually getting made as he kept hearing shouts and cheers coming from the kitchen.

In the final seconds of the game, one of the receivers—coached by Krew—made a catch and raced into the end zone to win the game.

Ryder rose to his feet and cheered, exchanging high fives with the other men.

After they kicked the extra point, the post-game show began, and everyone settled back into their seats. Ryder thought about checking on Zoe, but knew she'd be mortified.

It wasn't as if the kids had been left on their own during tonight's activities. David and Hadley had brought in their regular nanny as well as a high school "assistant" to watch over the group.

One of those assistants, a tall, skinny girl with glasses, showed up seconds later with a baby boy in her arms. Her gaze searched the room. When it landed on David, she stepped over to him. "He's really fussy. Mrs. Chapin fed him just a half hour ago, so he can't be hungry. I could see if she—"

"I'll take him, Avril." David jostled his son in his arms, but the baby continued to wail.

The cries made it impossible for the others to hear the commentary on the game.

"I'm going to take him outside. The fresh air might be just what he needs." David turned to Ryder. "Care to join us?"

"I could use some air."

Ryder stood by the rail while David paced, jiggling the crying infant. "Is he okay?"

"He's fine." David's gaze met his. "How are things with you and Zoe?"

"Good. I like being a dad. Two months ago, I would have said I couldn't do it. Now, I can't imagine not having Zoe in my life."

"I feel the same about Brynn. And now Carter." David smiled down at his son, who finally stopped crying, then back up at Ryder. "How about things between you and Trinity?"

How were things between them? Ryder thought of the secret that stood between them, one he'd never be able to share with her. Would it be a wedge between them in the years to come?

Ryder shook off the worry. "It's all good."

"You've had big changes in your life recently," David continued without giving Ryder a chance to speak. "I remember when Hadley and I got together. At the time, we were both dealing with so much."

"How did you navigate the chaos?"

"Very carefully." David chuckled. His eyes grew soft as the baby in his arms wrapped his hand around his finger and gnawed. "For us, it took getting all the secrets out in the open for our relationship to take off."

"Some secrets have to be kept." Ryder wasn't certain what had gotten into him, speaking this frankly.

Maybe it was seeing the baby and thinking what it would be like to have children with Trinity.

Maybe it was feeling the heavy weight of the secret every minute of every day.

Whatever the reason, when David's gaze sharpened, Ryder wished he'd kept his mouth shut.

"I'm not one to give advice," David began. "I'll just say that in my experience, secrets, when they come out, destroy trust."

"What if they don't come out?" Ryder kept his focus on the water and away from David's probing gaze.

"They have a way of coming out." David gave a humorless laugh. "Even when they don't, the act of keeping something hidden stops you from sharing freely with the other person. All that to say, if Trinity means something to you, think carefully about keeping secrets from her."

"Are you two going to be hanging out here all night?" Wyatt stood in the doorway. His gaze shifted from Ryder to David. "Problem?"

"Ryder was keeping me company while I got Carter to calm down." David's smile was as easy as his tone. "What's going on inside?"

"Hot cherry pie with ice cream to celebrate the win."

"Count me in," Ryder said, his voice hearty.

He thought he'd done a good job of masking any worry the conversation with David had stirred, but something about Wyatt's assessing gaze had him wondering if the only one he was fooling was himself.

CHAPTER TWENTY-THREE

"It was a wonderful party." Trinity leaned her head back and sighed. "I never knew baking pies could be so much fun."

Ryder slanted her a glance. "I sure enjoyed eating a couple of slices."

"They *were* good." Trinity chuckled. "Everything was perfect."

He nodded. "Do you know Brynn texted her parents to see if Zoe could spend the night?"

"I was standing beside Hadley when her phone dinged." Trinity gave a little laugh. "For a second, I thought it was the oven timer."

"I wonder if I should think about getting Zoe a phone."

"Has she asked for one?"

"In a roundabout way, but I'm sure a formal request will be forthcoming. It seems like most of her friends have one."

Trinity kept her tone noncommittal. "Is that the only reason you're thinking of getting her one?"

He turned and lifted a brow.

"Because most of her friends have one?"

"Not just that." Ryder's brows pulled together. "I'd like to be able to contact her—and for her to contact me—if either of us are running late. Then there's the whole safety issue."

Trinity's stomach clenched. "You're referring to the PI and her grandfather."

"I'd feel better if she could call one of us if she feels threatened."

"A phone sounds like an excellent idea to me."

"I'm glad you agree." Reaching over, Ryder grabbed her hand and brought her fingers to his lips. "Your opinion matters a great deal."

A languid warmth spread through Trinity's body, reaching to the very tips of her toes.

Tonight, she'd felt as if she had a family of her own. When Zoe had run into the kitchen, she'd shown the girl how to make a lattice crust.

Just like my mother showed me…

When Trinity had sat beside Ryder at the table, and he'd smiled at her while they ate pie and discussed the game, she'd felt like part of a couple.

Yes, for the first time, a happily ever after with the man of her dreams appeared to be within reach.

~

The car's headlights swept over the silhouette of a man when Ryder pulled into the drive.

"Did you see that guy?" Trinity's fingers wrapped around Ryder's arm, her voice hushed and urgent. "Is it that PI?"

"Not him." Though Ryder hadn't gotten much more than a glimpse, the man was bulkier and not nearly as tall as the PI, who'd topped six feet by several inches. "It could be a new tenant. Or someone else Swanson sent."

Trinity's face blanched. "You mean to hurt you?"

"I won't let that happen." Ryder gripped the steering wheel, and his mind spun.

"Should I call Cade?" Trinity's phone was in her hand, her finger poised. "I have his number programmed."

"No. Not yet. Let me see what this guy wants." An uneasy sense of dread weighed heavily on Ryder's shoulders. He almost wished the skinny investigator was standing there instead.

He'd pushed open the car door when Trinity grabbed his arm. "You're not going to confront him alone."

"Stay here." He shook her off, then closed his door firmly, sincerely hoping she'd do as he'd asked—heck, as he'd ordered—but that hope dissipated when he heard her door open.

Since Ryder hadn't closed the garage door, the man moved into the light.

Distinguished-looking was Ryder's first impression. The man was older than he expected. Late fifties would be Ryder's guess. He had an abundance of salt-and-pepper hair in a stylish cut and piercing blue eyes. "Ryder Goodhue?"

"Who are you?" Even before he asked, Ryder knew, and ice filled his tone.

Trinity moved to stand beside him.

The tightening of the older man's jaw was the only acknowledgment that he'd noticed her presence. His attention remained firmly fixed on Ryder.

"I'm Geoffrey Swanson. Jenna's father. Zoe's grandfather."

Ryder heard Trinity's quick intake of breath.

"Why are you here?" Ryder demanded.

"We need to talk." Geoffrey swiped a dismissive hand in Trinity's direction. "Alone."

Ryder experienced a surge of hope. This might not be as bad as he'd thought. Trinity would go inside, and he could speak with Swanson privately.

"I'm staying." Trinity placed a hand on his arm.

Ryder knew Trinity meant the gesture as a statement of solidarity, and he loved her for her concern, but he wanted to speak with Swanson alone. He had no idea what the man was about to reveal.

It took all of his self-control to keep his face expressionless. Actually, all he hoped was that he didn't look guilty. He thought of Zoe and the secret he could never share.

He wasn't foolish enough to believe that if the truth came out, Trinity would give him a pass just because he hadn't actually "lied" to her. Ryder had no doubt that, in her mind, a lie of omission was still a lie.

The greater good, he told himself. Which was making sure this monster never got near Zoe.

Trinity's reaction could not be his main concern. That was keeping Zoe safe.

"Where's the girl?" Geoffrey glanced around as if expecting the child to materialize out of thin air.

"Her whereabouts aren't any of your concern."

"She's my granddaughter."

"Well, I'm her father." Ryder lifted his lips in a tight smile. "Let me start out this discussion by saying I know what you did to Jenna. She told me all about you. Which means I'm not letting you anywhere near Zoe."

A vein in the man's forehead bulged, but he held on to control. A politician, Ryder thought. One who knew how to present himself to the public.

"Let's take this inside." The man's tone brooked no argument.

Ryder glanced in the direction of the Barn. Even from this distance, he heard Scully yapping.

"If you want to talk, we'll do it here." Ryder gestured with his head toward a picnic table. "I have a dog to let out first."

Ryder didn't wait for Geoffrey's response. Frankly, he didn't care if the man stayed or left.

Trinity hurried to catch up as Ryder swiped open the door

and strode into the lobby. "What is he doing here? Isn't your lawyer and his lawyer dealing with this?"

"They're probably not moving fast enough to satisfy him. I bet he's hoping to intimidate me into allowing him to visit Zoe." Ryder kept walking to his unit. "I'll let you know what he says."

"I'm not leaving you to speak with him alone."

"I can handle myself." He unlocked the door, and the dog bolted out into the hall. "Sit."

As Ryder retrieved Scully's leash, his mind raced. He needed to convince Trinity that it was best for him to speak with Swanson alone.

"I love Zoe." Trinity spoke softly beside him. "I want to be part of the conversation. The three of us are a team. Unless…I misunderstood."

His heart swelled, then pushed up to lodge in his throat. After clipping the leash on Scully, he stood and looked into her luminous blue eyes. Cupping her face in his hand, he kissed her with all the love in his heart. "You didn't misunderstand. You, me, Zoe, we *are* a team and a family. I love you."

Ryder had finally said the words. He wanted her to know how he felt, wanted there to be no doubt, in case tonight was the night she cut him out of her life forever.

He loves me. Trinity savored the words as she took the leash from Ryder and stepped into the cool night air.

Swanson stood by the picnic table, irritation evident in his posture and by the way he kept glancing at the expensive watch on his wrist. He'd shown up out of the blue, yet clearly expected everyone to jump when he said jump.

She'd thought it might take Scully a while to find the perfect bush, but he found the right one immediately, then wagged his tail and gazed up at her as if to say, *I'm done.*

The animal's quick actions made Trinity happy, because she didn't want to miss anything Swanson might say to Ryder. With a man like him, it was always good to have a backup set of ears.

"I'll get right to the point." Geoffrey took a seat on the other side of the table from Ryder. He didn't give Trinity a second glance when she slid onto the bench beside Ryder. "This will probably come as a great relief to you. I've located Zoe's biological father, and he's willing to take responsibility for the child."

Zoe's biological father? "He can't be—"

Ryder's hand closed over Trinity's under the table, and the rest of what she'd been about to say died on her lips.

She reminded herself this was Ryder's battle. He was up to the challenge. Her heart continued to beat rapidly, but she made every attempt to keep her features calm. Showing weakness in front of such a man was tantamount to waving a white flag of surrender.

"I'm Zoe's father." Ryder spoke with an equanimity that had Geoffrey's eyes firing. "My name is on her birth certificate. It was me who Jenna mentioned in her will, not some unknown guy you've managed to dig up."

Of course, Trinity thought. Geoffrey had gone looking for someone who would claim to be Zoe's father, to try to force Ryder's hand on custody.

"Bradley Kosmicki is willing to swear that he and Jenna were in a monogamous relationship when Zoe was conceived."

Trinity's heart picked up speed in the ensuing silence. What if Ryder *wasn't* Zoe's biological father? Ryder's dark eyes never wavered. "Your stooge can swear all he wants, but it's not going to get him—or you—anywhere. Zoe is my daughter, not his."

"A simple DNA test should clear this up." Geoffrey's smile and pleasant tone didn't fool Trinity. "I'll have my attorney get samples from you and the girl."

"*The girl* has a name." Ryder's tone might have held a polite edge, but his eyes were hard and cold. "Get Bradley, or whoever else you may have in your back pocket, to give a sample. I'll work with my attorney, and we'll get a sample from Zoe."

"You need to give one, too," Geoffrey insisted.

"I don't have anything to prove." Ryder's tone was as dismissive as the hand that swiped the air. "You say this guy is Zoe's father. I know he's not. Do you know how I know? Because I am."

For a second—Trinity would have missed it if she hadn't been looking straight at the man—Geoffrey's confident façade slipped. Just a fraction.

"You'll doctor the samples," Geoffrey accused.

"I want this to be conclusive. I want you to realize that attempting to dispute my paternity is a dead-end road." Ryder's smile became a smirk. "Dig up as many guys as you want. It's not going to give you what you want."

"It's not me who wants Zoe," Geoffrey blustered. "It's Brad."

Ryder actually laughed aloud. "Yeah, that's why you're here and not him. How much did you agree to pay him if he signed his parental rights over to you? Not that he has any parental rights, because he's not her father."

Trinity slanted a glance at Ryder.

"I-I don't know what you're referring to," Geoffrey said.

"C'mon, Geoff. Do you think I'm stupid?" Ryder shot the man a pitying glance. "This is so obvious it's slapping me in the face."

"You're talking crazy. You—"

Ryder talked over the man. "Here's how I envision it went. You hired investigators to find any man your daughter might have dated anywhere around the time she got pregnant. This Brad pops up on one of your reports. The dates don't exactly match, but hey, you're desperate. You contact the guy and offer him money to swear he's Zoe's father and agree to sign his parental rights over to you."

Geoffrey's face reddened before he regained his composure. "Suppose I did hire a private investigator and had him look into you, as well. And suppose he discovered the fact that you and

Jenna were barely in contact around the time Zoe was conceived. Unlike Brad, who was involved with her for years. What would you say to that?"

Trinity inhaled sharply. Could Brad be Zoe's father after all? Had Ryder already known that?

"I'd say a lot can be accomplished in one night." Ryder shook his head, not bothering to disguise the disgust lacing his words. "Did you really expect you'd tell me these lies and I'd just hand over my daughter? Not happening now. Not happening ever."

The man's body language when he shifted, when his eyes wouldn't meet Ryder's, told her Ryder was on the right track.

Ryder jerked to his feet, nearly upending the picnic table. "We're done here. Have your attorney contact mine. Other than that, I don't want to see you anywhere near my daughter."

Geoffrey stood and straightened his suit coat. "You haven't heard the last from me."

"You dig up another guy, it'll be the same song, second verse." Ryder's dark eyes were as cold as February. "You're never getting Zoe. Like I said, Jenna told me everything you did to her."

For only a second, the man's composure slipped. Then the arrogant set to his features returned, and he sneered. "Lies from a troubled young woman who—"

"Troubled?" Ryder's voice rose. "Yes, Jen was troubled. She didn't expect her father, the man who should have been there to protect her, to rape her. She didn't expect her mother to cover for you and leave her swinging in the wind."

Ryder pointed a finger at the man. "You will never get the chance to hurt Zoe like you hurt Jenna. Get out of my sight. You make me sick."

Ryder held a hand out to Trinity, who took it and found it ice-cold. Without another word, they turned and strode toward the Barn.

"She's my granddaughter," Geoffrey called after them. "I have a right to see her."

A muscle in Ryder's jaw jumped, but he didn't turn or respond.

Once the door shut behind them, Ryder expelled a breath. "I'm so glad Zoe spent the night with Brynn."

Trinity only nodded. Was Ryder really one hundred percent sure he was Zoe's father? Having Zoe and Brad undergo DNA testing seemed risky to her.

Trinity followed Ryder into his unit. The second she unclipped Scully's leash with shaking hands, the dog made a beeline for his bed.

"I need a drink," Ryder muttered.

"Make mine a double."

The hard set to his jaw relaxed, and he chuckled. "I like your style."

When he opened his arms, she went to him, burying her face against his shirtfront. "What a horrid, horrid man."

"No argument here." Ryder stroked her back as he held her.

Trinity breathed in the familiar scent of him, reveled in the strength of his arms around her. This was not a man who backed away from a challenge. This was someone a woman—and a little girl—could count on.

That was only one of the many things she loved about him.

There were many questions she wanted to ask, but despite his strength and the way he'd handled Geoffrey, she knew Ryder well enough to know that the encounter had shaken him.

"I know what you need," she whispered in his ear, planting a kiss against his neck.

His lips curved, but he shook his head. "I never thought I'd say it, but I'm not in the mood for—"

"I'm talking about a backrub." Trinity didn't wait for him to protest—or to agree—she simply took his hand and tugged him down the hall. "It'll relax you more than alcohol would. Then we'll get some sleep."

He stopped halfway down the hall and turned to her, enfolding her in his arms. "Thanks."

She brushed her mouth over his and smiled. "For what?"

"For knowing me. For being here for me." Ryder's expression turned serious. "I want to say one thing again."

Her pulse began a rapid *tap-tap-tap*. "What is it?"

"I love you." His fingers slid into her hair, and his mouth closed over hers.

The kiss started out slow, a long dreamy kiss that showed no signs of ending. By the time he lifted his head, Trinity was ready to tear off her clothes and jump him.

"I love you, too." She murmured the words, her mouth only inches from his. Then she stepped back, expelled a shuddering breath and lifted her hands as if that could steady her. "Which is why I'm going to follow through with my promise. I said I'd give you a massage, and that's what I'm going to do."

Trinity didn't want to rub his back, or at least not just that part of him. She wanted to touch him everywhere. She wanted to kiss him until she was drunk on the taste of him. She wanted to feel his warm body pressed up against hers and have every nerve ending in her body quiver in pleasure.

"I've got a different suggestion." A hint of devilment danced in his brown eyes before he kissed her neck. "Let's take full advantage of this no-child-in-the-house night."

"You're tired," she stuttered. "Stressed."

"Not anymore ..." His mouth covered hers in another lingering kiss.

Trinity's pulse began to hum. With Zoe at Brynn's, there would be no need to rush. Instead, like a fine bottle of wine, they could savor, not gulp.

~

Ryder planted kisses up the side of her neck, satisfaction surging as her breathing turned shallow.

He closed his fingers around hers and tugged her the rest of the way down the hall, reveling in the heat and the connection. "Sex isn't all I want from you. I want you in my life and not just for tonight."

Her expression softened as they paused just outside his bedroom door. Looping her arms around his neck, she gazed up at him.

"It's not all I want from you either." Trinity's gaze searched his face. "It feels as if I've been looking for you forever, and now here you are."

For once, he was speechless.

Her baby blues glittered as she lightly ran a fingernail down his cheek. "You're what I thought I'd never find. A sexy, sweet, honorable man I can trust with my heart."

His hands weren't quite steady as he cupped her face, kissed her. He could kiss her all night, he realized. Would kiss her all night.

Trinity brought out a different side of him. Around her, he could be himself. She accepted and loved him—yes, she'd finally admitted it—just as he was, flaws and all. "I can't recall anyone telling me I'm sweet. Sexy, yes. Sweet, no."

She poked him in the side, then laughed at his *oof* and stepped into his bedroom. "The navy and gray color scheme is very masculine."

He stepped close. "That's me."

"I remember." Her eyes glittered now, and a watchful waiting filled her expression.

"I want you so badly."

"I like it hot and fast." Her lips curved as, this time, her fingers toyed with the top button of *her* shirt. "I also like it slow."

"Spend the night, and I'll give you both." Though he'd told

himself not to push, he couldn't help himself. Need for her coursed through him.

"Hmm, what to decide." The button popped open, and her fingers dropped to the next one. "Since I'm wavering, I guess it's up to you to convince me."

When she gazed at him through lowered lashes, mischief dancing in her eyes, Ryder took her into his arms. "That will be my pleasure."

CHAPTER TWENTY-FOUR

When Ryder's head lowered and those smooth, firm lips melded with hers, the need rising inside Trinity was not to be denied. She let herself drown in the kiss, sliding her fingers into his hair and drinking him in.

He smelled so good, and she knew every inch of the body now pressing against hers. It wasn't just Ryder's looks or his amazing body or his ability to kiss her senseless that sucked her in. He was a genuinely good guy, and each time she was with him, she found more things to love.

When they came up for air, he gently brushed a lock of hair back from her face with one finger. "In case you're wondering, I've got protection."

"If you didn't, I have condoms in my purse. I'm also still on the pill." She smiled. "Double the protection."

"I like a woman who thinks things through."

"I'm a planner," she admitted. "Right now, I'm planning to enjoy every moment of this time with you."

His arms were strong as they scooped her up and carried her to the king-size bed. His hands were gentle as they undressed her, while he kissed her, murmuring sweet words in between each caress. His mouth, ah, his mouth, it teased and tantalized until fire scorched her veins.

He'd shed his clothes, too, and his body was just as she remembered, all broad shoulders and lean hips. Sculpted muscles called to her and had her running her hands over them or kissing his smooth skin.

Ryder gave as much as he took, making sure her pleasure equaled his own. Each kiss sent a fresh wave of heat and longing coursing through her body, until she didn't think she could fight the need a second longer.

Apparently feeling the same, he rolled on top of her, his body hard where she was soft and oh-so-hot. His hands returned to her breasts as he rolled her nipples between his thumbs and forefingers, even as his mouth ravaged hers.

When his tongue slipped back into her mouth, it was as if they were joined together already. Trinity couldn't recall ever making love with anyone who so totally consumed her.

"I want you inside me."

She waited impatiently. The condom was barely on when she wrapped her legs around him, groaning when he entered her.

"You are amazing. Beautiful. Smart. Sexy." As he murmured endearments, he continued the in-and-out rhythm as old as time. He kissed her again, as if he couldn't get enough of her.

Trinity understood. She felt the same way.

They rode the waves together, breaths coming in short puffs as the tension built.

Trinity cried out, her fingers gripping his shoulders.

Still, he pumped, making sure she'd wrung out the last bit of pleasure before taking his release, then collapsing on top of her.

When he started to roll off of her, Trinity wrapped her arms around his neck and held him to her.

"Not yet," she whispered, giving the lobe of his ear a playful nip.

"I don't want to crush you."

"I kind of like being crushed by you."

He chuckled, a low rumbling sound. In one fluid move, he flipped their positions. "I like being crushed by you."

A warm flood of emotion she couldn't have stopped even if she'd wanted to washed over her. A strand of his dark hair fell over his forehead, making him look…sweet. And sexy as all get out. Surprisingly, it was the sweet that made her decision easy. Trinity lifted a hand, pushing at hair the color of walnuts.

Oh, how she loved this man. With gentle lips, she kissed the spot she'd bared. "I've decided."

He smiled, slow and easy. "What exactly have you decided?"

"I'm spending the night."

~

When Ryder woke the next morning, it took him a minute to remember what had happened. At some point, Trinity had tossed a cotton throw over his naked body.

Had he really told her he wasn't interested in sex? He had to grin. It hadn't taken much to convince him otherwise.

The smile disappeared when he recalled the encounter with Zoe's grandfather. Thank God he'd gone through Jenna's journals and knew, without a doubt, that whoever Zoe's father was, it wasn't Brad Kosmicki.

Worthless piece of sh—

Ryder stopped himself, unwilling to waste one more second of energy on a man who'd sell a little girl to the highest bidder. Because, no matter how you spun it, that's what Brad had done. Or, rather, attempted to do.

Did he know Jenna's father was a pedophile? Didn't matter. Brad knew he wasn't Zoe's father, but had still been willing to lie for money.

Jenna had been smart to boot him out of her life.

This morning, Ryder would call Beck. He would make

sure there were controls in place to ensure that any DNA sample given by either Zoe or Brad wasn't tampered with. Then this would be over. He could shove the whole issue of Zoe's parentage to the back of his mind and never think of it again.

As he showered and dressed, David's words returned to gnaw at him, much the way Carter had gnawed at his father's finger. Words about secrets destroying trust.

One secret, he told himself. That's the only secret there would be between him and Trinity. He knew lots of married couples with secrets, some big, some small.

His relationship with Trinity could handle this. He felt sure of that, because at the base Zoe's safety was at risk.

Ryder nearly felt normal by the time he showered. As he dressed, a plan took shape. He would call Beck, grab some food, then head over to Hadley and David's to pick up Zoe.

Though he didn't feel much like going to the Harvest Festival, he'd promised Zoe and Trinity they would go together.

As he strode down the hall, he decided a little family time was just what he needed.

Family.

That's what they were—Zoe and Trinity. His family.

My family.

He rolled the words around on his tongue and smiled.

His smile widened when he entered the kitchen and found Trinity sitting at the table with a cup of coffee, staring down at a pad of paper.

He hadn't expected her to still be here, but seeing her in his kitchen felt right.

She looked up when he leaned over and kissed her gently on the mouth.

"Good morning. Seeing you here sure starts my day off right." He shot her a wink, then headed for the coffeepot.

"How did you sleep?"

"Amazing." Ryder turned with a cup of steaming coffee in hand. "How 'bout you?"

"Restless."

Concerned, Ryder pulled out a chair and sat down across from her. "You should have woken me up. Was it the incident with Jenna's father?"

"Partially," she admitted. "I had all these thoughts tumbling around in my head."

Her face appeared drawn, and fatigue edged her eyes.

Ryder reached across the table and covered her hand with his. "If you'd woken me, I could have given you a massage."

That brought out a little smile.

"Something is bothering you." There was a strange vibe in the room, the cause of which Ryder couldn't immediately identify. "Tell me, and we can worry together. Or maybe even make it right."

This time, his teasing fell flat.

Trinity took a long, bracing drink of coffee, reminding him of a guy tossing back a shot of whiskey to gather his nerves.

Alarm bells began to ring, but Ryder still hadn't identified the fire.

"You're not Zoe's father."

Everything inside Ryder turned to ice. He managed to set his cup on the table without spilling a drop. "How can you say that?"

"Because of this." She shoved the pad of paper across the table and blew out a breath. "The dates don't line up."

Glancing down, he saw a timeline of sorts, beginning with when he graduated from high school. He lifted his gaze. "I didn't realize we'd discussed when I graduated from Good Hope High."

He wasn't able to stop the coolness from entering his voice. But darn it, the thought of her skulking around to gather information about him didn't sit well.

"You and I didn't discuss it. In the kitchen yesterday, Fin mentioned she graduated with you in 2004."

Unlike his, her voice was calm and polite. Probably the same tone she used with her clients. The thought made him suddenly furious.

"So...what?" He shoved the pad back across the table. "Because I graduated in a certain year, you've made some scribbles and decided I'm lying?"

He immediately regretted the phrasing of his comeback. It only served to remind him that he *was* lying, not only to her but to everyone.

She flinched, and he saw disappointment cloud her baby blues.

He'd been a toad, a jerk to someone he loved. There was no excuse other than that the panic boiling up inside him had him frantic to stop this conversation.

"Why can't you tell me the truth?"

She knew the truth. He saw it in her eyes.

But if he admitted it, even to Trinity, and it somehow got out, Geoffrey would insist he take a paternity test.

If that happened, it would be all over for him and Zoe.

He couldn't take that chance. As much as he loved and trusted Trinity, the fact that Zoe wasn't his biological daughter was something he would never admit.

Not to anyone.

"I agreed to let them compare Brad's and Zoe's DNA."

"Which only means you don't think Brad is her father."

Ryder narrowed his gaze. "I hope you don't plan to voice these false suspicions to anyone."

"I would never do that."

"Good." With one quick motion, he ripped the top two sheets off the pad and crumpled them. "Zoe is my daughter. Period. End of interrogation."

Trinity gazed at the wadded-up papers for several long seconds. "You don't trust me with the truth."

The sadness in her voice tugged at his heart.

He longed to tell Trinity, wanted nothing more than to confide all. But he could not, *would* not, take any chances with Zoe's welfare.

"You say I don't trust you." Ryder searched her eyes with a steady gaze. "Don't you trust me? To do right by Zoe?"

"You're a wonderful father," Trinity admitted. "Zoe is lucky to have you in her life."

Ryder expelled the breath he hadn't realized he was holding. He picked up his coffee and gulped. "Do you want to eat here or go out to breakfast before we pick her up? Knowing Hadley, she'll have already fed the girls."

"Ryder."

"Yes?" He offered her a smile.

"This isn't one of those situations where we can agree to disagree." Her gaze met his. "I want you to tell me the truth. Is Zoe your biological daughter?"

If only Trinity hadn't added the word *biological*, he'd have been able to answer honestly. Zoe was his daughter in every sense of the word.

Ryder steeled himself. Met her gaze. "Yes."

Trinity knew it was a combination of lack of sleep and profound disappointment that had tears springing to her eyes. Determinedly, she blinked them back.

He was lying. She'd grown to know Ryder so well over the past weeks that she could read him like a well-loved book. Oh, he played a good game of poker, looking her straight in the eyes and answering in a firm voice. But she saw deceit in those dark brown depths, and her heart broke.

Trinity didn't need to smooth out the crumpled bits of paper. The dates were burned into her memory. "You're thirty-two-years old. You graduated from high school in 2004. That surprised me. I thought it would be 2005, but Ami told me you skipped a grade. Zoe was born in June of 2008, so she was conceived in the fall of 2007. You said you dated Jenna your first year in college. That would have been 2004 to 2005. You said you didn't date again, only saw her for dinner off and on through the years. There's no way you were with Jenna in 2007 when Zoe was conceived."

Ryder didn't so much as blink. "So maybe I had an extra one-night stand with Jenna that I never told you about. What's the big deal?"

She searched his eyes. "Tell me the truth."

"Let me ask you a question. Have you told me about every single time you've had sex?"

Trinity blinked.

"I didn't think so." His mouth formed a thin, grim line.

Trinity flinched. "I know what you're doing. I know you're holding to this to protect Zoe. I understand you love her and want to keep her safe. I love her and want her safe, too."

"If you want her safe, then let this go."

"That isn't the issue anymore. I can't just let it go that you're lying straight to my face. That you don't trust me to be in this with you, to help you. If you can't be honest with me about something I already know, if you can't trust me enough to let me be part of this, then how can I trust that you'll always tell me the truth going forward?"

"How can you even ask me that right now?" Ryder blew out a frustrated breath and raked a hand through his hair. "I'm trying to save my daughter, a little girl who has no one but me, from a true monster, and you're asking me to stop doing that to prove I love you."

"Don't do that, Ryder. Don't try to turn me into some crazy woman making selfish demands. That's not what this is, and you know it. There is no love without trust. I expected you to trust me, to trust us. And you couldn't do that..."

Trinity stood and grabbed her purse. "I will do whatever I can to help Zoe, including keeping your secret, but I can't be with a man who lies to me, no matter what the reason."

She left the papers lying on the table. "In case I didn't make myself clear, it's over between us."

He looked so miserable that, for a second, she was tempted to turn back and ignore reality. She couldn't. Wouldn't.

That had been the main problem in her marriage to Miles. She'd let Miles turn conversations around on her and avoid issues for far too long. It took too long for her to be struck full force with the realization that her entire marriage to Miles and her relationships with his daughters had been built on a house of cards.

Honest communication? Discussion of feelings? At the end, there had been none of that left. When she'd walked out the door for the last time, she'd vowed she would do it all differently if she ever got the chance.

She would work hard to have a relationship built not only on love, but on mutual respect and trust. A man who would lie to her face wasn't a man she wanted.

"Have a fun time at the festival today with Zoe." Lifting her lips upward in the semblance of a smile took everything left in her. "I'll be going into Connections today and working on paperwork. If Zoe asks where I am, you'll be able to tell her the truth."

"She'll want you to be there with us." He stepped forward, and before Trinity knew what was happening, he'd taken her hands in his. "I want you with her. With me. I'm begging you, Trinity. Let this go."

How many times had Miles said a variation of that same thing to her? How many times had she given in?

"I can't." Trinity pulled away and felt her heart crack in half. "Not this time."

CHAPTER TWENTY-FIVE

"I don't see why Trinity has to work," Zoe grumbled as Ryder paid for two caramel hot chocolates.

As he handed one to her, Ryder considered telling Zoe it was over between him and Trinity. It wasn't just the words that Trinity had uttered, it was the disappointed look in her eyes that told him their relationship had come to an end.

"I wish she was with us, too."

"She's cool, you know." Zoe sipped the cocoa and glanced up at him. "Brynn asked me what I'd think if she married you, and I said that'd be dope."

Ryder lowered his cup and frowned. "Dope?"

Zoe rolled her eyes. "You know, beyond cool."

He said nothing, could think of nothing to say.

"I just wanted you to know." Zoe studied his face. "What's wrong?"

He needed to tell her about Geoffrey's unexpected visit last night. Things had been hectic this morning, so he hadn't had a chance to consider exactly what to say.

Once Trinity had left, as if sensing the tension, Scully had barfed all over the kitchen floor and then again in Zoe's bedroom. By the time Ryder had gotten the mess cleaned up, it had been time to pick up Zoe at Brynn's house.

Brynn had begged him to allow Zoe to attend the festival with her family, but with Geoffrey likely still in town, Ryder had wanted to keep a close watch on Zoe this weekend.

"Dad?" Zoe placed a hand on his arm, two lines of worry forming between her brows. "Tell me."

"Let's walk this way." He gestured with his head in the direction of the bandstand, which would eventually be set up for the Baggage Claim concert tonight.

At the moment, the area was fairly deserted. Ryder knew it wouldn't be long before Zoe ran across a friend who'd want to tag along with them.

"We've spoken about your mother's father."

Her lips, which had closed on the rim of her cup, released it. She met his gaze. "Why are you bringing him up?"

It was clear to Ryder that Zoe didn't want to discuss the man. Out of sight, out of mind. The problem was the guy wasn't out of sight. In fact, he could be lurking around the festival grounds even now.

Ryder had difficulty imagining Geoffrey had left the peninsula. "He was waiting by the garage last night when Trinity and I got home."

Zoe's eyes went wide. "What did he want?"

Gesturing to a bench under a large leafy tree, Ryder took a seat.

After a second's hesitation, Zoe plopped down beside him.

"He told me he discovered that another man, Brad, was your father. He said Brad agreed to take custody of you, then turn you over to him."

"I'm not going with him." Zoe's voice rose, shaky and reed-thin. "You can't make me."

"Hey, hey," Ryder soothed. "What did I promise?"

"That I can stay here with you forever."

"That's right." He set a reassuring hand on her shoulder. "This is a ploy by Mr. Swanson, Zoe. That's all it is. Brad isn't your father. I am."

Worry clouded Zoe's eyes. "Why does he think he is?"

She was too young to have to deal with all of this, Ryder thought. But it couldn't be helped. For her own protection, she needed to know the score.

"Geoffrey is used to getting his own way by any means possible." Ryder kept his tone matter-of-fact, hoping his calm manner would help Zoe settle. "It was obvious he tracked down Brad, who knew your mom around the time you were born, and made him an offer."

"But Brad isn't my father, right?"

Even though Ryder had assured her of that fact only seconds earlier, he explained it again. "Bradley Kosmicki is not your father. He didn't even meet your mom until after you were conceived."

Zoe blew out a breath. When she brushed a strand of blond hair back from her face, her hand trembled. "You're positive?"

"Not a single doubt." He smiled reassuringly. "So positive that I told Mr. Swanson I have no problem with you giving a DNA sample, because I can guarantee that you and Brad won't be a match."

Zoe's hand rose to cover her mouth. "I have to take a test?"

"Unlikely, but a possibility." Ryder offered a reassuring smile. "If you have to, it'll just be a swab of your cheek. No pain at all."

"What if you're wrong? What if Brad is my father?" Her eyes filled with tears. "What if he gives me—"

"No one is taking my girl from me." Ryder met her gaze with a firm, steady one. "Trust me when I say he isn't your father. If we end up having to do the DNA test to make Mr. Swanson go away forever, we will."

"I'm scared."

He set down his drink and wrapped an arm around her shoulders. "You don't have anything to worry about. I'm your father. It's my job to protect you. You can count on me."

She stared at him for a long moment, her searching gaze reaching all the way to his soul.

"Okay." She expelled a shaky breath. "Okay."

"Mr. Swanson may have already left the area," Ryder continued. "But this week, when you're with your friends, I want you to be extra vigilant about your surroundings and make sure you stay with your friends at all times..."

On a slight rise a short distance away, Trinity observed the discussion between father and daughter. Even from here she could see Ryder was doing his best to project confidence. From Zoe's responses, he was doing a good job.

To her sharp and assessing gaze, he appeared weary. She watched him rub the bridge of his nose as if a headache was attempting to form.

Trinity desperately wanted to go to him, put her arms around him and assure him she was here for him.

She kept her feet planted. When father and daughter pushed up from their seats, Trinity took that as her cue and headed in the opposite direction toward where she was parked.

Her car was in sight when Trinity hit an immovable object in the form of Gladys Bertholf. Always one for the dramatic, Glady had her hair, dark as midnight with a bold strip of white, partially covered by a scarf adorned with gold coins.

Trinity vaguely recalled someone mentioning yesterday that Gladys would be telling fortunes today at the Harvest Festival. This weird garb must be her Madame Gitana outfit.

"We need to talk." Gladys's pale blue eyes seemed even more eerie today. "A relationship hangs in the balance."

Trinity resisted the urge to sigh. "If you want to talk more about Albert, you need to make another appointment."

Gladys put a staying hand on Trinity's arm, as if sensing she was seconds from walking away. "It isn't about him. It's about you and Ryder."

Trinity stiffened.

"You aren't with him and Zoe, so clearly something is wrong."

"Thank you for your concern." Trinity's smile felt frozen. "I need to get to the office."

When she tried to walk away, Gladys tightened her grip.

Trinity whirled. "Let go—"

"Won't you tell me what's troubling you?" Gladys's voice was as soft as a mother's caress.

Trinity shook her head, and tears stung her eyes.

Gladys slipped an arm around Trinity's shoulders. "Okay, then don't talk, just listen. Can you do that?"

Trinity didn't know why, but she found herself nodding.

"The reason I matchmake isn't because I'm a busybody." Gladys paused, then added, "Of course, I can be that, too. But in my ninety-seven years, I've learned that love is the only thing in the world that really matters. I also know how hard it is to find. You love Ryder."

It was a statement, not a question, but Trinity answered anyway. "I do."

"And he loves you."

Trinity didn't respond at first, taking several seconds to find the words. "I was married before. I don't know if you knew that, but it was when I was young and—"

"Each relationship is unique. What I shared with my Henry is different than what Albert and I now share." Gladys's eyes met Trinity's. "The love you share with Ryder is special. He's not your ex-husband. It would be wrong and, frankly, not fair to paint them with the same brush."

"I'm so afraid of making another mistake," Trinity admitted.

"There are no guarantees in life." Gladys patted her arm. "A brilliant woman, and one I'm proud to call a friend, once told me that great opportunities are often brilliantly disguised as impossible situations. I believe if you look at your situation with Ryder, you'll discover it's not impossible, but rather, a great opportunity."

Oh, how Trinity wanted to believe that. But she was scared, scared of letting Ryder off the hook for lying to her, scared of setting up a pattern in their lives, scared of…failing.

"I'll leave you with a final thought."

Trinity inclined her head.

"Every relationship is just a big honking leap of faith." After brushing a kiss across Trinity's cheek, Gladys whirled and strolled off.

Trinity stared after her in disbelief.

Had Gladys really just quoted Lorelai Gilmore?

CHAPTER TWENTY-SIX

Ryder walked his daughter into the church, his thoughts everywhere but on the upcoming worship service.

He'd spoken with Beck yesterday about Geoffrey's unexpected visit. Though Ryder was eager to get the DNA test over with for Zoe's sake, Beck insisted that it would be best to wait until they were contacted by Geoffrey's attorney.

That's when they'd give their criteria that the test must be done through a properly accredited laboratory. When Ryder voiced his worry that Geoffrey might provide his own DNA sample—rather than Bradley's—Beck assured him an analysis of Zoe's DNA compared to a grandparent would show that they shared only twenty-five percent of DNA, instead of the fifty percent you'd expect with a father.

"Dad."

Ryder blinked and realized they were standing at the entrance to the church sanctuary, blocking traffic.

"I'll see you after youth group." Zoe offered a little wave, then veered off in the direction of her friends.

Ryder pulled his thoughts back to the present and watched his daughter's friends slide over to make room for her in the back pew.

He continued up several rows and chose a spot across the aisle. This way, he was in sight of Zoe should she need him.

Though Ryder hadn't seen—or spoken with—Geoffrey since their encounter Friday night, he still worried the man might have remained in the area, hoping for an opportunity to talk with Zoe.

Each time the doors at the back opened, Ryder turned. Trinity arrived just before the first hymn. Ignoring the available space in his pew, she gave him a slight smile as she continued down the aisle and chose a spot near the front.

When he glanced in her direction near the end of the service, she was gone.

While Zoe was in youth group, Ryder sat in the car. He couldn't bring himself to go to Muddy Boots, where he'd be surrounded by happy couples. The more he thought about the position that Trinity had taken, his frustration grew.

It wasn't like he'd told her a bunch of lies, after all. Just the one. Though it was a big one…

A knock on his side window had him jerking his head up.

Trinity.

Ryder couldn't stop his smile as relief surged. She'd sought him out. It appeared she understood. Or, at least if she didn't fully understand, she'd decided to trust him. "Good morning. You look lovely."

"Thank you."

There was politeness in her tone, but no warmth. The relief flooding him went as dry as a parched riverbed.

"I have a question for you."

"Would you like to sit?" He reached for the door handle, but never took his eyes off her. "Or we could take a walk?"

"No, but thanks for asking."

Ryder wasn't about to conduct a conversation through an open car window. Not when this might be his final opportunity to convince her to give him another chance. Pushing the door open, he stood.

Trinity took a couple of steps back, putting more distance between them. For the first time, he noticed she clutched her purse so tightly the tips of her fingers were white.

Somehow it made him feel better to know he wasn't the only one off-balance.

"I'm going to Green Bay today. I thought I'd do a little shopping, have lunch, maybe check out the zoo or the botanical gardens." Trinity paused. "I'd like for Zoe to spend the afternoon with me. If that's okay with you."

Zoe. Not him and Zoe. Just Zoe.

He swallowed past his disappointment. "Have you mentioned the possibility to her?"

"In passing. Last week." The wind caught a strand of hair, and she lifted one hand to hold it back.

Ryder was struck again by her beauty. But there was so much more to Trinity McConnell than her looks. She was smart and funny and kind. He missed her fiercely.

"Zoe thought it sounded like fun when I first brought it up." Trinity lifted a shoulder and let it drop. "She may already have plans for today."

"No plans." Ryder didn't mention he didn't have plans either. There was no need. He wasn't invited.

Simply because he was hurting, he found himself wanting to tell her his daughter couldn't go. But that would be beyond petty. Zoe would enjoy spending time with Trinity.

Besides, he'd feel better knowing Zoe was out of town with a responsible adult, rather than doing something in Good Hope with her friends where Geoffrey might spot her. "If she wants to go with you, it's okay with me."

"I appreciate it."

"What's to appreciate?" His tone came out light, but his smile felt forced.

"I worried that because things didn't, well, work out with us, you might not want her spending time with me." She offered a smile. "I'm happy to know that isn't the case."

"The truth is I haven't told her we're not together anymore." Ryder hadn't been able to make himself do it. Hadn't been able to find the words.

Trinity's brows pulled together. "How did you explain me not riding to church with you this morning?"

Ryder reviewed in his mind the hectic moments leading up to them rushing through the doors of the church at the last minute. "It was a crazy morning. We got here shortly before you did."

"Oh."

He didn't know what significance to read into the utterance, so he didn't try. "If you're planning to leave from here, I'll wait with you."

She hesitated for a seemingly endless second. "I'll meet up with Zoe back at the Barn. Are you planning to head straight home after youth group?"

"You might as well wait with me."

This time, her hesitation fired his temper. Dear God, couldn't they even be friends? When he spoke again, his tone was clipped, and he found himself gesturing with his hands. "Look. We live just down the hall from each other. Even if you don't want anything to do with me—"

"Don't put words in my mouth." Her blue eyes flashed. "I never said I don't want anything to do with you."

Anger mixed with frustration. He flung out his hands. "What did I do, Trinity, that was so awful that you don't even want to be my friend?"

"I fell in love with you, Ryder." Her voice shook with emotion. "I trusted you. Until I found out that while you professed to trust me, you didn't. You lied to my face."

"The reason doesn't matter?"

"Everyone has good reasons. At least from their viewpoint."

Ryder tried to interject, but Trinity held up her hand to stop him and continued.

"I told you before, trust and honesty are the most important things to me in a relationship. Both were in short supply in my marriage. When Miles didn't want to discuss something, he'd tell me I just had to trust him."

"We're not talking about your ex. What happened with him isn't relevant to us."

"Isn't it? You say to trust you, but you don't trust me. That's what hurts. Especially since I work in a field where everything a client tells me is always kept confidential. I know how to keep my mouth shut. Yet you chose not to confide in me."

It wasn't anger now that rolled off her, but sadness. "Don't think this decision was easy for me, because it wasn't. I know the connection we shared was unique and not something that happens all the time…" Trinity's voice faded to a whisper, and she paused to take in a deep breath before continuing. "I see no reason why we can't be cordial, but it's going to have to be at a distance."

Why?

Had he voiced the question aloud, or had it simply welled up from the depths of his tortured soul?

She must read it in his eyes.

"I need to get over you." Trinity spoke slowly, as if choosing her words carefully. "I can't do that unless I put distance between us."

This was really the end. He could feel it. See it in her eyes.

Ryder grabbed her hand. "Trinity, please. I—"

She jerked back. "Don't touch me."

Her voice, sharp and brittle, cracked like a hard slap.

Ryder dropped his hand from hers. "As soon as Zoe is out of youth group, we'll be home."

She gave a curt nod and, without looking back, strode in long, purposeful strides to where her car was parked on the street.

Ryder kept his gaze on her as she pulled away from the curb. The empty space she left there matched the empty place in his heart.

He was turning away when his attention was captured by a dark sedan with tinted windows also parked on the street. It might have been a coincidence that it pulled out only seconds after Trinity did. Another coincidence that it turned in the same direction.

Ryder pulled out his phone and called Trinity. The call went immediately to voice mail.

"There's a car following you. Dark sedan. Don't go home. It's too isolated. Go somewhere public. Call me."

He followed up his call with a text, but had little hope she'd see it until she was home.

Ryder had a good idea who was in the car. Either Geoffrey Swanson or someone hired by him. For what purpose?

He wished he'd gotten Zoe a cell phone. Then he remembered Zoe had programmed Brynn's number into his phone. The girl probably wouldn't take a call while in youth group, but she'd see a text.

Zoe is to go home with you.

Almost immediately, the return text flashed.

K.

Tires spun and gravel flew as he pulled out of the lot in pursuit of Trinity and the mysterious black sedan.

Trinity stepped out of the garage, rolling her shoulders to relieve the tightness. Just being that close to Ryder again had brought an ache to her heart.

If he'd screamed at her or—

But, no, she corrected herself. Ryder wasn't a man to scream or to try to shame her into changing her mind. His dignity had only made her love him more. Could Gladys be right? Was it possible to—

"Miss McConnell."

Trinity's heart slammed against her chest with the force of a solid hit with a bat. She thought of pepper spray, then remembered she'd left it on the kitchen counter when she changed purses.

After the initial shock, she realized she knew the man. "Mr. Swanson. If you're looking for Ryder, he's—"

"I know where he is." Geoffrey Swanson's sharp-eyed gaze remained on her.

As her heart continued to race, Trinity reassured herself she was a grown woman, not a child. She refused to be cowed. "What is it you want?"

He lifted his hands, palms out, and offered a solicitous smile. "Just conversation."

She didn't wish to speak with him, didn't want to have anything to do with him. Yet, he was here, and perhaps she could find out something that Ryder might find useful.

Just as Ryder had done the previous evening, she motioned to the picnic table.

Grimacing at the dirt on the bench, Geoffrey waited until she sat, then reluctantly took a place on the opposite side of the table.

"You are aware Ryder Goodhue isn't my granddaughter's biological father."

Trinity's counseling experience had her schooling her features. "That's news to me."

Geoffrey leaned back and studied her with what could be described only as shark eyes. "Now, Ms. McConnell, there's no need for you to lie for him. From what I observed this morning, you're no longer a couple. Is it because of the girl? I understand. If I was a successful career woman, I wouldn't want to mother someone else's child either. All I'm asking you for is the truth."

When he paused for breath, she didn't bother to ask him how

he knew she and Ryder weren't together. He'd obviously witnessed their exchange in the church parking lot.

"Are you finished?" Trinity asked in the cool tone she'd perfected for male clients who behaved offensively toward her.

"Goodhue told you he isn't the father. Why he wants to keep the girl, I don't understand, especially since she isn't his flesh and blood." Though he managed a fairly convincing sorrowful expression, his eyes remained razor-sharp. "The child should be with family."

"Zoe," Trinity emphasized her name, "*is* with her family. She's with her father. Which is exactly where she's meant to be. The last place she needs to be is with her grandfather the pedophile."

Dark red slashed his cheeks. "Lies by an emotionally unstable young woman."

Trinity's phone buzzed. She pulled it from her purse and saw several missed calls and texts. All from Ryder.

He's here, she texted back, then set the phone on the table. She smiled at Geoffrey. "Ryder is on his way."

"I'll have you subpoenaed." Geoffrey's finger tapped the table. "You're not Goodhue's wife or his therapist. You'll be forced to tell the truth, to admit under oath that he told you he isn't the child's biological father. That should be enough, at least for the judge I have in mind, to issue a court order to force Goodhue to take a paternity test."

"Don't you already have a paternity test scheduled for some other guy?"

Geoffrey waved a dismissive hand. "That fool was the best I could find. Now he tells me he didn't even meet Jenna until after she was pregnant."

Something, Trinity realized, that Ryder must have already known. "Having me testify will be just as big a waste of time."

She glanced at the driveway, at the sound of a car fast approaching.

"Not a waste—" Geoffrey began.

"A waste." Trinity laughed and watched his face darken with anger. "I'll tell the truth. I'll testify that the only thing Ryder has ever said to me is that he's Zoe's father."

And suddenly, she realized the benefit of Ryder withholding the truth about Zoe's paternity. Not cool that he lied, but this time it would work in everyone's favor.

CHAPTER TWENTY-SEVEN

Ryder stood with Trinity and watched the dark sedan roar down the driveway. He shifted his gaze to Trinity. "Are you sure you're okay?"

"Perfectly fine." She flashed a quick smile, but her eyes held shadows.

"I'd say have a seat." He slanted a glance at the picnic table. "But I think we've both had enough of that table."

"Forget sitting. I need caffeine. Right now, I'd kill for a strong cup of coffee."

Ryder offered a hesitant smile. "I happen to have some fresh beans at my place *and* a clean spot for you to sit."

The sedan had sped away before Ryder had gotten out of his car. But he didn't care about Geoffrey. His only concern was Trinity, who, thankfully, appeared unharmed.

"Strong coffee and a seat without bird droppings." Her lips quirked upward. "I believe I'll take you up on that offer."

On their way inside, Ryder called David and told him he'd be over shortly to pick up Zoe. When David asked if Zoe could join them for lunch, Ryder said yes.

He refrained from plying Trinity with questions, waiting until they were at the table, with cups of strong, steaming coffee before them.

Scully lay contentedly on his bed, happily chewing on the bone Ryder had tossed him.

Ryder brought the cup to his lips, keeping his gaze fixed on Trinity. "Will you tell me what happened?"

Trinity laid it out for him. How Geoffrey had pulled in behind her car, his request that they talk and his assumption that her relationship with Ryder had fallen apart.

"He thought I'd start dishing the dirt." She took a long gulp of coffee. "When that didn't happen, he threatened to subpoena me. Said I'd have to tell the court what you told me, and when I did, you'd be forced to take a paternity test."

He met her gaze.

"He didn't like hearing that the only thing you've ever said to me is that you *are* Zoe's father." Trinity let out a breath. "I assume my testimony would make it difficult for him to find a sympathetic judge to order you to take a paternity test."

"Not only difficult, but I believe impossible." Ryder experienced a surge of satisfaction. "Not only did Jenna put me on the birth certificate and name me as Zoe's father in her will, I've claimed Zoe as mine. All ways to assume paternity."

"If you'd told me..." Instead of finishing the thought, she took another gulp of coffee. "I see now why you didn't think you could. Or should."

Ryder gave a humorless laugh. "Well, I can't say I imagined a court case being a factor."

"Do you think Swanson will keep trying for custody?"

Ryder shook his head. "While he isn't a man who likes losing, he's smart enough to see this as a dead end and not worth his continued efforts."

"What are you going to do about Zoe?"

He cocked his head.

"What will you tell her?"

Ryder shouldn't have been surprised her mind had traveled down this road. Her concern for his child was just another thing he loved about her. "Zoe knows that her grandfather's claim about Brad Kosmicki is bogus. When she's eighteen, if she wants DNA proof that I'm her biological dad, I'll tell her the truth and take a test. I'll emphasize that, no matter what the test shows, she's my daughter and always will be."

Tears blurred Trinity's eyes. "How'd you get so smart?"

He grinned and felt his heart lighten, just a little. "I've been hanging out with a very clever—not to mention extremely sexy—clinical psychologist."

She offered a watery laugh and swiped at tears.

"Where do we go from here, Trinity?" If she wanted him to keep his distance, he would. But the mixed messages she was giving off had him hoping. "Are we going forward together or going our separate ways? It's your decision."

Trinity pushed to her feet and strode to the counter. She needed a moment to settle her rioting thoughts and emotions. When she turned, resting her back against the counter, she discovered that Ryder was on his feet and only inches away.

He didn't reach for her. For that, she was grateful. It was difficult to think when he was close. Logical thought would be impossible if his hands were on her.

Trinity had a lot to say, and it was important she get it all out.

"I'm like Geoffrey in one regard—I don't like to fail. I failed in my first marriage. My biggest mistake wasn't the fact that Miles had children. It was how I handled the challenges in our relationship."

Ryder's dark and assessing gaze never wavered from her face.

Swallowing past a sudden dryness in her throat, Trinity pushed forward. "Miles and I skirted around issues, pushed them aside as if they weren't important, even when we knew they were."

The energy pulsing inside her made standing still impossible. Trinity slipped past Ryder and began to pace. "At the time, I was busy with my studies. It seemed easier to let difficult discussions slide. In the end, we slid past the point of no return."

"Is that what you think we were doing?"

"It would have been so easy to brush aside the fact that you lied to me. Push it under the rug. What I now realize is that comparing the two situations didn't do justice to either of them." She met Ryder's gaze. "I'm sorry. I was so caught up in the past that I couldn't see what was in front of me."

"I'm the one who's sorry. I didn't explain myself—"

Ryder was close now. So close she only had to raise her hand to still his unnecessary apology with the tips of her fingers.

"Some things you need to speak about to get resolution," she said. "I don't believe there's anything left for us to say."

When confusion furrowed his brow, Trinity realized she hadn't been clear.

She looped her arms around his neck. "I know everything about this situation that I need to know. I know you're a good man, a wonderful father and the man I love. While I'll never be a fan of lies of omission or outright lies, I can accept that you did what you thought you had to do to protect your daughter. I don't like to pretend something didn't happen, but in this instance, can we pretend I didn't walk away?"

He stared at her for a long moment. "No."

Startled shock flashed through her. Trinity blinked. "No?"

"I don't want to ever forget that you're a woman who's strong enough to stand up for what you believe is right." He trailed a finger down her cheek, a smile lifting the corners of his lips. "And strong enough to reconsider and shift gears."

Ryder pulled her close and held her tight.

When their lips met, everything inside Trinity melted. This was love—the pain, the joy and the happiness.

"One big honking leap of faith," she murmured against his lips.

"What did you say?"

Lifting her head, she smiled into his eyes. "Let's go pick up our girl."

EPILOGUE

The wedding of Trinity McConnell to Ryder Goodhue was held the day after Thanksgiving at the Ding-A-Ling. When Trinity originally brought up the possibility of getting married at the bar, Ryder had had his doubts.

Now, seeing the magic local florist Lindsay Vaughn had wrought, he realized there was an intimacy about the venue that made it the perfect choice.

Chairs that had been set up for the ceremony had been returned to the tables that were temporarily pushed to the side. The reception, complete with a buffet and drinks on the house, was in full swing.

"The night I arrived in Good Hope, you were standing right over there." Trinity glanced in the direction of the gleaming bar, which now held a smorgasbord of tasty temptations. "Now, here we are, barely three months later, and you're my husband."

Ryder captured the hand that sported a large emerald-cut diamond and brought it to his lips, pressing a kiss against her knuckles. "I can't imagine my life without you in it."

"I feel the same." Her blue eyes sparkled, matching the underskirt of what she called her twirl dress. The cocktail-length dress, white with swirls of blue and tiny threads of silver on the skirt, billowed out when she twirled.

Family and friends had been encouraged to dress casually for the ceremony and reception. Ryder couldn't bring himself to get married in a polo shirt, but after the ceremony, he removed his suit coat and tie. He now stood beside his bride in dark pants and a shirt with tiny blue stripes that matched his new bride's eyes.

Like Ryder's parents, Trinity's family, including her two sisters and younger brother, had arrived the day before Thanksgiving. Though Rafe had been estranged from his family for years, Ryder had hoped to see his brother. But he was a no-show.

Ryder pushed aside his disappointment. This was his wedding day, a time for celebration and joy.

He and Trinity had more to celebrate than joining their lives together. On Wednesday, they'd watched Zoe's face light up when the document arrived advising the application to change the last name on her California birth certificate had been approved.

This had been the final step in her journey to become Zoe Swanson Goodhue. They hadn't heard from Geoffrey or his lawyer since the confrontation at the Barn picnic table. It appeared the man had realized he was fighting a battle he was destined to lose.

Zoe wasn't the only one with a name change. Ryder had been fully prepared for Trinity to remain a McConnell, but she'd surprised him. She'd told him she liked the idea of having the same name as him and Zoe, as well as any other children they might have in the future.

"You know, if we'd waited, you could have had an outdoor wedding with all the frills." Ryder would have married her the day after he proposed. He'd also been okay with waiting and doing it up big next spring or summer.

To his surprise, she'd not only chosen the day after Thanksgiving, but a rather nontraditional venue for their nuptials.

"I didn't want to wait until spring to start our life together." Trinity cupped his face in her hands and kissed him. "Besides, this way, Wyatt and Greer won't have to share that time with anyone else."

"I don't believe they would have minded, but I'm glad we didn't wait." Ryder tugged her close. "Not being together under the same roof with you for even this long has been torture."

Though many couples moved in together before marriage, with a tween daughter at home, he and Trinity had decided not to go that route. The hardest part was they'd also decided they wouldn't sleep together unless Zoe was out of the house.

He'd felt like a teenager again, trying to keep the fact that he was having sex a secret. Ryder smiled. Actually, the sneaking around had added an air of excitement.

Now, they were married. After a short honeymoon trip to a nice warm beach, he and Trinity would come back to a shared bedroom.

Ryder slung an arm around his bride's shoulders and brushed a kiss against her hair. "This was a great choice. The decorations make such a difference. I never thought the Ding-A-Ling could look...romantic."

Romantic, as long as you ignored the zing of darts, the crack of a cue against a ball and the *ding-ding-ding* from pinball machines in the back room.

"It's incredibly beautiful and romantic." Trinity smiled, taking in the white ceiling drapes and the balls of flowers hanging from the ceiling. "Best of all, there's plenty to keep the kids occupied."

Her gaze lingered on the pool table, where Zoe played a game of eight ball with Callum.

"My father and Wyatt seem to be having a blast tossing darts with David and Steve." As he gazed in that direction, Ruby and Katherine caught his eye and waved.

"Look at Gladys flirting with Albert." Trinity expelled a happy sigh. "Just goes to show love has no age limit."

"I agree, because I'm going to love you forever." He ran his hand down the sides of her arms, unable to believe that this brilliant, compassionate and lovely woman was now his wife. "In case I haven't said it enough, you look absolutely beautiful."

"You don't have to say it. The look in your eyes when you saw me walk down the aisle said it all." Trinity's voice held a husky edge, and desire flared in her eyes.

Ryder stepped even closer, wishing they were alone. Wishing he could—

"Congrats, again."

Ryder jumped at the touch on his arm.

Marigold gave Trinity a quick hug. "I ran into your daughter by the pool table a few minutes ago. What a sweetheart."

"We think she's pretty great." Ryder rested his palm against Trinity's back, finding it increasingly difficult to keep from touching her.

"Zoe is amazing." Pride filled Trinity's voice. "I was thinking the other day that I was just a little older than her when the McConnells adopted me."

Trinity's eyes seemed to seek out her mother, who was having an animated conversation with Greer.

The two women, Ryder knew, had instantly bonded over an intense—and lengthy—Thanksgiving dinner discussion about the needs of foster kids.

"Cade and I have considered fostering." Marigold's eyes took on a faraway look.

"It isn't always easy," Trinity acknowledged, "but it's a way to really make a difference in someone's life."

"We're also considering..." Marigold's voice trailed off as she narrowed her gaze. "Is it my imagination, or is Oaklee flirting with your brother?"

Though the question was directed to Trinity, Ryder turned in time to see Oaklee walk her fingers up Phoenix's arm. Trinity's youngest brother had taken casual to a new level, showing up in a graphic T-shirt and jeans with holes.

Oaklee's dress, a vivid orange, hit just above thigh-high boots. With her hair now multicolored and spiky and his piercings and tats, the two looked like a match made in alternative-rock heaven.

It was only on second glance that Ryder noticed what Marigold failed to see—Oaklee casting furtive glances in Ethan's direction, as if to gauge his reaction.

Ryder was about to mention the observation when he found himself distracted by the sight of the two women behind the bar.

"Look." Ryder nudged Trinity and pointed. "Both of your sisters are now serving drinks."

"I specifically told Sage we hired a bartender so she can enjoy the party." A fond smile lifted Trinity's lips, and she chuckled. "She simply cannot resist showing Amber Lynn how to mix the latest drinks."

"Amber is also a bartender?" Marigold's brows knitted together in confusion. "I thought she was a teacher."

"She is," Trinity explained. "But Sage loves to share her knowledge of the latest and greatest. It appears she's bringing Oaklee behind the bar to show her, too."

Ryder smiled, taking it all in. Friends. Family. Community.

He was a lucky man.

Once Marigold had stepped away, Ryder wrapped his arms around Trinity.

"I realize now that when we went around the table yesterday and said what we were thankful for, I left off something."

Trinity inclined her head, her tone teasing. "What did you forget?"

"I'm thankful for the bad weather in Chicago when we first

met." He brushed his lips across hers. "That night set the wheels in motion. If we hadn't gotten to know each other then, we might not have ended up together. That would have been a tragedy of epic proportions. I can't imagine my life without you in it."

Before he even finished, his wife was shaking her head. "I firmly believe I'd have found my way to you even if I'd stayed in Omaha and only came here to visit Wyatt. Some things are meant to be."

Trinity wrapped her arms around him then and pulled him close in a hug that said *I love you* louder than any words. "You and I, Mr. Goodhue, were meant to be together."

"Meant to be," Ryder murmured, the words feeling oh-so-right on his tongue. "You're right. Nothing would have kept me from finding you."

She lifted her face, and when his mouth closed over hers, Ryder poured all the love in his heart into the kiss.

As the kiss ended, he caught sight of Zoe across the room watching them. She smiled and gave him the thumbs-up.

Ryder grinned.

Yep. Meant to be.

Thank you for coming along on Trinity and Ryder's journey. As you probably know if you've read very many of my books, you know I love adding children whenever I can (especially little girls). Probably because I have a wonderful daughter and three amazing little granddaughters. I love it in this story where both Ryder and Trinity showed their character by how they focused on Zoe's needs.

Many of my readers have told me they'd love to live in Good Hope. So would I! Never fear, we'll be coming back here again and again.

The next book in the series brings together Clay Chapin and Bea Appleton. This book is a reader favorite and I bet you'll love it, too. Grab a copy of this uplifting story today! (or continue reading for a sneak peek) Bachelor Games in Good Hope

SNEAK PEEK OF BACHELOR GAMES IN GOOD HOPE

Chapter One

Clay Chapin strode into Book & Cup, the small bookstore he liked to frequent on the edge of Good Hope's business district. When his girlfriend, Stella Bryant, texted she absolutely must meet him at four, he'd paused before responding.

With Stella insisting on meeting so early, Clay had been forced to scramble. As he made every effort to keep his personal and professional lives separate, he didn't want her stopping by the school where he was the principal.

He briefly considered meeting her at Muddy Boots or Blooms Bake Shop, but even in early May, those shops would be hopping. Whatever Stella had to say must be important and likely required some privacy.

Book & Cup had gotten the nod. The place was close to his work and never seemed to do much business. Clay often stopped here after the school day ended. He'd grab a coffee, find a table in the back and pull out his laptop.

Every three or four visits, he'd buy a book to take home with him.

The bells over the door jingled as he pushed it open. Beatrice Appleton sat on a stool behind the counter, a cup of coffee in front of her and an open book in her hands. Last year, when owner Judy Koontz had grown weary of running the bookstore, Bea had assumed the day-to-day management duties.

Bea had attended Good Hope High with Clay's younger sister, Greer. As Greer and Bea hadn't run in the same social circle, and Bea had graduated early, Clay's memories of her during those years were hazy at best.

Today, Bea's mass of light brown hair was pulled back in a messy twist. Her graphic tee showed a stack of books and proclaimed "My Weekend Is All Booked."

Clay smiled. He liked this tee almost as much as the one she'd worn the last time he'd stopped in: "If I can't take my book, I'm not going."

She glanced up from the large leather-bound tome. Her dark eyebrows lifted. "This is a pleasant surprise. You never stop by on a Thursday."

Because he was meeting Stella, who likely wouldn't see the charm of the shop, Clay made his smile extra warm.

"My girlfriend, Stella, will be stopping by around four." Clay jerked his head toward the back of the shop. "If you could send her back to my table when she arrives, I'd appreciate it."

Curiosity flickered in Bea's blue eyes, but he knew she wouldn't dig. "Sure. No problem."

As always, Bea's calm demeanor soothed and steadied. Clay liked that she didn't seem to feel the need to fill every second with aimless chatter. If he asked about a book or a series, she'd give her opinion.

They also talked about current events. Clay found her extremely knowledgeable on a wide range of topics.

"Want coffee?" Bea's expression turned speculative. "Blueberry muffin is today's featured flavor."

"You know how I look forward to my jolt of caffeine." He

rubbed his chin and pretended to ponder the option. "Is the blueberry any good?"

"It's a book club favorite."

"Then you might start seeing me on Thursdays."

"I'll get you a cup." She favored him with a quick smile that lit up her face. "I'll send your girlfriend back as soon as she arrives."

"Thank you."

"You're welcome."

Clay made his way to his favorite spot at the back of the store. He wished he knew what was up with Stella.

The urgent need to meet was definitely a puzzle. Clay placed his laptop on the familiar scarred wooden table situated between Science-Fiction and Horror.

He'd barely settled in when he caught the enticing scent of blueberries. He glanced up to see Bea approaching, a cup of steaming coffee in one hand.

"You looked like you could use this. I already added the cream." She set the cup carefully on the table. Her lips quirked. "We're fresh out of whiskey."

He chuckled. "I'll make do."

The fact that Bea didn't hurry off told Clay customers were in short supply today. Not totally true, he reminded himself. On his way in, he'd held the door open for a group of ten to twelve ladies exiting the store.

Clay offered Bea a persuasive smile, knowing Stella wouldn't show for at least another fifteen minutes. "Join me?"

She hesitated. "You're meeting someone, remember?"

"You can keep me company while I wait."

She considered his offer, then sat.

Clay settled back in his chair, wrapping his fingers around the ceramic mug. He wore what he thought of as his school uniform—gray dress pants, a cotton shirt that buttoned up the front and a tie.

The kids loved his novelty ties. This morning, Harry Potter

had gotten the nod. Though the dress code at school was decidedly casual, Clay had grown up with a father who wore a suit to work every day and felt underdressed without a tie. Silly ones had quickly become his thing.

Bea cocked her head. "What did you think of the Gladwell book?"

"*Blink* made me think. I'm glad you suggested it." Clay sipped the coffee and found he liked the taste. He'd been surprised when Bea had handed him a copy of *Blink*. The book hadn't been on his radar when it was originally released in 2005. As he'd read it, Clay realized the content was still relevant today. "Though I'm having difficulty with Gladwell's assertion that intuition beats out our rational brain, the premise is intriguing."

They spent the next ten minutes discussing the book and Gladwell's suppositions. As always, Bea's comments challenged him, and the discussion turned spirited.

She sat across from him at the table, her blue eyes appearing violet in the light from the store's vintage fixtures.

It was at moments like these that he wondered how he could have only vague memories of her during his high school years. Especially since he remembered her twin sister, Brittany, so vividly.

Yes, it was odd, he thought, gazing across the table as she made a stabbing gesture with one finger to make a point, that he'd never noticed her. He liked the way her eyes sparkled when she pressed a point.

The jingle of bells over the door had Bea shoving back the chair with a clatter and springing to her feet. "That's probably your girlfriend."

"Or a customer," he murmured to her retreating back. He glanced at the clock on his laptop. It was still too early for Stella to make an appearance.

Shifting his gaze to the screen, Clay focused on the proposed additional safety measures the district could implement before the start of the next school year. In his mind, student safety was paramount.

He was deep in the middle of an article on best practices when the next jingle of bells barely registered. Seconds later, Stella's husky, confident voice shattered his concentration. Closing the laptop, Clay pushed back his chair and stood.

Stella stepped out between two stacks of books.

"You found me," he teased, then leaned over and brushed her cherry-red mouth with his lips.

"Trust me. It wasn't difficult." She chuckled, but two lines formed between her brows as she surveyed her surroundings. "This seems an odd place to meet."

"It sounded as if you wanted to speak privately." Clay gestured to the chair across the table. "This is about as private as it gets when meeting in public."

Stella cocked her head as if listening for voices or movement. "I believe you and I are the only customers. I don't know how this place stays in business."

Clay had wondered that, too, on more than one occasion. "You look lovely today. Is that dress new?"

Stella had a closet full of clothes. Which Clay figured was to be expected, considering she worked in a clothing store.

"It is." Her lips curved as she took a seat. "Thank you for noticing."

Clay sat across from her. Leaning slightly forward, he gave her his full attention. "What's up with the sudden need to meet? I admit I'm intrigued."

Her chestnut-brown eyes settled on him.

"When we met, I misjudged you. That's on me." She puffed her cheeks, blew out a breath. "I once had high hopes for our relationship."

"Had?" Clay took her hand, playing with her fingers. "Not anymore?"

She slipped her hand from his and sat back. "That's why I'm here."

The fact that she didn't offer him a teasing smile had unease slithering up Clay's spine. Still, he kept his tone light. "Now I'm seriously intrigued."

Stella moistened her lips with the tip of her tongue. "I'm not sure where to begin."

"Why don't you start by telling me one thing that's turned out differently than you hoped?" Clay kept his gaze firmly fixed on her expressive face.

"Well, when we first started dating, I thought we'd go out more."

Whatever he'd expected her to say, it wasn't this. He and Stella usually spent both Friday and Saturday nights together. Sundays were reserved for family. Though he always invited Stella to go with him to church and family dinner, she refused more often than not.

"We go out every weekend," he reminded her.

"I meant to nice places. Last weekend, you said you were taking me out for a special dinner. I was super excited. I bought a new dress." A tiny smile hovered at the corners of her lips as if she was recalling her anticipation. Then her eyes went flat. "You took me to Egg Harbor."

"Mexican food is a favorite of yours. Everyone knows Sombreros has the best Mexican food on the peninsula." Clay adopted a teasing tone. "You adore their pomegranate margaritas. I remember how upset you were when they took them off the menu. I'd heard they were back on and thought it'd be a nice surprise."

"It was a nice surprise," Stella grudgingly admitted. "But I thought, I hoped, you were taking me somewhere a bit more upscale, like that Asian fusion place in Green Bay. I've told you numerous times I want to go there and see for myself if the buzz is warranted. Remember?"

Now that Stella mentioned it, Clay did recall those conversations. "The new place. The one on North Broadway."

"Yes." Her gaze remained firmly focused on his face. "It's been getting rave reviews."

"Apparently, the hype is well deserved. Wyatt and Greer ate there last week."

Stella's lips lifted in a tight smile. "Of course they did."

He wished she'd made it clear that going there was a big deal to her. And he wished he'd done a better job of listening. But he had a sinking feeling that whatever was going on with Stella went far beyond him not taking her to a new restaurant.

Clay felt like he was up to bat. The problem was, he wasn't sure of the rules. Heck, he didn't even know the game. He cleared his throat. "I'm having difficulty figuring out the point you're trying to make."

"Over Valentine's Day, your brother took his wife to Paris." Stella's tone held a wistful quality. "Your sister is going to Tahiti for her honeymoon."

All true, Clay thought, still having trouble making a connection. From her expression, he sensed she wouldn't make him wait long before clarifying.

"Why don't you and I go to Paris? Or Tahiti?" She gave a little laugh. "Heck, at this point I'd settle for San Francisco or New York City."

Clay cocked his head. Was that what this was about? She'd been bitten by the travel bug and wanted them to see the sights together?

He reached across the table and covered her hand with his. "You know it's difficult for me to get away when school is in session. But the semester is winding down. My summer is pretty booked, but I'm sure I can fit in at least a quick trip to Chicago."

Stella sighed. "You just don't get it."

Clay thought he'd hit a home run, but the edge in her voice

told him he'd struck out. He glugged lukewarm coffee, wishing for whiskey. "Enlighten me."

He considered himself an easygoing guy, but he didn't much care for game-playing. That's exactly how this felt.

"I remember the day you strolled into my shop looking for a gift for your mother. Right away, I liked what I saw."

Wary now, Clay merely inclined his head.

"I asked my co-worker who you were, and she told me you were one of the Chapins, the family who owns the banks." She hesitated. "I admit I was surprised to later discover your sister is the one with her fingers in the banking pie."

Clay shifted in his seat.

"I like you, Clay." Stella's expression turned earnest. "I like your smile and how you're always happy and upbeat. Plus, you're seriously hot."

The last comment had him chuckling. This was good, Clay told himself. Whatever was going on, the air must have needed cleansing. Every couple had difficult times. Was this the watershed moment that would lead to a deeper intimacy between them?

Bring it on, he thought.

"In addition to your hotness, your privileged background is a point in your favor."

Okay, he could live with that. Just like he could live with the fact that her initial attraction was because she thought he was hot. Clay couldn't help but smile.

Appearing nonplussed, she gazed at him. "That doesn't bother you?"

"The way I see it, a person is the sum of their parts." Clay smiled. "My family heritage is part of the whole."

Relief washed over her pretty face. "I thought you'd be angry."

"I appreciate that you feel comfortable enough with me to be honest." He resisted, barely, the urge to reach across the scarred tabletop that separated them and once again take her hand.

Clay could tell this conversation was important to her. He wanted to encourage more of this openness, rather than shut it down.

Too many times in the months they'd been together, physical intimacy, whether a touch, a kiss, or more, had taken the place of honest communication.

He thought of Bea and their brief chat about Gladwell. Honest dialogue was a way to build true intimacy. Clay resolved to make more of an effort in that direction.

"...my parents' lifestyle."

Clay realized with chagrin that while his mind had been wandering, she'd been talking.

So much for keeping the communication channels open.

He cleared his throat. "What does your parents' lifestyle have to do with our relationship?"

Though he'd kept his tone easy, her dark eyes flashed. Like a bird with her feathers ruffled, Stella drew herself up and tossed her hair back over her shoulder. "I was about to explain."

Because he felt bad for not listening, Clay didn't point out that her tendency to get easily riled stifled, rather than encouraged, honest dialogue.

"My parents like to camp." She spoke without preamble.

Clay brightened. "I love to camp."

Stella muttered something under her breath. "Their idea of a perfect vacation is a fishing trip to Canada."

"We could go there this summer." Clay made no effort to curb his enthusiasm. "I know the perfect spot. It's—"

Stella held up a hand, cutting him off. She closed her eyes for a second, breathed out. "My parents are satisfied with yearly fishing trips to Canada and hosting backyard barbecues. That's fine. For them. Me, I prefer more exotic locations and activities."

When she hesitated, he offered an encouraging smile.

"Let me just say, I have zero interest in staying in a cabin or a tent. Even less in holding a fishing pole or baiting a hook." She brushed a strand of hair back from her face, then leaned forward. "I want to experience the best the world has to offer. I want to stay in luxury hotel suites. I want to dine in the best restaurants. Based on your background, I assumed the love of the finer things in life was something we shared."

One beat of silence. Then two.

"Why are you telling me this?" He gave her the benefit of the doubt, because he didn't want to assume.

"I don't believe we're on the same page." Stella blew out a breath, shifted in her seat. "I'm not sure we ever were."

"I enjoy spending time with you," Clay told her.

A ghost of a smile lifted her lips. "We've had some fun times."

"We have," he agreed.

"Unfortunately, the kind of life we each ultimately want is very different." Sadness skittered across her face, then vanished as she squared her shoulders. "After considerable thought, I feel it's best that we don't see each other anymore."

Clay studied the face of the beautiful woman who'd captivated him all those months ago. Stella had a certain type of man in mind for herself.

That man wasn't him.

He also had a certain type of woman in mind for himself. One who understood that his passion wasn't traveling the world and staying at five-star resorts, but educating young minds.

A woman who embraced simple pleasures as well as the finer things in life.

That woman wasn't Stella.

"You're right." Clay pushed back his chair and stood. "It's best we go our separate ways."

When she rose with that easy grace he'd always admired, Clay extended his hand. "I hope you know I appreciate your honesty. I wish you only the best."

Stella's fingers lingered on his for a heartbeat longer than necessary before she withdrew her hand. She cocked her head, and puzzlement filled her eyes. "You don't seem upset. I thought you'd be upset."

Had she thought he'd try to convince her to give him another chance? Perhaps had even envisioned him begging?

If so, that would only show she didn't know him at all.

To find out the rest of the story, pick up a copy of this feel-good holiday romance today! Bachelor Games in Good Hope

ALSO BY CINDY KIRK

Good Hope Series

The Good Hope series is a must-read for those who love stories that uplift and bring a smile to your face.

Check out the entire Good Hope series here

Hazel Green Series

Readers say "Much like the author's series of Good Hope books, the reader learns about a town, its people, places and stories that enrich the overall experience. It's a journey worth taking."

Check out the entire Hazel Green series here

Holly Pointe Series

Readers say "If you are looking for a festive, romantic read this Christmas, these are the books for you."

Check out the entire Holly Pointe series here

Jackson Hole Series

Heartwarming and uplifting stories set in beautiful Jackson Hole, Wyoming.

Check out the entire Jackson Hole series here

Silver Creek Series

Engaging and heartfelt romances centered around two powerful families whose fortunes were forged in the Colorado silver mines.

Check out the entire Silver Creek series here

Made in the USA
Coppell, TX
12 May 2021

55376093R00163